FESTER

THE SHADOW BLOOD TALE

FESTER

THE SHADOW BLOOD TALE

ZAVEN BOSWELL

For information contact : feignedshadows@gmail.com

Book and Cover design by J.W. Rose

ISBN: 978-1-968956-02-8

First Edition: July 2025
10 9 8 7 6 5 4 3 2 1

To Jenna, for supporting me in my dream with

your passion, wisdom, and inspiration

1

Why have they not returned yet? There has never been a time when both of them left me here alone. Perhaps they disappeared because I failed to meet their expectations or angered them by mocking their ridiculous lifestyle. This is my life, after all. I'm not them. I'll continue to wait here and hope they return.

The lanterns provide an eerie glow to this abandoned sanctuary: a dirty, creepy cave beneath the feet of my hometown. Two stone pillars lead the way to a bloodstained wooden door I refuse to go near. However, my parents think it's their duty to safeguard the mysteries behind that door and hide this location from any of the residents above.

To withhold a secret like this forever can be miserable, but it's also a convenience. My conversations with the locals are limited to only the necessities: shopping, sleeping, and bathing. I have never been fond of people or the chaotic lives they invest in. The only ones who have my approval are my parents, Ashen and Flare, who taught me everything I need to know to guarantee my survival. Still, their lives are a waste of time as well.

I give them one week to come home before I set off to experience the world. Perhaps it's time I create my own destiny.

*   *   *

Word is spreading around concerning the invasion in Lirium, the overseeing kingdom of this region. The king's son, Enzo Malfester, supposedly gathered a large enough force to take over—descriptions of destruction, death, and unrest clutch onto all these rumors. For a world at peace, it's ridiculous how someone must ruin it for their personal gain.

Now I don't know where I can go. Is anywhere safe assuming this information is accurate? I could travel in a single direction and discover where it takes me, but who knows how wise it is to move outside of the kingdom's control. My knowledge of the world is limited apart from Dalgin, my hometown. So, it's only a matter of time before we all suffer the influence of this new monarchy.

*   *   *

It's almost been a week since Ashen and Flare's departure. I hope they haven't encountered trouble from Enzo's reign. At this rate, they may already be dead.

Supplies are rising in price, and my money won't last much longer. There are patrols forcing compliance concerning the new leadership, which disgusts me. This place is already falling apart. The only reason I'm still here is because this place is hidden near the outskirts of Dalgin; boulders and vegetation act as cover for this unordinary abode.

I place a hand on my heart and reflect on any helpful advice my parents might offer in this situation. After considering my many conversations with them, I recall a hazy memory of my father informing me that if he did not return, I must seek my mother for what I must do. So, I asked my mother, Flare, and she said something about entering the door . . . or to protect the door. Who knows. This is one thing that always frustrates me, all their safeguarding-the-door nonsense. Doubtful there can be anything remarkable behind there. I don't understand why they must ruin a wonderful family life by embracing their duty to ridiculous extents. I get this cave is our home, but this is taking the fear of trespassing too far.

3

I'll allow them one more day. Otherwise, I will assume they're dead, discover what's behind the door, and start a new life elsewhere. I have already spent enough time here.

*   *   *

I pack my money and clothes into a bag and hoist it onto my shoulder. There's nothing else of value I can bring, for anything that does not help me survive is a waste of space when moving into a new life. I'm upset my parents left me, but now I must assume they're dead. The only burden left to relinquish before I depart is to open the bloodstained door.

Approaching it, I tolerate my first surge of excitement ever since I was younger. The feeling is awkward, unstable, and annoying, but I cannot suppress it. I pause at the door and take a deep breath. A part of me doesn't care about what's inside, but uncovering its mysteries may reveal more about my parents. After all these years, I can't say I know much about them apart from their responsibility. What terrible secrets—secrets kept for generations—can I find within?

I press my shaking hands across all the rough edges and notches I can find, gripping, pushing, and pulling them. Nothing budges. I run my hands over everything again, giving extra care to those spots I may have overlooked. Still, nothing happens. Excitement shifts to anger, and I punch the bloody door with all my strength. Pain floods my knuckles and spreads across my hand, and I snivel and release an inhuman noise born from my unhealthy mix of rage and agony. Once again, the door refuses to move an inch. I whip around, done with this horrendous piece of crap, and come face-to-face with a burly man wearing a gray hood and rags. My heart freezes as I see his mouth curve into a smile—his only visible facial feature.

"That was quite the display, foreigner," his voice is deep, stunning me. He's a real threat invading my home. This is the first incident in the past sixteen years. After all this time, I thought my parents were too paranoid for their own good, but now I understand why. If men like this desire to cause harm, we need to be ready to eradicate any intruders.

He continues, "A bit gross how you touched all those bloodstains, but I commend you for trying. Still, you should know there's only one way to unlock this door." The man shoves me away from the only thing my family cares about. "If only your parents could see you now."

2

A creepy man invading my home and carelessly dishonoring my parents' wishes. He must be stopped at all costs.

Pulling my knife from my pocket, I point it at the cloaked man. He backs away and loses the cocky spark in his smile, but maintains his composure despite my threat. Scowling, I refuse to let down my guard. With the current crisis concerning Lirium's invasion, he is probably here to defile this sanctuary.

"Enough of the brave girl act. Put down the knife, Phoenix, and tell me where your parents are."

"You are not the one to ask questions here, especially after entering a wolf's den." I smile back at him, and I see his fade entirely. "How do you know my name? Who are you?"

He opens his cloak and rests his hand on a plain sword hilt. It's a smug attempt to strike fear into me. "Those are questions I cannot answer, Phoenix. It's best if you never know. But if your parents are nowhere to be found, I must inform you that they are dead." He bows his head as if giving peace. "It is unfortunate."

"What do you know of them?" I growl.

"I know everything. Now, enough games from you, foreigner. Let me pass so I can do what I must."

He inches toward me, and I jab my knife at him. The man dodges out of the way, and I somehow miss and lose my balance. Next thing I know, he draws his weapon and points it at me—a blade much shinier and larger than my own.

I restore my bearings and declare, "You will tell me everything: how you know who I am and what happened to my parents. I will cut it out of you if I must. By setting foot in here, you have tainted this cave with your presence. You are unpermitted to enter this door for the sake of my family's history; I take it upon myself to be the current protector of this sanctuary."

3

This is my first real opponent, but Ashen and Flare have taught me everything I need to know when it comes to combat. If he truly knows everything, I may be able to cut some information out of him. I will then kill him to send a message to others.

"So, the cycle continues then," the man states with a definite frown. "Yet, you do not understand what they have been hiding from you all this time. What are you trying to protect?"

"My parents' legacy." I feign an attack which causes him to recoil in fear, then I take the opportunity to dash toward his flank. Next, I smite his ribs, and blood splatters onto the already-stained door. The man growls with discomfort and spins his sword in a one-eighty-degree blow, a swing capable of decapitation. I'm aware of the incoming danger, so I duck and rush into him, striking his knee.

Blood spews onto my clothes and skin, and I must refrain from vomiting. The man's wail as he crumbles to the floor worsens the feeling. I bend down and inhale a slow, deep breath, and contemplate the past.

I have never fought to kill a human before. Instead, I only practiced with training dummies and, on occasion, my parents. We used sticks so nobody would bleed—which I appreciate. The bulkier sticks hampered my movement, so I stuck with something small. This is when my father gave me a knife, a weapon I must only use if there was no other option. Nonetheless, I have been itching to use it on someone up till now.

I approach the fallen man and point my knife at him, satisfied with my victory. "Tell me, who are you? What do you know?"

"Call me Jerrick," the man speaks through uneven breaths. "As for what I know, now is not the time."

"Well, Jerrick, then it's time you paid the price for your trespass. Goodbye."

My heart leaps as I muster up the courage to strike him down. He's defenseless, so I drive my weapon toward him to finish the job. Before my knife reaches its prey, Jerrick reveals some unknown vigor and seizes my blade inches from his face. Blood pours from his palm and drips heavily onto the floor, and he stands up with intense effort, judging from his facial expression. I refuse to release my weapon as he towers over me, and instead, I try to yank it free. Although, no matter the amount of force I apply, the knife stays with him.

He produces a deathly yell as he tears my weapon away, leaving me in awe. Stricken by what's left on the man's hand, I taste burning bile, which leaves a nasty aftertaste as I swallow it.

Afterward, he gets up and proceeds to the stained door, places his bloody palm on it, and enchants an inaudible sentence. I cannot stop him, so I watch, helpless. I'm so worthless. Why does blood have to make me feel this way? How can someone like him steal my weapon right in front of me?

The door disappears into naught. Jerrick stares at me. I return his gaze. Both of us may pass out at any moment. He is so gross with his affinity to harm.

Jerrick whispers, "Come with me, and we shall discover

the fate of your parents." His words sound genuine. He seems too weak to be a threat. Besides, he still has my knife, and I'm curious what lies beyond this boring room.

He doesn't waste time to examine what's inside the dim passageway, he just dives in, and I somehow struggle to keep up with a limping man. We turn occasionally, and I make an effort to create a mental map of where we're going. He does not glance at the other paths we pass by; it's almost like he understands the layout or has an unwritten map. My only navigational tools are the lanterns that line the rocky, thin passageway, keeping everything somewhat lit. Still, even the flames reveal no end to the twists and turns. We are in a miserable, claustrophobic labyrinth.

Flicking his hand upward, Jerrick passes me my knife. The sharp object fumbles into my hand, but I catch it without cutting myself. I smile at him. His life belongs to me. Now I can get rid of him and discover the mysteries of this place alone.

"I know exactly what you're thinking, Phoenix, but there's a reason why I trust you with that weapon." Jerrick stumbles. I expect him to fall due to his leg or lack of energy, but he catches himself and continues his vigorous pace. "You are lost within this maze, and you need a guide. The artifact at the end of this tunnel also requires two people, coincidentally enough."

I snort and plan my vengeance despite his logic. He's only buying time. He cannot find excuses to save himself forever.

We continue with haste, and the air develops a foul scent. It's difficult to tell if something rotten is oozing from the walls or if an animal died further ahead. Before long, the stench becomes so nauseating, I must cover my nose with my shirt. On the other hand, Jerrick appears immune to it, probably because he is rotten himself.

We round the final bend and set foot in a grand, circular room. An excess of lanterns lines the walls, illuminating the space like a cloudless, sunny day. The middle of the chamber has a slight incline where a stone platform rests. Four identical pillars surround the platform, each being a simple stone structure.

Without concern for his safety, Jerrick proceeds toward the middle platform. I refuse to pursue any further. Something about this place is silent, unnatural, and evil.

"Stop! Look!" I yell at him, and he pauses long enough to see what I see. The platform bleeds red from the earth's bowels, and soon, the disgusting color climbs up the pillars and approaches the ground where we stand. I want to run. I've seen enough. I turn back, and the door is nowhere to be found. My heart skips a beat from the realization of my demise. Spreading until the whole ground is eclipsed in the horrific red hue, it's like we are inside the stomach of a beast. I rush to Jerrick and grab his cloak.

"What do we do? There's no way out! I thought you said you knew what was here!!" I yell at him but find subtle comfort in not dying alone.

He doesn't spare me a glance. Instead, he touches my shoulder and claims, "It's a test. It will determine who is worthy and who must die. With any luck, we shall survive and retrieve what I desire."

As if on cue, a demonic shadow rises from the middle platform. Its head is the shade of night, and its eye sockets are nothing but empty holes left to be filled. The creature opens its mouth and smiles, baring nasty sharp teeth—long and uneven. The demon's body is shapeless and thorny and extends and retracts between Jerrick's and my height. Long arms stretch from the chaotic torso of the terror and end with sizable dangly fingers.

The creature zooms toward Jerrick and me, grinning wider until its mouth touches its empty eyes. "What have we here, hmmm? Haven't seen a visitor for such a long time."

The demon's voice resonates like it is on the verge of laughter, but it has a bite on the tongue. Every word it pronounces helps me understand death, like the void is speaking to me, calling for my heart to stop. "Such a reunion with the living must be celebrated. For you two, I will call myself . . . Dureizen." It grips us in a hug, and the shadowy thorns threaten to puncture my skin.

I struggle to lift my knife in an attempt to strike the demon. Despite my efforts, my muscles refuse to obey. My arms are becoming numb and my lungs are empty. The only thing I can do is stop resisting, and let the escalating pressure of the embrace kill me. Dureizen must understand my predicament, for it releases us and lingers over me. The demon stretches until it almost touches the ceiling, thereafter angling its inordinate face close to mine. I shut my eyes and strive to quell my beating heart. My anxiety only intensifies.

"Blonde hair, hmmm, resembling light but pale in the eyes of darkness," Dureizen's voice echoes, penetrating my skull. "Brown eyes. Even though they are closed, I can see deep in your soul, a soul of putrid black and withheld love. I could make those eyes red, yes. Your skin is soft, a body that has not experienced the misgivings of life. I would even go as far as . . . saying you are the same as me—stuck in a makeshift prison for most your life. However, you have fresh blood on those clothes, the blood of another in this room."

Dureizen cocks his head like a curious bird and turns his gaze to Jerrick. I dare not look away from the demon. I can only imagine the fear my companion feels.

"Ah, you are a mischievous one indeed," the creature begins. "You are—"

"Say nothing about who I am," Jerrick declares. "Nobody can know the truth."

It emits a dark laugh and says, "Your secret is safe, lost one. One who has no home, one who has no life, one who seeks nothing but everything out of his grasp. Your life is ticking away as we speak. Why do you stand and bleed out without bandaging yourself? Do you intend on being a scarecrow eaten by the birds?"

The demon returns to the middle platform and shrinks until it is the size of us. Subsequently, one of Dureizen's hands transforms into a knife, and it cuts off a large thorn from its body. A deep crimson oozes from the shadowy wound, and Jerrick grunts with displeasure and falls to the floor.

"Behold. This is the power which you seek, hooded man called Jerrick. The power to manipulate the loss of blood to power. Check your fatal wounds."

I stare at the injuries on Jerrick's body seaming back together, and some of the blood in the dirt returns to his body. The process is sickening to watch, yet fascinating.

"Why did you heal him?" I blurt out. Since Jerrick can move and walk freely again, he will no doubt seek his revenge against me.

"Why indeed," the demon responds. "One of you will die soon anyway, and it is pointless to conduct a sacrifice when both of you intrigue me. Now, be blessed with my power!"

Dureizen picks up the severed thorn and dissolves into the air. I lose sight of the creature, although my gut warns me of approaching danger.

"Jerrick, I think we should—" Before I finish my sentence, Dureizen manifests behind him and bares his teeth. "Look out!" I scream, but it is too late. The demon stabs the thorn into his back and fades away to nothingness.

On instinct, I approach Jerrick out of concern as his mouth becomes agape with agony, yet there's no noise. I feel his heart. Everything is normal about it, and his breathing is calm. This makes me nervous. The demon must have put a curse on him. If I kill Jerrick now, maybe I can save him from the suffering, protect myself, and escape?

I thrust my knife forward, but Dureizen's long hand

appears from nothingness and grabs my wrist before it reaches its target. The rest of the demon then appears before me. It puts a finger to its lips and snickers.

"You murderous little thing you. I hope you never change." Dureizen reveals the thorn and stabs my heart. My body goes numb, and I go blind, like a dream without visions. I can only rest in this endless purgatory until my body allows me to wake.

4

Jerrick is an enigma. He's a stranger who arrives the day I'm about to leave home and encourages me to meet a powerful entity foreign to this world. Furthermore, no matter how much damage I inflicted on this man, he hasn't put a scratch on me. Who is he?

I have spent most my life secluded from others. I have done nothing except prepare to inherit my parents' role. So, what does Jerrick gain by dragging me along with him? Why did my parents care about protecting a demonic door? Did they know Dureizen was beyond it?

And what does the demon, Dureizen, want from Jerrick and me? The creature seems too powerful to need others to do its bidding, especially from people like us. Perhaps this is the adventure I've been seeking? Not like I have another option.

I awake to a sound best described as munching on rocks. My eyes shift into focus, and my mind temporarily aches while struggling to comprehend where I am. I last remember encountering Dureizen and being put into a death-like trance. Now it appears I'm back home in my prison. Sitting next to me, Jerrick is eating the last of my leftover food, stale bread.

"This isn't yours to take!" I shout and snatch the half-eaten bread away.

"I was going to buy us fresh food when you awoke, but eat the stale bread if you prefer."

My stomach growls and gnaws my body, so I bite into the teeth-breaking dough. After the sharp edges of bread slide down my throat, I ask, "What happened? How did we escape?"

Jerrick shuts his eyes, and instead of answering my question, he dares to say, "I'll tell you everything if you promise to stop torturing me with this knife."

He produces the small weapon from his gray cloak and tosses it to me like in the labyrinth. I catch it with ease. His offer is intriguing, but I still cannot trust him. Nonetheless, we have witnessed a lot today, so I guess that should count toward something.

"I will only kill you if you're plotting against me. How's that?" My answer seems to satisfy him, even if it's untrue.

"Good." He leans back, and I notice the stubble growing across his face for the first time. "Get comfortable. After this, we are leaving Dalgin."

I consume another crisp chunk of the crunchy bread and nod. There is nothing left in Dalgin for me. It will always be my home, though I see no reason to protect a demon like Dureizen. The door leading to his chamber is no more anyway. A single room is all what's left of my home.

Jerrick stops wasting my time and explains, "In Dureizen's chamber, you passed out on the floor beside me, still holding that knife. I never mentioned it before, but your blade is special. Mined and crafted from black steel, a material found in an unknown, concealed location in the world, gives the knife renown for its unique properties. A phenomenal weapon, indeed. From my understanding, your knife once belonged to the old king before he was overthrown by his brother, Enzo Malfester. Krolas Malfester was the original owner, and somehow it got passed down to you. Keep this weapon close, and do not lose it. Only royal weapons are known to be created with such fine material."

Testing the edges of the fine blade, the weapon almost penetrates my skin, even with the lightest touch. No other knife has threatened me so, considering the cooking and carving knives in shops. If what Jerrick says is true, I'm better equipped for combat than any of the knights in Lirium—where the royal family resides. I'm proud to wield such a special gift from my father. I wonder how he obtained it. There are many things I don't know about my parents, and at this point, I will never discover their secrets. They will only be known as guardians.

Jerrick continues, "Furthermore, I see hope for you, foreigner. I doubted Dureizen would allow you to live, so I brought you with me. You increased the probability of my survival. The demon killing both of us was an unlikely outcome because of its lack of visitors in years."

"So, you planned to kill me? For what? Afraid you can't take on a little girl if she challenges you?" I snap at him, my body trembling with anger.

"No, I can't take you on in a fight. We established that."

"So, I'm right about you being weak."

"NO." Jerrick clears his throat and repositions himself. I have him cornered. "You are a skilled fighter; I'll give you that. But Dureizen is understood to fancy sacrifices. We are not the first who have met this demon, Phoenix. Still, the fact that he did not kill either of us burdens me."

"I don't understand why people would want to meet Dureizen. Why did you come here?"

"Allow me to conclude my story, and you will understand." Jerrick waits until I finish the last bit of bread, then he continues his tale. "We were confined in Dureizen's chamber with no escape route. But energy flowed in my veins. I knew we got what I came here for. The demon had blessed us with its power, the power of blood magic.

"I was prepared to do what I must, so I cut myself with my blade and willed an exit to appear. Then behold, the entrance to the chamber returned, and I grabbed you and evacuated. Halfway back, I felt shaky and discovered my body would not heal its wound. Despite my newfound powers, there was an oversight I caught before it became too late: healing after using a spell. Clearing my mind and relaxing the damaged muscles was vital. Afterward, I willed my injury to mend. My body then patched itself up like Dureizen's demonstration. Blood magic is limitless and is about will and understanding, at least from what I have gathered so far.

"We soon got back here. You did not want to wake up, so I ate your leftover food. All old and disgusting, might I add. This leaves us where we are now."

My stomach is sick from acquiring this power. Blood is disgusting. I could hardly watch Jerrick bleed from his injuries. To master this magic is already impossible for someone like me.

"If other people visited in the past to meet Dureizen, where are they now?" I wonder aloud. "If we really have this demon's blessing, what are we expected to do?"

"The ones with blood magic have a purpose. A goal individuals must fulfill." Jerrick pauses, seeming to consider his upcoming words. He then sighs, "After these magic users complete their task, Dureizen extracts their power. Nonetheless, I'm just curious about where your path will lead. You're special enough to survive Dureizen's test, so now we will travel together to help achieve my purpose. Maybe you will find yours along the way, foreigner."

"And what do you plan on doing with this newfound power? Also, stop calling me foreigner. What gives you the right to call me that?" I glare at him. Helping a man like Jerrick can only mean trouble.

"I am from Lirium. Although it is a neighbor to your home, Dalgin, it is far superior than anything this town can offer. Despite this, when Enzo Malfester stole the throne and began causing havoc, I had no choice but to come here. Krolas Malfester must've been killed, and someone must rise against this tyrant."

He's from Lirium? I've only ever heard about it, but judging by what people say, it seems much grander than a small town of thirty people or so. Still, Dalgin is my hometown. I never left here. There is tranquil peace in an area like this. Well, there used to be peace. Now that Enzo's guards have arrived: higher prices, inordinate taxes, threats, and fear have made this serene setting fade. If I can help Jerrick overthrow Enzo, maybe everything can return to how it was. Perhaps I can discover what happened to my parents, and maybe I can find my purpose in life.

Jerrick's eyes loom in the darkness under his hood as I

contemplate his words. There will be no trust in this adventure to save Lirium, but I will follow him for the greater good and discover the meaning of my life.

I open my mouth to speak, but Jerrick interrupts with, "It is time to shop for supplies." He gets up, and I follow his example. "Although I can travel back home without food or water, you weighing me down will have its disadvantages. Let's be off, foreigner."

I roll my eyes and follow him outside. I will never return here until his mission is done.

5

A new adventure begins with a stranger I don't know and a power I can't use. Nonetheless, I must find my purpose.

Dalgin is a place of desolate desires:

- *The town is found in the middle of an expansive, grassy plain.*
- *The only distinctive scenery is a small forest where my underground home exists.*
- *The temperature is perfect, and it rains once or twice a week which keeps the greenery vibrant.*
- *There are about twenty-five wooden buildings—shops*

and residences—and a handful are vacant.

Everything here screams loneliness. It used to be alright, despite always being a small town. However, this town is no longer able to warrant expansion. Many new houses being built to accommodate the growing population have stopped midway due to people moving away. Others like me, sick of the small-town life, relocated to Lirium to meet new people and obtain better opportunities. They are long gone.

The ones who remain in Dalgin are content with their limited opportunities. With so few people living here, it must become boring speaking to the same shopkeeper or friend. I would disappear too if it wasn't for my duties, but now I'm free from that curse. Now I have a new plague, following Jerrick to his home in Lirium.

"Our current task is to find food and water; show me where they're at," Jerrick grumbles.

I roll my eyes. "Guess I'm going to have to get used to this attitude sooner or later."

We stop in the middle of town, and Jerrick turns to me. "I can dump you over a cliff for all I care. There is little reason why I need a small girl berating me around. Foreigner, you get back here this instant."

I walk away from him to calm my nerves. I'll leave it up

to him if he wants to follow. I couldn't care less about supporting a man like him. I can find my purpose alone.

When I'm far away from Jerrick, I sit behind one of the vacant houses. I breathe slowly, deep breath after deep breath. Closing my eyes, I consider all the changes in my life within the last few hours.

Since my parents disappeared, I was already planning on departing. Then, of course, Jerrick comes in and fights me, dragging me along with him to learn blood magic, something I have no desire to use. Now I have to travel with him? I still see little reason for teaming up. The kingdom is his problem, and though saving it and my home may be ideal, I am not above running away. Jerrick didn't have to enter my life and chain me to his passion—overthrowing corrupt kings.

A sharp object scrapes against the house with a sickening sound. It is close, about an arms-length away to my right, but I see nothing. I stare at the spot to decipher what might have generated the foreign sound. Maybe someone lives here now and hit something against the wall? But still . . .

I turn away and see a teenage boy—about my age—with dark eyes standing before me and smiling. My heart skips a beat, and my hand struggles to grab my knife.

A flash of metal near my stomach catches my eye, and I

push away from my assailant. Once there's some distance between us, I see he wields a strangely familiar black knife. I fumble through my pocket and succeed in producing my black steel knife. Somehow, our weapons are identical.

"Where did you get that?" I ask and stare at his knife. That weapon almost pierced my flesh.

The boy runs his fingers through his brown hair and plays with his weapon. "Name's Zier: descendant of a god, a nightmare among cryptic dreams, your emanant demise. In fact–" He charges at me and catches me off guard, knocking me to the ground with immense power. "You're my new target."

He ignores my question, but like Jerrick, he is no match for me. I propel myself from the dirt and rush him with lightning speed. The newcomer raises his eyebrows, and his mouth becomes agape with agony as I slash at his chest and draw blood through his black and red leather armor. He doesn't fight back. I backstep, leaving some space in case he becomes desperate. I'm sure he can't recover, but I don't want to risk it. I'm close enough to appreciate my work.

"At least Jerrick made things interesting," I mumble under my breath and focus on the anguish evident in his face. It makes it easier to not focus on his blood.

"Most people accept their fate or run . . ."

I glare at his black eyes. "Why would I run from a loser like you? You're weak, just like everyone else."

He smiles and strokes his wound. From there, he presses his hands together and pulls them apart, creating small strands of crimson liquid between his fingers. "For one hundred years, I've been ready to stop the cycle, and it will end with you."

"Phoenix! Stay away from him!" Jerrick runs toward me, his gray cloak fluttering and hampering his movement. "He's a demon! He will take everything from you!"

I'm skeptical of his belief and return to Zier. His face is foreign, striking fear in my heart, for I've seen nothing so unnatural. The whites in his eyes are pure black, staring into my soul and invading my body. His massive, awkward smile has long, sharp teeth jutting out of it in both directions. Additionally, he continues to play with his blood and cocks his head to the side. The horrific image burns into my mind.

The air grows colder, and the sky darkens. Unmoving, his body dematerializes until there's nothing left. I know he continues to watch me—wherever he is.

"Old man, you know nothing of me," Zier's triumphant voice echoes in the sky. "And Phoenix, you and I will meet again. Till then."

I shiver as my body cools from the inside out. The sun appears again, and the icy world melts into warmth. My face must show despair because Jerrick takes my hand and says, "Let us get what we need and leave. This place is no longer safe for us." Then he leads me to Dalgin's town square, where its townspeople—confusion apparent on their faces—watch us as if we have the answers to the world's darkest chill.

6

How does Jerrick know Zier's a demon? What does it mean for me? Did I fall into Zier's trap by defeating him? Zier said we will meet again, and I believe it.

Jerrick and I don't speak to each other for the remainder of our time in Dalgin. Random people try and ask us if we know anything about the weather change or the commotion when encountering Zier, and we ignore them. Despite their antagonizing, Jerrick is able to buy supplies from the shop without much issue. When they upcharge him a ridiculous amount, likely due to Enzo's takeover and influence, he pays them like money is nothing. It's clear we both want to get out of here.

I keep thinking Zier will appear before me again. If our encounter is anything like before, I can handle him without much problem. However, who knows what he has up his sleeves. For all I know, killing him will only make him reappear stronger.

With an entire pack of supplies, we depart Dalgin. I occasionally look back at my homeland. It disappears further into the horizon every time. It's surreal. Although I barely knew anyone during my time there, it feels wrong to leave it behind. That place is all I've ever known. Everything beyond is a mystery. Out in the rest of the world, a new king is drunk with control, towns and villages must be more significant and unique, plenty of new sceneries only nature itself can devise, and many creatures beyond my imagining are a few of my expectations. Meeting Dureizen and Jerrick started my journey; without them, I would be guideless in this new world.

I can think of better guides than Jerrick, though. His strange and unknown demeanor makes him arduous to admire. If he proves untrustworthy in the future or stands in my way, I won't hesitate to end his life. I'm more important than him anyway. I can defeat Enzo myself if I decide to.

Together, Jerrick and I approach a large mass of trees. I look back once more and see Dalgin is but a speck. My heart pounds with homesickness from the sight. Why can't I just forget about it and move on?

"We will stop here for the night," Jerrick states.

I stare at the darkness under his hood and try to make out his face, but I fail again. "It's not even dark yet," I tell him. Judging from the sun's position, we will have an hour before sundown. "We can keep going. It would be best to get as far away from home as possible."

My words cause my heart to sink to my stomach. I'm cautious of Zier, but I also want this homesickness to expire. Distance is the only cure I know.

Jerrick shakes his head. "No. With two people this late in the day, I will not risk us traveling through Zwelis."

"Zwelis?"

"This forest. We can make it through before dark, but it would be difficult. One slip up and we will lose our way, stuck in an ambush prone zone. I don't trust nocturnal animals. Besides, after we pass through tomorrow, we only have a few hours before we reach Lirium. I also want to discuss Zier with you. Dalgin was not the place meant for such a discussion, but here before nightfall, I can disclose all my information regarding this demon. Least be told, I was not expecting him to show up this early. Now, sit down and make yourself comfortable."

I do as he says and pull my knife from my pocket. It feels great to have something only royals have. Regardless of its use over the years, I feel the blade's edge, and it's as sharp as ever. However, Zier corrupts my image of it. Could this be the actual weapon, or does he possess it? Is Zier royalty to some extent? These questions stir in my head.

Looking up, Jerrick takes out his sword and sits across from me. He shifts around, seeming to get comfortable, then slices his hand. I jerk my head away from the sudden action but force myself to return it. In his palm, a small fire is lit. It sparks and shines with the intensity of life. The beauty enwraps my gaze, and I watch it as he sets it upon the grass between us. The fire does not spread. It stays contained like a magical orb of passion.

The fire crackles as dusk fades in, and the shadow under Jerrick's hood lengthens. The fiery magic's glow stays ever-vigorous and provides a makeshift shelter from the dark.

"Zier is a demon, that much you know," Jerrick breaks the silence. I nod and listen. "Although he is a demon, he used to be man. Dureizen found him and transformed him into what he is now."

"Who is he? Why is he considered dangerous?" Though the idea of demons is scary, he was weak to my blade . . . I think.

Jerrick pauses as if he's unsure of the answers. I can't blame him, though. Considering Dureizen and Zier's example, these creatures can be very complicated. They are capable of anything.

After a moment, he continues, "Zier's duty is to return the blessing of blood magic to Dureizen."

"Why is that so bad? It's not like I plan on using it anyway. Maybe I want him to take it."

"You will use your power, foreigner, and I will teach you. You will obtain control over your fear of blood."

"But . . . I—" How does he know I'm afraid?

"Nonetheless, if you let him take it, you may as well die where you sit. For over one hundred years, people have obtained this blessing. Likewise, when those magic users complete their duty and return their power, they vanish from the earth. They may be alive. They may be in hiding. Or the obvious answer, Zier kills them. Despite how strong blood magic is, Zier can kill anyone. He has never failed his duty."

"So, we already have a death sentence . . .?" I shiver and

move closer to the fire.

Jerrick replies soothingly, "We always have a death sentence. Nobody lives forever. We can try and escape death throughout our lives, but it will always catch up."

"Why is Zier already showing up? We just met Dureizen."

"That I do not know. Our task is to end Enzo's reign, and we have yet to enter Lirium. If I must guess, he may be targeting you as a test. You did not meet Dureizen with a complete goal in mind, right?"

I look down and sigh. "I did not." I want a new life to discover my purpose, but I doubt that's an actual goal. Not as admiring as saving a kingdom.

"I thought so. Who knows why you lived, but I'll take your assistance."

Staring behind me, I sense someone is watching, yet nobody is there. The sun is almost below the horizon now, with only a few moments of daylight left. When night arrives, Zier will observe me while cloaked in the unknown.

Jerrick chuckles, "You may be hunted down for the rest of your days, but I think you proved yourself enough for now. From my guess, Zier will not return for a while, and if he did, he might be crossing Dureizen's wishes. Besides, I will help protect you if it comes down to it."

"Well, let's talk about something else. What do you do for fun? What was your childhood like?" I don't care about his answers. I just want to get my mind off demons and magic.

"I grew up poor. Had a broken family. I learned about the world through research and schooling from educators my parents hired. Aside from those matters, some combat training and reading passed the time. Pretty boring life up till now."

I nod. "Sounds a lot like me. Just a boring life. Although, being pursued by demons isn't much of an improvement."

"Demons, and don't forget our goal of killing Enzo and curing the throne."

"I know . . . I know. It's just—"

He passes me a waterskin. I take a few gulps of the fresh water and hand it back to him. "Thank you," I state.

"We better get some shuteye. It's almost dark, and we have a long day tomorrow." He stands and examines the environment around us.

"Jerrick." A chill passes over me like the one in Dalgin. "Zier said something to me before he disappeared." The man turns to me as if waiting for an answer. "Zier said he wants to break the cycle he's in. He wants to use me for that, but I don't understand what cycle he's talking about."

Jerrick nods and says, "Do not let it consume you. You can't trust their kind. They play games to mess with others and only care for themselves."

"I know, but maybe it has something to do with me not wanting to learn magic. Maybe this information caught him off guard, and he wants to kill me quick?"

"Phoenix, stop. He is inducing fear in your head. Besides, you will learn magic whether you like it or not."

"That's to be determined. But just in case, is there something we can do to ensure he won't kill me in my sleep? I know he might not return for a while, but I'd feel safer."

"Fine, foreigner. I was already planning a precaution anyway."

He looks around again like he didn't just insult me, and the murderous rage inside me swells. How much I hate that word, foreigner. If Zier returns, I hope he kills Jerrick instead to free me of the word.

At last, Jerrick explains, "I will keep the fire burning through the night unless my wound heals itself when I'm asleep." He holds up his hand to show the small amount of blood trickling from it. I look away. "As for your demon problem, I have an idea. If you cannot handle blood, turn away."

Following his command, I stare at the ground near him. The shadows from the falling sun stretch far. Likewise, the black creatures connected to us become three times our height. These black beings are much more prominent than those from artificial light. Underground, they can never receive these dark shades unless only one lamp is lit. I focus on them as I hear Jerrick scream in pain, his shadow hunching over. It looks like he cut his arm, but I refuse to focus on my peripheral vision. Instead, his shadow shifts and expands. It then stretches and creates a sizeable barrier around us. The light from the sun fades, and my shadow brightens and reflects only on Jerrick's immense shadow.

I'm reminded of home. The fire burns ever brighter when the sun cannot reach us. Around us, the darkness is a sizable dome and continues to swirl like it has a mind of its own. The movement is disturbing. This thing is unnatural.

Jerrick grunts. Curious what caused the noise, I chance a glimpse, ignoring my better judgement. I lock eyes on the red. His arm is bleeding profusely, but his other hand hovers above the wound. His gash is shrinking, and the excess blood is returning to his body. It's sickening.

"There," he grumbles. "I have modified my shadow to

do my bidding. The concept always excited me as a boy. Now Zier will have difficulty finding us as we blend into the darkness—a darkness which acts as a barrier. Also, we can keep the fire without concern of who might see us."

"What about oxygen?" I ask.

"No different from outside. It is a shadow."

I lie down and get comfortable on the crisp grass. Having a softer bed pleases my skin, and I feel my body drifting away into sleep. As an afterthought, I comment, "Please don't tell me I'll have to hurt myself like you did. . . ever."

"You may have to one day, but if you are afraid, we will work you to it. Phoenix, I know we have an uncertain path ahead, but if we work together, our force may rival a demon's."

Sighing, I face away from him. I just want to get my mind off this subject. Maybe I'm not ready for an adventure like this. Why does magic have to involve blood? Many thoughts plague my mind and cause a headache, converting sleep into an unpleasant experience.

7

This is becoming a life I'm forced into, not the adventure I dreamed of. With my parents dead or gone, what choice do I have but to follow Jerrick around on his quest? A part of me wants to say goodbye and escape from him. Still, Zier is following me and will always do so until I die. Without Jerrick's guidance, I might die in a matter of days.

Why did Dureizen give me a power that I cannot use? This 'gift' is useless, shortening my life like a sick joke.

I awake after what feels like a few hours of rest. My head has a splitting headache, my eyelids are heavy, and I feel like I'm dreaming. All this is because he entered my home and made us meet Dureizen.

Pulling the knife from my pocket, I stare at the sleeping man. He is facing away from me, and I generate no sound as I stand and approach my prey. All I must do is kill him, and if I do, will that solve my problems? It may, especially if I refuse to use magic. Perhaps I can negotiate with Zier to leave me alone? Although, a deal with a demon never ends well, but it may be worth a shot.

I raise my knife and freeze as he turns around and stares back at me with dim, cold eyes. He shakes his head in disapproval.

"Phoenix," he starts, "I wonder about you sometimes."

I grit my teeth and drop to the ground next to him. Why can't I just do it? I accept every opportunity, and I still fail to do it.

He continues, "How are you feeling? I believe you have undergone a ton of stress now that I consider it, and I want to see if there's anything I can do to help you."

Still watching him like a wolf, my eyes shift into a glare. "Unless you can get rid of this migraine you caused, you can do nothing for me."

"Well, let me see." He gets up and rests a hand on my forehead. Before I can question his intentions, my headache fades until it's just an irritating memory. "How's that? Not sure if it did anything, but I thought to try it."

I blink a few times from the abnormal feeling of pain being sucked away in seconds. "I feel better. Thank you."

"Don't mention it. As I said, we will start small for you, and perhaps you can cure your own headaches by the end of the day. We begin your training today."

"Today!?" I shake my head, and my stomach churns. "I'm not ready to harm myself. I never will."

He grunts and punctures his bloody finger deeper with his fingernail, and the shadows surrounding us vanish into his body. The sunlight burns my eyes, and I must shield them from it. A few seconds later, I notice his other hand touches his bloody finger and palm, and his wounds fade to nothing. The fire also reduces into an ember and eventually gives up on survival.

Smiling under his hood—no doubt proud of his accomplishment and superiority over me—he boasts, "Just like that, Phoenix, the wound can last as long as you wish. But since you are so afraid to begin, let us move on. We do not have all day."

We eat a small meal of Dalgin apples and drink water to wash it down. Afterward, he stands up, and I mimic his action.

He leads the way into Zwelis, and I follow close behind.

Everything is wrapped in shadows as we enter the forest. The plants only reach our knees while the trees tower over us—multiplying the further we progress. Dead branches break under the weight of our boots. The clamorous birds scream louder with every step we take. Woodpeckers hammer on trees, and I wonder if they will succeed in tearing one in half. The leaves rustle above us, something scurries away, and the faint, resonating flow of water overbears every annoying creature the closer we get. This place is wildlife's best friend. No people, a playground for animals, and an environment where food, water, and shelter are a walk away. It's noisier than Dalgin, but I can get used to this.

We approach a small river. An overhang of rocks in the stream causes the water to plunge and create ripples. The current is slow, so it should be passable without much issue. Nonetheless, Jerrick holds up a hand to stop me.

"Observe," he says. I expect him to say more, but no more words follow.

Examining the water's edge, I try to notice anything unusual. When there's not, I seek out some fish in the prominent blue. There is none. There's nothing here in this barren river besides rocks. I understand I've not seen my fair share of nature while dwelling in a cave for most my life, but nothing is out of the ordinary. Nevertheless, watching the water move in strange and beautiful ways is captivating. It calms my nerves.

After a moment longer, I stare at him, evident confusion touching my face. "What is there to see?" I ask, forcing my uncertainty to affect my tone.

He sighs, "You're something else, foreigner. I am assuming you only considered how nice the river looks."

"No."

He looks at me and strives to test me by asking, "Well, what did you find?"

I hesitate and examine the water again. "Animals come here to drink?"

"And?" he pushes further. When I don't respond within the first two seconds, he adds, "How are we going to cross this stream?"

"By walking through it." I wait a moment to see if my answer is correct, yet he doesn't respond. "We will walk through it and not fall. Also, we will try not to get very wet."

He sighs at me once again and shakes his head. "What can we manipulate with magic to make this process easier?"

"Anything we want depending on how much blood we lose?"

"Yes and no. After studying magic for years before visiting Dalgin, I have learned the ins and outs and the dos and don'ts of its nature."

"And where did you learn them? Surely they are not lying around for anyone to read," I challenge. I catch him off guard as he looks away. It feels great to get back at him for asking me a trick question only he knows. As he stays silent, I ask, "Why did you learn about all this anyway? Preparing for some apocalypse? You mustn't have known about Enzo's takeover beforehand."

"Enough, Phoenix. If you require an answer, the kingdom of Lirium had suspicions about Enzo well before your time. As for where I learned all this, it was at the library in the castle."

I smirk. "You must have been a servant before Enzo took power. No doubt made only a couple coins judging by your clothes."

"Hmph. Let's return to business and not discuss Jerrick's deep dark past."

I got him good. Vengeance is mine for all those times he's called me foreigner.

"As for crossing this river and trying to make the process easier, nothing can be done," he continues his speech and attempts to ignore my ever-present smile. "Definite rules in magic make certain things like this impossible."

"Like what?" He really did ask me a trick question.

"Blood magic cannot affect existing nature unless it is a living organism. Furthermore, you can create nonliving things to some extent, such as fire or earth, but it takes a lot of practice and can backfire easily. Producing objects is usually not worth the risk as it requires a lot of energy—also known as blood and focus. If it did come down to it and you wanted to learn how to replicate an element, understand all elements of nature are difficult to materialize."

"But I saw you make a fire yesterday! You can't tell me how risky it is and barely bleed a drop! Besides, it was our first day with the power."

"Are you done?" Jerrick questions. I quiet down and wait for more blatant lies, but I'm curious what more he has to teach. "The fire I formed last night was a product of experimentation. I understood how difficult it would be from my readings, and with the bit of blood I spent, I could only produce a flame small enough to fit my palm. I could keep it energized because I have trained all my life to focus on specific tasks and not sway from them and become distracted. Even conversing while letting the fire continue is no burden for me.

But conceptualize this: creating a pebble compared to a boulder is a whole new concept.

"Also, if you paid attention, I manipulated my shadow to become an obedient being. Since it is connected to me, a living thing, I can utilize it. Doing something like this took a lot of blood and focus, but I will never have to do it again. Of course, it will only move once I spend blood—only a trickle compared to its original summoning. Nonetheless, I do not have a shadow at this time."

"Fine, fine." I roll my eyes and confirm there is no shadow with him, despite the many trees blocking where it should be. I stare at the darkness under his gray hood. "I have one question about magic if I am to learn it. How do you heal yourself?"

"An actual good question for once. You can heal yourself or another with any blood loss, even if that blood was initially used for another spell. This means you can heal any wound with the same blood you spill. What helps me is placing a hand over my injury and focusing on the process."

I nod and observe the stream again, taking in all the information I just learned. From what he tells me, I can do and create anything I want with my power, aside from tampering with the world around us. Living creatures are an exception, supposedly, but I wonder if we can't harm or affect them directly. However, healing magic would not make sense then; Jerrick's shadow also proves we can manipulate ourselves and others.

"So, what about the living? Can we afflict magic on them?" I ask since he seems to know all the answers.

"Why do you ask? Want to kill all the animals and me?"

Anger boils inside me until I see a smile under his hood. It's a joke. I take a deep breath and answer, "If we are to confront Enzo, I want to know how difficult killing him will be."

"Difficult enough. Enzo's a trickster who should not be overestimated. If he can take over a kingdom and influence others to join him, we are not in for an easy battle. Blood magic has its limitations."

He shuffles down into the stream like a happy, young boy, then takes his time to find his footing. Once standing in the water—only reaching up to his knees—he looks back and tells me what I dread: "We are going to get a little wet. No use wasting magic here. There's much more for you to learn up ahead."

Reluctant, I follow him, careful not to fall face-first into the water. He will answer my question later.

8

Jerrick expects me to learn magic, probably so I can help him achieve his goal, but what about mine? Still, sorcery is enticing, and I suppose I can fend off Zier with it. What other choice do I have? Living a short life isn't ideal.

We succeed in crossing the river. My chest down to my feet are soaked. Jerrick claims they will dry as we walk, so I continue to accompany him and struggle to ignore the irritating sensation.

Deep in Zwelis, the trees are much thicker and seem to span for miles. Huge bushes and tall grass tower over me alongside our path. The animals are monsters here; the endless cacophony of birds, squirrels, and other animals scurrying around is a bit much for me. I can shut it out enough to where it isn't too bothersome, but sleeping here may actually be a nightmare.

We arrive in a spot where the trees design a near-perfect circle around us. The grass here rises to our knees. This patch of land seems like an excellent site to build a new home—but who wants to live here with all this noise? Furthermore, traveling to town for supplies would be a nightmare.

Jerrick holds his hand up, and I stop.

"Time for another lesson, I suppose?" I ask.

"Yes. What do you think magic can achieve in a location like this?"

"Nope, not playing this game again, old man. Just tell me whatever you want so we can move on. Like you said, we don't have all day."

He purses his lips and shakes his head. "Fine," a tinge of annoyance clings to his voice. "But this is where I need your assistance."

I frown at the word 'assistance.' It's clear anything he wants from me must require cutting. Still, I'm unsure if I'm ready to use spells, but I'll at least listen to what he has to say.

"Concerning your question about using magic on the living, any spell is technically possible." I'm happy he confirms this, finally. "In fact, despite the limitations of not using elements that already exist in nature, we can accomplish much with blood magic. Every one of us magicians have a specific power linked to us. The official term is called link magic. This ability will always be advantageous in battle, regardless of the situation. Observe."

Jerrick releases his sword from the scabbard resting on his hip. The weapon is stained with a bit of blood from previous magic uses. If his blade is already decorated like that, I can't imagine how it will look after a week.

Slicing his arm, he raises his wound toward the sky. Without delay, his hand glows, and a reddish flash—almost like lightning—shoots out of it. The spell travels in zigzags high into the air. It must fly well above the trees before fading away to nothingness.

He holds his mouth open like he's astonished of his achievement, and I realize I'm doing the same. We shut our mouths simultaneously, and he sheaths his weapon and heals his wound. Overall, I think I'm starting to get over the nauseous feeling of watching him partake in magic, especially considering its limitless capabilities.

Then he declares, "Well, Phoenix, now it's your turn. When you use your magic, bring to mind everything about who you are. Adjust those thoughts into strength."

Never mind, I don't think I can get over blood. My face feels hot, and my body shakes. "I don't want to," I stammer.

He moves closer to me and drops down on one knee. "I need you to do this. If you cannot, you are useless to me."

"Then so be it."

"Phoenix, you must. I need to see what kind of magic your body uses so we can advance. If you fail to get over yourself, you are dead weight to me."

I open my mouth to object, then I realize if I don't travel with him, I'll be in more danger in regards to Zier. Without Jerrick, there's no way I can find my purpose anytime soon.

Grasping my black steel knife, I examine its clean-cut edge and swallow hard. This weapon will cut into my skin on my own accord. The blood I will lose will cause me to vomit. Still, I shove those thoughts away and bring the blade closer to my arm.

"Remember," Jerrick's words halt my progress, my knife-hand shaking violently above my arm, "you can heal yourself after you display your link magic. When you do, clear your mind and concentrate on the recovery process. Now do it!"

My knife presses against my skin, and the smallest amount of red liquid leaks out of me. I want to faint. Nonetheless, I raise my hand to the sky, mix-match my emotions, and visualize my vigor detaching itself from me. Understanding myself and my past manifests an awkward feeling, disturbing imagery, and potent rage within. Detaching from others while people formed friendships, working with my parents to protect their . . . questionable duty. Training, being afraid, uncertain of my goals, not sure what has become of my parents, how I may or may not be glad they're gone, what Dureizen and Zier see in me. I try not to get sick from blood loss, so I strain my eyes and focus on my hand and the bright sky which will witness my sorcery. My heart beats harder, and I feel intense might overflowing within me, and I release it all with one massive burst of anguish.

A small mass of purple-blackness releases itself from my palm. Instead of shooting into the sky, it sinks like a waterfall before me.

"What was that?" Jerrick's voice sounds condescending.

My failure leaves me miserable. After dumping all my emotions, feelings, and memories into this spell, I only get a wimpy, blackish waterfall. How useful is that? It probably doesn't do anything. Besides, this 'attack' requires too much time to devise. I must also be within striking distance to use it. Never going to be practical.

"Why can't it be as good as yours!" I shout and scowl. "Your link magic can actually be used in combat. You're telling me mine is much weaker than yours!? I'm stronger and better than some servant from the castle. Challenge me any day, and I will always win."

I stomp away from that fool and wipe the wetness from my eyes. "What has anyone ever seen in me anyway? My parents only raised me to take their place and protect a blood demon."

He follows and stands behind me. "You are a curious case indeed, foreigner. In my knowledge of history, nobody has ever had a power such as yours. For some reason, Dureizen thought it was ideal to grant you his blessing. Do you have any idea why?"

"Just to make me suffer and find a nonexistent purpose."

"Dureizen does not function like that. No, you are unique, and I wonder what you will become. Perhaps your magic has a unique property when used on the living?"

He gives me time to reflect, and I inspect my knife. Over the course of its use, there's no blood stains on it. The color gleams a perfect black. It must be because of the material it's made with. Still, this feature means nothing for me, someone with no actual powers.

Putting away my weapon, I move my hand to my bleeding arm and focus on recovering my skin. I do my best to relax my body. Deep breath after deep breath, the horrible feelings and intrusive thoughts rid themselves of me, and my mind becomes clear. I concentrate on the recovery process, a seamless action judging by Jerrick's demonstration, and yet, nothing happens.

"Do not worry about healing now," he disrupts my thoughts. "You are still bleeding, and I want you to try something." I turn around and see he's pointing at a tree. "There is a stick bug I want you to demonstrate your link magic on. Remember, concentrate on yourself and everything about you, and then shift those feelings into a spell. Go ahead, move."

I obey his command and approach the tree, locating the hidden bug after some searching. I focus on my past, my current situation, and who I am, and I feel sick from it like before. Then, I hover my hand above the stick bug, and an insignificant portion of purple-blackness leaks out of my palm again. The instant the spell connects with the bug, it dies and falls to the ground. My lips twitch into a smile.

Jerrick frowns. "Could it be that your magic is some form of death? If it is so, remind me to never get close to you. Except—"

"Except what?"

"Look."

I search for the bug hiding within the grass it landed in. All my darkness has dissipated, making it easier to find the results of my spell. Magic probably dissolves after a few seconds, which is good to know. Nonetheless, there's no bug to be found. Could my death spell destroy beings and—oh no.

The stick bug stumbles along the grass like a drunk returning home—in this case, the tree. I grit my teeth in frustration.

"Pathetic." Jerrick shakes his head at me. "Truly pathetic. Perhaps we can still utilize your magic, but as it stands, your abilities are too unorthodox compared to mine. Trying to teach you is going to be a miserable task. So, we will have to experiment with what works best for you. There may be loopholes which can increase your usefulness in combat."

"Fine, whatever. Let's get moving."

"Not yet."

I glare at him with all the rage I can muster. "And why not? So I can practice here and fail forever? So I can feel more inferior about myself? I won't amuse you."

"I don't care about what your feelings are on the subject. There are a few things I need to tell you before we move on. But first, please heal yourself so you can stop bleeding, Ms. I Fear Blood."

Out of my frustration, I forgot that I'm still cut. Maybe anger can allow me to use blood magic easier? I hope this works. I touch my arm and focus on healing, clearing my mind. Still, nothing happens.

"What am I doing wrong?" I ask.

"Keep trying. Make sure you clear your mind."

"I already did, and nothing's working."

"Try harder. It's not difficult, Phoenix."

"Then you do it if it's so easy. Healing is impossible."

He nicks his finger with his thumb and lays a hand on my injury. My arm feels ticklish as it patches itself up, and when he uncovers it, no mark is left behind. As to prove a point, he heals himself afterward without needing a second cut.

Jerrick frowns under his hood and comments, "You really are useless."

"Shut up. I'll figure out how to heal soon." I doubt I will, but I want him off my back. "What are we doing now?"

"As we stand, we are approximately halfway through

Zwelis. When we arrive in Lirium, we will only depart the kingdom once our mission is complete. As for now, the best time to teach you the rules of magic is here, outside. Does that sound fair to you?"

"Go on. I'm ready for another spiel." I sit and relax after all this traveling.

"Good. You know we can use spells on living creatures. Furthermore, you can also affect someone directly without using your wimpy powers."

"Really?" I perk my head up with newfound interest.

He continues, "The link magic within you and I is our basic spell. Additionally, sorcery has minimal limitations after you understand the rules. You come to realize you can tamper with anybody you see. With enough blood loss, you can tear off somebody's skin or inflict a curse of some sort—like a disease. In fact, the more blood you lose, the more potential and control you have, and your enemy will fatigue themselves trying to dodge your attack. If your will does not falter and your mind is clear, the sky is the limit. That being said, do not overdo it and kill yourself.

"As we can affect animals and creatures directly without our basic spells, it is easier to influence visible objects. I can heal you without much issue because of this, especially when

I am close. Although, it is difficult to use spells on fish underwater or worms underground. The same goes for stopping somebody's heart since we cannot see it. The feat is possible only if you take the risk and can perfectly imagine your target. For now, let us avoid anything too advanced."

I consider what he says and wonder about my parents. "Can we bring back the dead? They are close to the living." My heart hurts as I can already guess the answer, but I want to hear a confirmation.

Jerrick shakes his head. "No, Phoenix. Even though they were once alive, no record exists of anyone reviving the dead. Once something dies, they become an inanimate object. I'm sorry."

Nodding, I ask, "Are there any other rules to magic? You said there weren't many limitations, and I'm starting to believe that's a lie."

"There are no more rules. Now it comes to practice and trial and error with our skills. I must test my capabilities and enhance my skills in combat. You must learn how to turn your spells into something useful which cooperates with your battle style. Somehow."

Before I can ask any more questions or force Jerrick to spill secrets on how to become a proficient spellcaster, he starts walking away from me. His pace is brisk like he's chasing someone. Could it be Zier? Why would he want to follow him? I stand and try catching up to Jerrick as he disappears into the depths of the forest. The tremendous amount of bushes and trees block my field of view, but I follow the discernable rustling noise and catch sight of his gray cloak. When I finally approach, he shifts into a run, faster than any old man I've ever seen.

"Hey, wait!" I yell after him, but he ignores me and breaks into a sprint.

Why in the world is he running away? I'm beginning to believe this has nothing to do with Zier. Is it possible Jerrick's trying to get rid of me after acknowledging my lack of skill?

My legs ache from the uneven ground. Constantly shifting my footing isn't ideal, but I must do so to avoid tripping. I can barely keep Jerrick in sight as he dashes past the vegetation. Maybe he wants me to use magic to catch up? Still, that may not be possible unless I can use a spell to influence my ability. Since I'm a living being I can see, I say it's worth a shot.

I seize my knife and hold it next to my arm. Letting the blade hover above my skin is difficult while running and dodging everything blocking my way. I don't want to accidentally nick myself. I don't want to do this, but I will if I must. Like he said, I need to get over my fear someday.

Cutting a tiny sliver of skin, I use the blood oozing from the scratch and focus on my body. I imagine my skin transforming into an unstoppable force. Anything in my way will not hinder me, and I will acquire speed because of it. I must catch him.

My body savors the developing, unnatural sensation shielding my skin. I'm revamping my being into something superior. I feel light as a bird, invisible armor protects me and doesn't hinder my movement, and from my perception, I can smash my way through any hazards blocking my path—except trees, of course. Gaining speed, I squint my eyes as I dash through a bush as large as me. I expect to crash into its thorns and thick branches, but when I pass through, I feel ticklish like feathers are brushing against my body. Afterward, I find that I'm only inches away from Jerrick, so I prepare to ram him.

This is what you get for forming dreadful emotions inside me. I release the air deep within my lungs with so much force, my voice cracks as I yell and tackle Jerrick. I knock him down, and we land in a large forest clearing about two-hundred feet in diameter. He groans, and my mission is complete.

I grin and take many deep breaths to bring back oxygen into my lungs. "Let that . . . be a lesson I'm not as useless as you believe. Bet you can't do that!"

We both get up, and he looks at my wound. Then he responds, "As I'm impressed, you still can't heal yourself, can you?"

Since the speed and strength magic works on me, I have broken the barrier locking away my healing spell. My hand covers my arm, and I imagine my skin weaving together and the blood returning to my body. It feels tingly, like when Jerrick healed me. After the sensation dulls, I remove my hand, but the bloody injury remains.

"It's not possible," my voice quivers. "Why can't I heal my wounds?"

9

Is there a trick to healing that he's not telling me? I know it's not as simple as he makes it out to be. If I must use this power, is there a way to avoid healing myself? Now I just sound absurd.

"So, you're saying you can use magic to enhance your body, but you cannot do the easiest spell in the world?" Jerrick growls. "I should not have expected anything more. After discovering your common spells were useless, I should have left you behind. I do not need an incompetent distraction."

"I'm just as annoyed as you! I don't understand what I'm

doing wrong! What if you just heal me after I use spells?" I suggest.

"And distract me even more? I will have to check on you every second to see if you are bleeding out."

"Then I won't use it. I'm a good enough fighter as is."

"I—"

I step closer to him and rest my knife under his chin. "Well?"

Jerrick turns away like he doesn't care about my perfect reasoning. Who needs magic when you can out-skill everyone else? He only needs it because he's weak.

He looks at me after walking halfway across the forest clearing, then presents his empty hands like he's sick of arguing. "You are lucky Enzo does not have Dureizen's blessing," he remarks. "History claims that two spellcasters have never challenged one another in a duel. The results may be catastrophic. Nonetheless, today will mark the first encounter."

"What are you talking about? Want to fight me again and lose?"

"No, Phoenix, I am saying this is your final chance at redemption. If you defeat me, we travel together. We will take on Enzo, and I will have you become my apprentice so you can learn how to heal and use magic proficiently. If I win, I'm leaving you to rot, and you can deal with Zier yourself. This is your last chance to prove you are worth my time."

I accidently swallow some air, and my saliva grinds down my throat until it reaches my stomach. Whatever happens here determines my future. If I lose, I will be free from Jerrick, live my life, and travel where I desire. But this outcome means Zier will capture me sooner than later. If I win, I will continue to follow Jerrick, and I can learn more about the world, become proficient in spellcasting, and find my purpose along the way. Perhaps he can teach me how to hide from Zier with a shadow too, so I can search for my parents without being hunted?

"Are you ready, Phoenix?" Jerrick shouts so loud to where the birds fly out of the trees. Everything in the forest heard him.

I clear my head and know what I must do. "Yes," I tell him, "I'm as ready as I'll ever be."

"Wrong. Can you tell me the rules of magic once more?"

Taken aback by his sudden question, I stammer, "Well . . . I know how to use link magic and manipulation . . . and we can't use spells that affect nature which already exists."

He rests his hand on his forehead, and I wonder if I said

something wrong.

"Phoenix, let me go over the seven guidelines again. Pay attention:

"Someone cannot affect existing nature unless it is a living organism.

"Reviving the dead is impossible, for they are unliving.

"You can kill people directly only if your will is strong and can envision your target.

"Unlike fish underwater or worms underground, it is easier to affect things you can see. Also, it is challenging to stop somebody's heart because it is hidden.

"You can create elements to some extent, but the skill takes practice and can backfire, so it is usually not worth the risk as it requires a lot of energy. Working with nature of any form is tricky whichever way you want to look at it. However, there are some rule breakers, like nature connected to a living thing—such as my shadow.

"The more blood you lose means greater control and capability, as long as your mind is clear and your will does not falter.

"You can heal yourself, or another, with any blood lost. Even if the blood was used for another spell, it could be used again to recover.

"I trust you will take this lesson to heart. These are rules we all abide by as magicians, and reckless acts can lead to severe consequences. Any questions before we begin?"

I take a deep breath and calm my nerves to the best of my ability. I feel as if my magic flows better this way, and I don't want Jerrick to see how tense I am. Shaking my head, I prepare my weapon and charge at him, ready to dodge his foreseeable attacks.

"Then let us begin," he declares. He pulls out his blade and makes the first cut.

10

Running away is not an option. It's time to show Jerrick he was wrong to judge me.

As I expect, a bolt of red lightning flashes toward me, and I dodge out of the way and continue sprinting. A small amount of blood drips from Jerrick's arm, but I can care less about that now. I'm stronger than blood.

I reach him and slash his chest. At the last moment, his arm blocks the blow, and my blade does not puncture his skin. I'm in awe until I see more blood trickling down his other arm. He must've made the injury last second. Switching my tactics,

I release my blade and drop below his knees, then I grab my knife and swipe at his legs. This time I succeed in making him bleed. Still, I'm sure he can recover from any attack.

Jerrick's growl of displeasure echoes through the forest clearing as he falls. He then reaches out and grabs my wrist. Before I can react, a strong force knocks me away from his grip, and I fly high into the air. I'm in no pain from the blow, but I soon find myself free-falling in the sky—about thirty-feet high. I may die when I hit the ground.

Through my panic, I slice a portion of my arm and plead for a soft landing, focusing mostly on my legs. I just hope it works. My feet hit the ground with a thud. My legs rattle from the impact. There is a bit of pain, but it's fine. I can still stand.

"You are reckless, Phoenix," Jerrick calls to me. "To save yourself, you need to make a significant cut. A small one will not always save your life."

I check my arm and realize he's right; my cut is no more than an inch wide. The force of the fall might've been too much for a small scratch to handle.

Looking up, it seems he had cured his wounds while I was in the air. It's a clever tactic, but still annoying to deal with. This is a losing battle if he continues to heal when I can't.

"However, the blood you spill is enough to test something

out," Jerrick acknowledges. "Seeing as we are the first magicians to battle against one another, I want you to try deflecting my link magic with a new, same-size cut."

"I'm not going to participate in your stupid games. You just want to hurt me."

"If you do not deflect my magic, you are not coming with me to the castle."

I growl at him. Of course, he must make up some stupid rules along the way. "Fine. What do I need to do?"

"Considering my magic is part of a living thing—that being me—then another magician has the potential to manipulate and shift my spells how they desire. It should not require much blood, as you are not creating anything, just redirecting it."

Before I can argue with his logic, red lightning flickers through the empty space between us and barely misses me. So much for playing fair. I look at him and see no blood loss on his part, perhaps he sliced his finger or another spot I can't see from this distance. It seems like he can always use spells easily while I struggle to do anything.

"C'mon Phoenix, just try and catch it!" he playfully yells. He is going to get it after I entertain his little magic trick.

He holds his hand out again, and I'm ready this time. I make a small slit on my arm, next to my other wound, and I reach out to prepare to catch his spell. I use all the memories of Jerrick and everything I know about his secretive self to try and understand his unique qualities. The most prominent concepts I understand about him is that he's quirky and determined, perhaps leading to the chaotic nature of his lightning. I realize it's not much to go from. All I must do is hope for the best.

The attack he launches at me is swift. I must determine where it may end up. Meanwhile, I imagine the spell being escorted toward my hand, and before I know it, the red lightning strikes my palm and tangles itself in a self-contained ball. The makeshift sphere stirs with demonic aggression, and I struggle to contain it. In seconds, the energy whisks away into nothing. No trace is left behind, and I slump my shoulders and breathe slow.

"Good job," he nods and gives his approval. "This shows it is possible to exploit other people's magic. Redirect it toward me this time."

"I have to do it again?" I ask with evident annoyance. He pays no mind to me and launches another attack, and I have just enough time to shift my thoughts to him.

Like before, I catch his spell, which swirls with uncanny determination. Considering my last attempt, this energy will disappear if I hold it for too long, so I struggle against the weight in my hands and outstretch my arms toward Jerrick. I think about the attack returning to him in the same aggressive manner. I imagine this awful man receiving a taste of his own power.

The spell leaves me with immense force, causing me to stumble backward to keep my balance, and it tears through the air with incredible speed and ferocity. Jerrick drops to the ground to avoid the spell, and the attack disappears before reaching the trees.

"Why did you dodge it!" I yell at him. I'm sick of his games. Still, it's nice to know how to deflect spells to some extent—even though the trick is useless in real battles.

"Can't have you defeating me too easily, especially during a test. Now you know more combat techniques aside from your pathetic spells." Jerrick stands. There is a slight movement from his hand, and I prepare for whatever trick he has up his sleeve by slicing a bit of my arm. If I keep the injuries close together, it may lesson my fatigue. Rather not die from blood loss and lose this battle.

A strange blackness molds beneath him. It grows and shifts as it expands across the grass like a storm cloud's shadow.

"I knew it," I mutter under my breath. His shadow stretches across half the clearing, and as if the ground cannot withstand such a great mass, the darkness ejects off the grass and towers over Jerrick. I have just enough time to dodge out of the way as it lunges toward me like a wild animal. I trip and fall, and I bruise my arms from the impact. The darkness swirls just overhead, and I'm glad I wasn't standing a second longer.

"You are a formidable opponent, Phoenix," Jerrick says as his shadow returns to him. "So far, you have exceeded my expectations, but you have so much to learn before you can match up to me."

His shadow, albeit larger than life, mimics Jerrick's physical details:

- The hood covers its face with an over-layering darkness.

- Small protrusions from under its nose and down to its chin recreate stubble.

- Its cloak travels down to its legs.

- Ankle-high boots give the shadow a strange lower mass.

- The figure is skinny on the exposed parts of its skin—forearms in particular.

I never gave much attention to his attire because it's so plain. Nonetheless, seeing it on a shadow is surreal. Darkness is not supposed to have features.

The strange mass lunges at me again. Using my blood, I use the same technique from when I ran in the forest, and my feet feel lighter, and my body becomes indestructible. I dash around the shadow, and it fails to catch me by a long shot. If I can approach Jerrick before his companion returns, I can end this battle here and now.

I push myself to my limit and sprint toward the man—who's moving his hands as if calling his ally back. He's too slow. My blade, quick to strike with inhuman speed, screeches with the intensity of steel on steel. He parries it and leaves me off balance. Something grabs my leg and forces me into the air, likely his shadow, and I panic and cut a large portion of my arm. My body is numb from the gash, but I can't let it end here.

With all my strength, I let the flurry of magical energy overtake me. I shall fight his ego and confidence with my willpower. All this time, all my life, will not be for nothing. I'm alone, and unless I can do something to change my path, I will forever be a nobody.

Dark powder puffs out of my body and surrounds me,

trickling toward the ground where Jerrick stands. He laughs, and my hands ball into fists after hearing his mockery. However, the laughter dies, and he seems to lose interest in me. His shadow melts back into him, and I fall. My bloody arm hits the ground first, radiating so much pain that I scream. He does not seem to care.

I nurse my arm and stand up. The dark powder still surrounds us, but it's fading fast. No idea what Jerrick's doing, but a victory is a victory, and I will make him pay for everything.

He stares in my direction, perhaps he is looking at me from under his dark hood, and I sink my knife into his stomach. I am ready for retaliation, for him to kick me back and cast another spell, but he just stands there and slumps his head toward the wound. Releasing my knife, I keep it inside him as a reminder that I'm the victor—whenever he comes around. Maybe he realizes how pointless this battle is.

"Brother I . . ." he speaks. I watch him, unsure of what he's playing at. "I'm sorry. Father too. I should have known and done something sooner. Perhaps talk to him."

The black powder disperses into nothingness, and I snap my fingers at him. "Hey, what are you talking about?" I question.

He shakes his head and says, "I don't know. I feel uncertain about myself like a wave crashed into me and made me feel so. You think your magic did this?"

"I don't know."

"If it did, your link magic is weak but has a strong affinity to emotions. Spells like this are unheard of but can be useful, I'm sure. Just as you won our battle, I lost sight of myself."

The excitement from not having a useless power roars within me, but it's impossible to focus and celebrate with my arm bleeding so profusely. I point at it, and he runs his hands across it and begins healing it for me—the knife still inside him.

"Perhaps I have been too rude, Phoenix. I'm sorry. Like you, I have nothing left; my only purpose is to cure the throne of the evil which has taken it. I know you are missing your parents and have never had much of a life before, but I'll help you build a brighter future after Enzo is gone. We can do whatever you want. We can escape Zier and . . ."

"We'll see," I interrupt. "After what you put me through and the secrets you're hiding, I'm unsure if I want to travel with you after I find my purpose."

"Fair enough, but the offer is on the table. You are strong enough to follow me if you please." He finishes healing my arm until it feels as good as new.

He grimaces as I pull my knife out of him. "That's revenge, and now that we're even, I'll follow you at least until Enzo's gone. He's causing too many problems for me to live peacefully. Maybe I'll even stick around if you tell me everything you've been keeping secret. I want to know about my parents, my knife and how my father may have gotten it, who you are, and what you're hiding under that hood."

He heals himself much faster than healing me, then offers, "I can do all that back in Lirium, maybe once my mind is clear when Enzo's dead, but I can also teach you more about our newfound skills. You know the basics, and though I cannot help you with your linked darkness spell, at least I can try to understand its properties and determine how we can use it in combat. Nonetheless, you already seem to be on your way, morphing a useless spell into a powder. It just cost you a lot of blood."

"I'm done with harming myself for a while, thank you. How much longer until we are out of Zwelis?"

"Just another mile or two, then a short walk to Lirium."

"Do you have a place where we can stay? Surely, Lirium is crowded with guards who don't want people assassinating their king. Or were you planning on marching to Enzo the moment we arrive?"

"I have a makeshift residence, and we can go over plans once we get there. Until then, let's take the rest of this journey easy. Thanks to you, I have a lot to consider before we arrive."

I nod and notice his shadow is still gone. I don't think I killed it, but it must stay within Jerrick until he summons it again. Suppose I decide to travel on my own after saving Lirium from tyranny. If so, I must learn how to manipulate my shadow to protect me.

Before I can ask about the process, he turns away and gestures for me to follow. I do so, and we exit the forest clearing. After all this, I will better understand my future, and knowing this simple fact causes me to expose a brief smile.

11

What can I expect when we arrive in Lirium? I've heard stories of a magnificent castle with regal leadership. A city where everyone prospers behind the protection of the outer walls. A beautiful landscape where the sun shines, revealing a warm, pleasant atmosphere.

I've always imagined visiting Lirium. The details sound so perfect, and though I've heard rumors about Enzo's reign destroying its beauty, I cannot imagine all the kingdom's pride turning to dust within a week or two.

We exit the forest and step onto an expansive, grassy plain. The hills roll across the landscape, and no trees exist from this point—a welcome change from the last few hours. The sunlight warms my face and arms. The air is so fresh, and I'm ready to begin my life anew.

Never traveling outside of Dalgin has hindered my chances of exploration, not to mention my parents never let me leave. Seeing this landscape, I can see why they left Dalgin—if not only for supplies—and catch a glimpse of the outside world. If they are still alive, despite Jerrick's assumptions, they may have forgotten me and gone to live the rest of their lives elsewhere. The idea makes me angry. How can they forget about their only daughter?

Off in the distance, about three-hundred meters away, a large structure reminiscent of Lirium's description basks in the world's glory. Many stone towers reach high into the sky like they are striving to grasp the sun. All these structures connect to a large base with strong fortifications: high walls, knights patrolling the balconies, and ballistae ready to stop those who desire an invasion. There's also a drawbridge allowing access to the city surrounding the castle. I'm glad so many people recount their tales about Lirium, for if they didn't reveal information on its defenses, I might've pushed the idea of marching our way to Enzo and defeating him on his throne, an idea Jerrick would laugh at.

The castle and the city below must fabricate the entirety of Lirium. Many dirt roads branch out from the kingdom, which must lead to other residences, but perhaps Jerrick's right. There's no way another location can live up to such grand expectations. Here is the kingdom of the world.

A multitude of knights in shining white armor travel on the roads. Their armor reflects the sun's rays with enough potential to cause blindness. They all have wagons led by muscular horses, though some are leaving the city instead of arriving. I'm curious as to why no travelers are using these roads, and I believe we might stick out like a newcomer in a small town. One, we don't have a wagon. Two, we're not knights. Perhaps it's a coincidence? It may be the time of day?

"This kingdom used to be so much more," Jerrick breaks the silence.

"How so?"

"Our knights never left the castle unless we were threatened or in war. Now they are the only ones who leave and enter Lirium. Travelers and merchants are not welcome, and those who try to escape are captured and imprisoned, damaging trade and morale. Also, from this distance, we should overhear a faint sound of chatter and the daily activities of workers, but I discern nothing. Something has happened to the people here, where seldom few do their required jobs and instead mope around and lie in misery. It's a phenomenon I do not understand. How can Enzo allow this to happen?"

I try and comprehend any noise from Lirium, but he is right. I hear nothing. The only sound I can detect is the horse-drawn wagons.

"Wait," I say as I notice something doesn't add up. "Why do you keep calling me a foreigner when we are just a walk away from the castle? Dalgin isn't too far, and surely you don't call everyone a foreigner, do you?"

Jerrick's expression remains unchanged. "Dalgin is a foreign town to those who live in Lirium. As you can see, our two homes are divided by Zwelis, a sizable forest. Sure, we could take the time to cut down the trees and create a makeshift road so carts could travel and offer supplies for trade, but why would we do that? The only territory we would arrive in is Dalgin, a small and useless place where nobody has money, and the only motivation for an invasion would be for evil. There is nothing notable beyond Dalgin in the south, at least nothing we have explored yet. Still, our resources are better used elsewhere."

"You're cruel. Yet, you traveled there for power, which only you knew about, or else I would've met more intruders.

You're the first one. Answer me why."

"You assume I saw an interest in visiting Dalgin, foreigner. Nevertheless—"

"Stop," I growl. "Get on with the truth before I cut you open."

He sighs, knowing I can end him if I desire to. "Fine, Phoenix. I knew about Dalgin because, during my off time as a servant, I liked reading many books in the royal library. That place had old collections from ages ago. It was like a ghost town because people never wanted to read in their free time. Everyone spent endless hours doing their paperwork and jobs and training, ending with them all becoming exhausted, which then they retired to their quarters. Our ladies were busy seeking suitors and provided a suitable castle to live in. The royal family always had important political matters to attend to. And outside of them, the only other people with access to the royal library were servants. Still, even those people spent their time romanticizing fantasies over histories."

"So, with the first sight of danger you ran away to Dalgin. You weren't afraid to be executed by Enzo Malfester for ignoring your duties?"

"There is more to life than being a servant." He shakes his head. "I was afraid, you could say, but when I learned about the existence of blood magic, I had to make the trip. It's a coincidence Enzo's takeover occurred shortly beforehand, but the chaos and disloyalty helped me escape undetected."

"Doesn't answer how you knew about my parents. You claimed they were dead because they disappeared."

"I know about your parents from the lore I read. Your home had guardians protecting Dureizen ever since the demon got sealed away on his own accord. Ashen and Flare are the final guardians I read about, and I assume those are your parents, correct?"

I look down. My feelings for them will always be a mixture of love and hate for what they did to me.

"I thought so," he continues. "We can expect them to be dead since they are no longer protecting your home. Being a sentinel was their duty forevermore. Leaving you in charge means they have passed their duty down to you."

"What if somebody else enters the cave while I'm away? Does this mean we could encounter another spellcaster in the future?"

"I doubt it. As I said, only we know about Dureizen's whereabouts. Nonetheless, I'm sure you appreciate being one of the strongest people alive. I cannot imagine living in a world where a dozen magicians are roaming around."

"True. . ." I remark. A world with many others like me, where I might not feel so alone. Although he's probably right, it might be better if this cursed blessing is never obtained by the wrong hands. The more people with power, the more dangerous this world will become.

I look at Jerrick and ask, "Why are we standing around here when we could make our way to the castle? How do you plan on getting us inside?"

"Oh, I thought you liked doing nothing and enjoying the scenery? This is your first time away from Dalgin, I'm sure."

"I can appreciate the world as we move on. I'm ready to get in and defeat Enzo. Then I can move forward in life."

"Well, you're going to have to wait," Jerrick states. "A friend of mine, when he eventually arrives, will escort us inside. His name's Rufus, and he is a knight disloyal to the new king. In the meantime, is there anything more you wish to discuss, preferably a not so heavy topic?"

My mind wanders toward animals Dalgin may not see very often, but this subject is too simple. I consider the weather, but this is also too common of a discussion—Dalgin locals seem to talk about it at least once daily. Then my mind wanders to our travels, how we explored Zwelis—a forest I had never seen much of—and now recognizing the beauty of

Lirium. Despite the corruption taking hold of the kingdom, it's far more impressive than anything I've ever seen. I ask, "What's the world around us like? Any other significant towns or locations I should know of?"

"Now, there is a topic I can tell you all about. As I said, the only notable locations in the south are Zwelis and Dalgin. However, to the north, we have more towns and villages that are great for trading. Further north, we will hit the ocean, where there is a trade port called Sivertin. We always get a great assortment of supplies from other countries there."

"What kind of supplies? Isn't Lirium able to be self-sufficient?"

"It is, it is," he says with urgency. "What trading with other countries does is help the economy and morale of our people. We rarely need any wood, stone, weapons, or food, but what they trade with us are goods we cannot find here. Coffee is a magnificent product from overseas, along with art, gems, and toys for children. One of my favorite items we received is a book called, 'How to Live With My Out-Of-Control Partner,' something I've been wanting to reread ever since I met you."

I raise my eyebrow and mutter a simple warning, "Watch it."

He smiles and continues, "Alas, I left it in the castle, so it may be some time before I can return to my studies. Still, I'm hoping Rufus brings me the copy I requested.

"Anyway, back to your question. To the east, we have more towns and villages we trade with. If you continued to travel in that direction, you would reach numerous mountains which conceal the Trivaskle Kingdom. Lirium and Trivaskle coexist in peace, despite our limited communication due to the hike to reach one another. Still, there has never been conflict between the two kingdoms."

"Never heard of Trivaskle, but it sounds like it may be worth visiting since they're friendly."

"I recommend the trip. I've traveled there once. I will spare you the details of what it is like, for the kingdom is too fascinating for my words to give it justice. Once this is over, we can visit."

"I'm sure. So, how about the west?"

"To the west, there is a city called Crystalline. They are too advanced for their own good, and I don't trust them. It's a dangerous location where unfortunate events occur. They are kingless, unguided; if you ever want to see it, you do it yourself."

I raise my hands in the air as a sign of surrender. He

doesn't acknowledge me and instead gazes at the dirt road away from the castle. Following his gaze, I notice what he is watching. There is a knight in the distance, leading a large wagon off the road and toward Zwelis. The knight is heading in our general direction.

"I thought you said carts can't travel through Zwelis?" I ask. As usual, I have my doubts concerning Jerrick's words. "Unless, is this Rufus?"

He doesn't answer me. The bold individual in shining armor continues to approach us. He's riding near the front of his wagon while a single, large white horse pulls the luggage. I turn and see Jerrick is also watching him. The man leans forward next to me—as if doing so will allow him to see everything perfectly. He is a statue as he stares and waits, for if the knight is coming for us, it might spell trouble. At last, he grimaces and shakes his head at me.

"That's him all right, the old man himself," Jerrick seems to say more to himself than to me.

"Who?"

"Rufus. He's not going to Zwelis. As I said, taking a cart through this forest is impossible, though I would like to see him try. No, he is heading our way."

"About time." I didn't know what else might intrigue a

good conversation with Jerrick. My goal was to let him ramble on until Rufus arrived, and I'm happy my plan succeeded. Still, I'm curious about Crystalline. A location he hates might lead to a good time.

The silence between us grows into an uncomfortable shroud as we watch the knight approach us with minimal speed—taking him time, no doubt. It seems it will take Rufus a while to reach us, so I move away from my mentor and return into the forest outskirts. The shade provides excellent relief from the sun. It may take a week or two to become comfortable in broad daylight for the entire day. Furthermore, I want to see how Jerrick interacts with this so-called knight who is disloyal to Enzo Malfester. If he is wrong about this man being Rufus, or if things go horribly wrong, he will suffer the consequences, not I. Here, I am safe from the awkward silence and danger.

At last, the knight arrives and dismounts his horse and stands before Jerrick. I wait for my suspicions to become reality. Still not moving an inch, Jerrick is as still as a scarecrow, with his jacket fluttering from the mild breeze. Neither of them says a word.

I look back and observe the dense trees for any frightening creature or unnatural occurrence. Behind one of them where the greenery muddles with each other, I believe I see a shadow stalking me. I focus on the anomaly, and it wavers. I blink. It's gone. The hair on the back of my neck rises, and a part of me wishes to investigate what it might've been. Jerrick and I must not have much time to escape if the shadow is Zier. I exchange glances between Jerrick and the silhouette's previous location. I'm at a loss for what I should do.

A bold voice echoes, "For dishonoring the new king, you are under arrest." I turn my gaze to the knight and involuntarily remove my knife from my jacket pocket. This may not end well.

"Rufus, we don't have time for your shenanigans," Jerrick responds to the threat.

"Very true, sir, but that is what I would've said if we weren't working together. I'm ready to return to the old ruling of Krolas Malfester, which can only be done if we succeed in a timely manner. Did you obtain what you were looking for?"

"Yes, Rufus. Though there is a better time to demonstrate. During my travels, I picked up some pocket change I was not expecting to drag with me. May I present my new companion, Phoenix, who is also blessed with magic—though not as skilled."

I storm out from behind the trees and forget my fears as anger takes control. "Just because I told you not to call me a foreigner doesn't mean you can make up worse names for me. Additionally, I beat you during our sparring match."

"A sparring match I let you win," Jerrick spats.

The knight removes his helmet and reveals a man with brown, medium-length hair and a patchy short beard. He is free from any scars and blemishes, making me believe he has not seen much combat or hardship. He appears to be in his thirties.

"Phoenix, right? My name is Rufus, an old friend of nasty ol' Jerrick here." He holds a hand up apologetically toward the man, who does not respond. I like this guy who stands up to Jerrick and is polite.

"Yeah, I'm Phoenix. Nice to meet you. How can you deal with Jerrick? He's always a hassle. Always has been a problem ever since he met me, trying to barge his way into my house."

Rufus nods. "It's something you get used to over time. Barged into my house on an occasion or two. But let me tell you, his attitude is a bit too much to handle sometimes, and his demeanor is just as bad, which I'm sure you got a strong sense of what that's like in your short time together, and don't get me started with his—"

"We can continue about how terrible of a person I am when we return to Lirium," Jerrick disrupts. "We are not far from the castle. If anyone looks out this way, they will see us all squabbling about in the middle of nowhere."

"You heard the man, Phoenix! Let's continue this conversation later and in more detail, of course. Everyone in the cart! And please don't mind the clothes and other goods in there. Just use them to stay low and hidden."

We get in while Rufus sits in the front seat, holds the reigns of his noble white horse, and waits until we're ready. There is a lot of random junk in the back of the wagon, and I must watch my every step. Large cloth piles line the outer rim of the cart, some of which reach the wooden ceiling. Trinkets such as wooden sculptures of animals riddle the floor with tripping hazards. Breakable glassware, metal, food, weapons—with and without scabbards—and other undiscernible random junk make me feel like there's no space for us. Jerrick nudges me forward so he can get in, and I fall over and hurt my arm on the sharp end of a sculpture. Lucky for him, I'm not bleeding.

"Where did you get all this stuff, Rufus?" I ask.

"Enzo wanted all this and for me to get it for him. I'm still a knight, after all. Disobeying orders will be the death of me."

I nod like he can see me and crawl further into the cart until I reach the end. I grab some of the clothes and cover my body until only my face is exposed so I can breathe. Looking over at Jerrick, he mimics me and lies still. Getting into Lirium might be difficult, and I hope we won't be spotted. We're lucky we have a friend on the inside who has a cart full of crap.

As soon as we relax, Rufus announces, "Alright, everyone, we are off. It will be a bumpy ride until we reach the main road."

Without further warning, the wagon jerks forward. Jerrick and I sprawl across the wooden flooring, trying not to slam into any loose cargo. Some more clothes fall on me, and I must shove them off. Jerrick tries to create more room by nudging the goods away from him, but it is futile. The cart hits a large bump, and I become airborne for a quick moment before smashing my body back onto the hardwood. I growl. This ridiculous method of transport should be more stable. Whoever designed this cart never tested it out.

"Not used to traveling this way?" Jerrick sneers.

I shake my head and reply, "Why would I want to? I'm sure as a servant, this is how you always got around."

"Not particularly."

We ride on for a while, and I constantly fear the cart crashing into another hole and bouncing like before, but it never does. Instead, the road flattens out over time, allowing me to relax again. Only now do I realize how much my body aches. Next time, I will take my chances getting caught by guards rather than being on this horrible thing again.

We ride along the smooth road for some time, and Jerrick and I are able to adjust into a plausible hiding spot under all this garbage. Once in position, him and I stay still and enjoy the ride into Lirium.

"Don't get too comfortable," Rufus says in a low tone, "King Enzo Malfester is waiting at the gate."

12

There is so much to this world I never knew about, along with the chaos people design. I never thought I would take part in it.

I freeze. Our entire mission can end at this very moment. Enzo may discover and kill us before we have a chance at retaliation. Do we stay still or prepare to fight? Jerrick and I could jump out and surprise Enzo, but a lucky strike from any of the knights will kill us. My nerves are begging me to shake, and some objects near my legs shift and create subtle, unnecessary noises as I adjust my position. I will get us captured if I fail to calm down.

Jerrick is a statue. He's facing me and plays dead, and I need to do the same. A few deep breaths and contemplation should help me mimic his ability. Breathe in, then out. In, and out. Inhale, exhale. All will bode well. I just have to trust Jerrick and Rufus' plan.

Still, stowaways in a wagon never fare well upon discovery, at least from what I understand. Chances are, the knights will investigate the cargo, as they do with everything coming in and out of the castle, and this is when Jerrick and I will be apprehended. I will fight with my last dying breath if this happens. Still, I have little confidence in survival. I will only make it so far with this many knights and Enzo to command them. My experience in battle only fares against individuals.

I trust Rufus knows what he's doing and will get us through. However, can we ever fully trust him? He is a knight, after all. Enzo is the new king. Where do his loyalties lie? Certainly not with an ordinary servant like Jerrick. I get a few minutes with Rufus, and he escorts us into a death trap.

"Rufus, my beloved knight, you have just missed Agnes by mere minutes," Enzo seems to announce to a large audience. "So, how was your trip to Kuemarin? Did you retrieve everything I require?"

"Everything and more," Rufus speaks in a bold tone. "I will deliver all the goods to your chamber once I pass through, after which I will see my wife, Agnes, who I presume is resting at the castle."

"Yes, yes. After I confirm you have what I desire, I will let you have the rest of the day with your wife. So, tell me, any casualties?"

"None, just as you asked." The confidence in Rufus' words gives me hope regarding our safety. It bothers me, however, how all these goods were stolen from another town. What is Enzo planning with all this useless merchandise?

"Good, good," Enzo states. Everything goes silent, and I'm anticipating Rufus or Enzo to say something more. Every awkward second that passes, my mind delves deeper into fear. Please allow us through without a cargo search.

My heart is pounding out of my chest. I'm afraid everyone can hear it, including Enzo. I stare at Jerrick, who remains unmoving. He makes no indication that I'm being too loud. Maybe it's all in my head. Perhaps I can only hear my heartbeat so well because it's inside me. Either way, I take quiet, deep breaths and stay motionless, suffering in the anticipation of our fates.

"Check the cargo," Enzo declares. "If you lied to me and I do not acquire what I need, you can say goodbye to this life. Forever."

The wagon doors burst open as my heart simultaneously skips a beat. They are bound to discover us. Any vigilant inspection will amount toward our capture. We aren't even well hidden! The newcomers knock over some clothes and rummage their hands around the cart. After some seconds, I don't believe they will jump in with all this clutter.

Jerrick remains unconcerned under his cowl, a face I know I cannot match. Someone touches my foot, and I recoil involuntarily, but I stop myself before I move more than an inch. More things fall from the side of the cart, and I beg that they presume they touched a pair of shoes Rufus snagged in Kuemarin. Please don't think I'm in here.

The doors close, and a ruff voice states, "Everything's in order, King Enzo. Many goods from Kuemarin have been retrieved."

"Excellent, Rufus," Enzo says. "You are free to enter. Please enjoy the rest of the day after you drop everything off at my castle."

We move once more and pass through the gates. I let out a sigh of relief. Who knows how long I've been holding my breath.

"Jerrick," I try to get his attention so he stops acting like he's dead. "Jerrick, we are through. I can't believe it."

"Quiet," he spats. "Talk when we arrive at our destination."

I shut up and am left alone with hazardous thoughts circling through my head. Are we going to the castle? I wonder. Enzo was clear with Rufus' orders. He needs to go there before anything else, which might be where Jerrick wants to be, so we can end this tyranny before it gets out of hand. Enzo's been in power for a week, and the longer he brandishes his title as king, the more the lands will suffer. If Kuemarin is anything to go off, every town and village is being antagonized and ransacked. There's no way Enzo is buying everything. Where will Jerrick have us regroup until Enzo returns to the castle?

The wagon slows to a stop, and Rufus opens the doors to let us out. This time, Jerrick exits first, then I follow.

Rufus takes off his helmet and bears a grim expression.

"Too close for comfort," the knight explains. "I'm happy you and Phoenix weren't discovered. When he told the sentries to check the cart, I thought I'd never see Agnes again, and you guys would be killed."

Jerrick states, "We can dwell on it inside. Let's go." He grabs my arm and leads me to a sizable building. I try to look around the best I can while moving at this hectic pace. I catch glimpses of many buildings and houses along an extensive, winding road, where many people are trudging about. Some lie in the middle of the street, while others seem to have no goal in mind. Their moods seem unnatural for a location where there must be many activities, opportunities, and jobs available. Yet, it is clear that this small portion of Lirium houses more than three times the people in Dalgin.

Jerrick shakes his head with an annoyed expression, then yanks my arm, nearly pulling it from its socket. We arrive at the two-story building with minimal windows, and he unlocks the door with a key tucked within his cloak. We enter, and Rufus follows close behind us. I have no time to process anything as the door shuts. Now, we are by ourselves in a pitch-black room. It's silent here, and I wonder if we will stop Enzo or if Jerrick wants me to stay locked away while he does the dirty work, a prospect reminding me of my parents. Being left alone whenever they needed to shop or patrol outside, I never went with them anywhere. Instead, I was only allowed to leave for brief periods when both my parents were home.

My sore arm is let free, then a dim light materializes in Jerrick's hand, illuminating the lower part of his face. He looks menacing. "This is where we will stay," Jerrick's lips hardly move. He turns away and lights candles around the room, creating an ever-growing image of many wooden tables and chairs in a large open area. A staircase further in leads to a second floor, but Jerrick avoids it and lights the last of the candles.

My mentor continues, "Welcome to the abandoned bar, once housing a murderous fight ending with everyone dead but one, and that individual is me. This establishment has been closed since, forgotten about, and will be evermore. Welcome to our new home, where we will train and prepare to kill Enzo Malfester."

13

So, this dreary space is where we're living from now on? I guess it could be worse because it's similar to home. Dark, eerie, and will no doubt be stained with blood the more we train.

I'm curious how long we'll wait here? I left home because I was ready to move on from my restricted life, not to be forced into another. I wish to find my parents, discover my purpose, and explore the world. Everything is on hold until I'm free.

"Are we not attacking Enzo anytime soon, then?" I ask, even though I already know the answer.

Jerrick shakes his head. "No. Even though we are strong enough to end his reign, I need time to develop a strategy. Furthermore, there is something amiss going around. Many of the knights, except for Rufus and a few others, obeyed Enzo's every command the moment he rose to power. It is a situation I do not understand and need more intelligence on. If we defeat Enzo today, others may continue to worship him. Knights will overrun us, and everything will be lost. Let us not poison our fate."

"Rufus, do you know what happened to the old king, Krolas Malfester?" I ask. "Do you think he's dead or hiding somewhere?"

Jerrick turns to him, awaiting his response alongside me. Rufus stares at the floor, then begins, "No, Krolas could not be alive. Knowing how Enzo rules his kingdom, his brother was likely killed during the takeover."

"Which means we will have to decide on a new king once the job is finished," Jerrick chimes in. "It's going to be icky business restoring the peace, so we will need someone knowledgeable on politics and people's needs. My goal is a week of rigorous training with Phoenix so we can take on unexpected threats. All the while, Rufus, you will gather intelligence and determine the perfect time to strike—perhaps even finding a suitable new king."

Rufus puts a hand on Jerrick's shoulder. "I mean, I can take the throne. I think I may be a suitable king."

"No, Rufus. I have seen how you act within the castle. You would spend every minute of your off-time drinking ale with your wife. We need a king who prioritizes the kingdom and its people at all times."

"Do you suggest yourself, Jerrick?" Rufus asks mockingly.

"If it comes down to it. But my reign will run short, considering Dureizen and Zier. Give me about two days after taking down Enzo, and I will be dead and gone. I cannot position myself on the throne unless there is a way to get rid of blood magic and avoid these demons. This is another reason why I am not ready to end Enzo's reign. I need to have a little longer to remember, contemplate, and reexperience my life and my mistakes."

I consider their words. If we succeed in stealing Enzo's crown, Jerrick's purpose will be complete, and he will soon die. Without him, I don't know what will become of me. My path is dark and uncertain, and I cannot hold my own if demons track me down and attempt to steal my life away. After Enzo's death, what will my motivation be? Can I find a purpose? Would doing so protect me from Zier? If I take the throne and lead the kingdom to prosperity, can I live a lifetime, perhaps living forever?

"What if I take the throne?" I blurt out. "I can lead the people of Lirium and build a bright future such as Krolas did."

Jerrick shakes his head and claims, "Without the proper training, Phoenix, your dream is impossible. From my knowledge of how a kingdom runs, it would take you many years before you are ready for such a task. I would love to see you rule and discover yourself, but I don't believe the life of a queen is meant for you."

Rufus shakes his head and adds, "Jerrick, don't be so hard on her. You'd make a great queen, and if you had someone to show you the ropes and guide your choices, I'd say it's possible. Our only reasonable options are her and me. Who do you choose? Who'd make a better ruler?"

Jerrick grunts, turns away, then flaunts his hand in the air and commands, "Go grab the supplies from the cart. Phoenix and I need new clothes and would prefer food and drink before we starve ourselves. Phoenix, make yourself comfortable."

Rufus puts on his helmet and walks out without hesitation. I look down at my clothes and see a lot of bloodstains from battle and training. I didn't realize how nasty I got. It appears Jerrick isn't so gross, as his cloak likely hides many of his stains. Still, we are both in need of a bath and new attire.

I find a table nearest the door and try to get as comfortable as possible on an unsteady wooden chair—one of the legs must be loose. "Jerrick, is there a washroom here?" I question.

"Why, were you expecting one? I thought you cave dwellers never had such amenities to beg such a question. My expectation of you was to eat, sleep, work, and—"

"That's disgusting. Of course, my home didn't have everything I needed to survive. I still went out once in a while to bathe and sleep—a rock-hard ground is not comfortable for months on end."

"Fair enough." Jerrick finishes roaming around and sits across from me, leaning back his chair precariously. "Upstairs are our rooms, and despite the beds not being up to standard, they will work for our short time here. You will find the washroom in the back of the house. This place used to house a barkeeper who lived here."

"Who you killed."

"Don't dwell on the past," he tells me like needless

murder doesn't matter. "It is not like you wanted me dead before. We fight for a reason, and sometimes this means killing for our own protection. You know that. I needed this place for our hideout."

"Fine. So we all want to kill people. I know your story and mine, but what is Rufus'? Did he kill others to obtain those supplies?" I smile at the thought, but I'm unsure if those in Kuemarin deserved death. Dureizen is right about one thing: I'm a bit murderous. Nonetheless, I feel I'm only this way toward those who deserve it, nothing more. I should not smile at the deaths of those I've never met. So why am I doing so?

"Who knows his actions, but Kuemarin does not deserve ransacking," he claims.

"How so?" My head rests on my hand, and I watch him with a hint of curiosity touching my brow. I enjoy learning about the world, and Jerrick has been an excellent resource.

"Kuemarin, a town close to us in the east, is a peaceful residence that has done nothing but support Lirium. It has quite the history, too, if you want to hear?" I nod, and he continues. "The town was founded by a woman who loved the ocean. Rachel Kuemarin was her name, and she lived with her husband near the shore of Sivertin—the trading port. They both admired the sea, and their dream was to build a new home for their child near its beauty so they could all live peaceful lives. Still, fate had other plans, for nothing good can stay in this world. Life always takes what people deserve. Rachel deserved her husband and a happy life.

"Her lover went out on a fishing trip to celebrate the birth of their child. He wanted to catch so many fish to feed the whole town of Sivertin to celebrate. They must have loved life so much to be able to bring people together for such an event. However, instead of her husband returning home, he never came back. Days passed, and no word of his return reached Rachel, but she waited still. By the time her child grew to be about four—just old enough to care for herself—she gave up on their dream. Her husband was dead; staying close to the ocean just brought horrible memories to her soul.

"Out of her bitterness, she traveled further inland and forged a home to protect her child from the ocean. A few people felt for her and followed, maybe because of sympathy or a wave of shared anger. Together, they created a town from scratch, and King Krolas overlooked it and sent them supplies to assist their cause. Regardless of what happened, it is believed that her love for nature has turned toward hate, and the only thing she cares for now is her child and the kingdom which supported her."

"Quite the story . . . is she still alive? How long ago was this?" I'm curious if his tale is just legend or if there's some truth behind it.

"Oh, Rachel is about my age. This all occurred when Krolas Malfester came to power."

"And how old are you?" I ask. I predict he's in his thirties or late forties, but I have no proof.

"Old enough to rival Dureizen's age." He smiles.

I smile back. "So, older than a thousand years then?"

"Feels like it."

The door slams open, and a giant monster of cloth—breathing heavy like a dragon—blunders into the dim room. He staggers, and some clothes fall near the entryway. As if he gives up on any further movement, he drops everything altogether with a thud. The candles flicker from the gale force it brings, and the culprit of it all is none other than Rufus.

Jerrick laughs, "You did not have to bring them all, or at least in one trip."

Rufus takes a quick breather and rests his hands on his knees. Then he stands up straight and responds, "I needed to accomplish this in one trip, or else others would've found my activities suspicious."

"I would find it more suspicious to act like a monster, struggling to take more than a few steps," I snicker.

"A monster!? Is that what I looked like?" Jerrick and I nod in response. Rufus sighs, removes his helmet, and closes the door. "Fine, a monster it is then. Still, all the clothes for you two are here. Any preferences you want to see firsthand before I bring them upstairs, by myself?"

Jerrick ignores his plea and asks, "Got anything with a hood? That's all I will wear."

"Yes," Rufus responds haphazardly, trying to separate our clothes. "Everything for you has a hood."

"Then I don't need to see them. When you're done playing, you can bring my attire to my room upstairs."

I sense some negative tension between the two. I'd prefer to keep it from simmering much longer, so I approach the large pile of clothes and assist the knight. "I'll help you organize and put things away, Rufus," I mutter. "Also, I want to see what you got for me. I'm sick of wearing blood-stained garments."

"I'm glad you asked, Phoenix. Luckily during my visit to Kuemarin, Enzo wanted all types of supplies and clothing. A few things from my trip should fit you well enough. There's some leather armor—not too heavy to restrict your movement—and some black clothes to not reveal bloodstains as much. Of course, there are other colors and normal clothes you can wear when not performing blood magic." He lifts up a nice variety of garments with varying designs, patterns, and hues. Thanks to him, the number of outfits I now have is much more than I've ever owned.

"Thank you, Rufus." My mind wanders to who these clothes might've belonged to. Perhaps they were from a merchant or a defenseless family, but I see no blood on Rufus' armor. I want to ask him, but I don't want to start a confrontation after he's offering us so much.

I gather up my stack of clothes, and Rufus grabs Jerrick's, and we go upstairs and ignore my mentor's gaze. If he does not want to help his friend, I'll do it instead.

On the second floor, the wooden boards squeak with every other step. Rufus enters the first door we encounter and explains that my room is the next one at the end. I follow his instructions and walk into the vacant room, and the light from a single window allows me to see its contents:

- The bed is covered in pristine, white sheets, and not a single wrinkle is seen. It is standard in size but is a million times better than sleeping on cold, hard stone.

- A painting of Lirium's castle is hanging beside the bed, perfect for provoking magnificent dreams.

- A table and chair are in the corner, as well as some books and journals. I hope some of them are blank so I can write in my free time.

- A few candles are in the room to provide a perfect amount of light once the sun sets.

- The room's size gives me a sense of freedom, for this space belongs to me.

- There is a closet with a door to access it, like an additional room.

This place is perfect. I cannot imagine what the castle's interior must look like if this is how nice a commoner's room is in Lirium.

"Rufus!" Jerrick's anger resonates from below, "Once you are done, go and fetch the food outside. We need to survive, and I plan on raising a barrier soon."

I hurry and drop my clothes into the closet, leaving my favorite one out for me to wear later: a long, black dress with leggings and new shoes. The shoes I have now are old with wear and need replacing. Additionally, suppose I am to wear something during training or battle. In that case, I can instead wear my new dark-leather armor with black clothes. I'm happy I have clothing options now, and I'll change my current attire after I wash up and deal with Jerrick's attitude.

I return downstairs and meet up with my mentor. The main door is open, and I guess Rufus is outside, grabbing some food. When the knight reenters the bar, he brings a large wooden crate containing bread, fruits, vegetables, and waterskins. The waterskins surprise me because the bar already has drinks, but I won't complain. Besides, there is enough tension between Rufus and Jerrick, and I don't want to fuel the fire.

"Rufus, bring that to the storage room so I can lockdown this place," Jerrick commands. "The sooner the better."

"Very well." Rufus shuts the door, runs to the extra room in the back, and returns within seconds. "I understand I've overstayed my welcome. Perhaps next time I can visit longer?"

"Agreed. Once I fabricate a barrier, you will only find our residence if you remember it's exact location. You will knock three times where the door should be, and I will let you in. Keep me reported on events and if there are any changes in Lirium while we remain here. If there is a time to strike, let us know, and be sure to report every two days or sooner. If the third day arrives, we will no longer allow visitors. Am I clear?"

"Yes, Jerrick. I will return soon. As long as Enzo does not expect treachery, I will follow your command."

"Good, now be off."

"Take it easy out there, Rufus," I chime in before he leaves and closes the door with a single click.

Once he is gone, Jerrick unsheathes his sword, slices a small part of his arm, and his shadow emerges within the candlelight. He does not heal the wound; the shadow swells and latches onto the wall. The light tries to extinguish the darkness, but the fire's efforts are in vain, for the shadow darkens our new home and expands until blackness covers the walls, ceiling, and floor. I'm curious what the window in my room looks like now. Will any outside light shine through?

After Jerrick's shadow embellishes everything around us, I ask, "Why must you act so rude? Isn't Rufus your friend? He's done nothing but assist you with your goal. You think any other knight would help someone like you kill their king?"

"Rufus will never place his loyalties with Enzo, so I need not worry about him betraying us. Also, I could only create a barrier once he was done blundering about, for I see no reason to go through the hassle of moving my shadow more than once. Enzo expects him at the castle anyway, and the more time he spends here, the greater chance we will be discovered.

Does this answer satisfy you?”

“Sure, but you could have treated him better.”

“Fine. Next time I will apologize for my words. As for now, clean up and head to bed. We begin training tomorrow.”

“Already?” I ask. “The sun is still up, though.”

“Yes. Tomorrow will be a long, harsh training day, and I want you to be ready for it. Nonetheless, as long as you heed my warning, you do whatever you please.”

“And what are you going to do?”

Jerrick hesitates and stares at the shadowy wall. “I have some things I need to consider. I’ll be in my room if you need me.”

With that, he leaves me alone and heads upstairs. I follow him, grab my new clothes, and bathe. Afterward, I dress, eat food, and return to my room to discover what I can see from my window. I’m happy the darkness does not hinder the sunlight from shining through. This room is the closest to freedom I’ll be, until Jerrick’s done mourning and decides we’re ready.

I peer outside and see the streets are now empty. It’s strange. When we arrived here not long ago, I could’ve sworn many people were moving about. Maybe they all go to bed early, or there’s some event I’m unaware of? Still, at least from here, I can appreciate the town and all its glory.

Other buildings are the same height as ours, forged in stone, brick, or wood. The streets are made of rock and follow a coherent, curving path, unlike anything Dalgin has. All my hometown offered was worn dirt and grass in its scenery—no need for anything more. As for the castle, I can only discern one corner, no matter how much I bend or move. At least I have a painting of it above my bed.

I lie down on the pure white sheets and gaze at the castle painting. The various brush marks and linework is phenomenal. What might it be like to rule this kingdom, to find purpose in leading this region and its people to prosperity after Enzo is defeated. Despite what they tell me, I believe I can do it.

Still, am I ready to wield blood magic and train with Jerrick? I want to become stronger and take on any threat, something Jerrick can already accomplish just fine. In time, I might be able to use magic without thinking twice, but is a week of training enough time? Furthermore, am I ready to kill Enzo and deal with the consequences it brings? Only time and determination will tell.

14

A large rock mound rests in the center of a large, open area. Everything is covered in a haze, and I cannot turn my head away from what's in front of me. It's damp. It's cold. Nothing is welcoming about this abandoned sanctum.

"Father, I have returned. Did you wish to see me?"

A male figure moves from behind me and into my field of view. He looks familiar, with his brown hair . . . and his black and red armor. Blood drains from my face as I come to recognize this man.

Hollow eyes emerge from the mound and turn left and right like an owl. It then locks onto me, and I want to run, but my legs refuse to listen. Those nothing eyes stare at me and peer into my mind with unwavering awe. I watch back. My body aches and groans for me to move, but something keeps me still no matter how I struggle.

Finally, those dead eyes—blank and emotionless—shift into a vengeful rage as it notices the man before him. The creature presents an aura of damnation which boils within my heart. It's strange. I feel an understanding between us.

The creature rises and fills the room until it crashes into the ceiling, its spikey body providing eminent danger for those too close to the mass. The head of the demon looms toward the man, then it shuts one eye to match the rest of its body's inky blackness.

"Ah, my son has finally returned home," the demon says with interest. "What did you find of the poor, young Phoenix?"

"You'd be wise to keep her alive. She wields the power of death, misery, and destruction. She's a killer who longs for a purpose. It's so easy to see."

"And those black eyes tell me you perceive something more, Zier."

The man looks at my direction, and I wonder why they are discussing me while I'm in the same room. It's unsettling, and I wonder if I'm somehow invisible. Where is Jerrick when

I need him?

"There is more," Zier mentions, examining the demon. "She is unique. The power of death she must command has only been found in one other individual. Someone like her is an anomaly. Is there really no way to spare her?"

The black demon shrinks, and its body muddles and shifts into an identical match to Zier. He places a hand on the real Zier's shoulder and smiles lavishly.

"You feel a connection," the creature says. "A connection of a rare occurrence, for you also wield the power of death."

"Dureizen." Zier pushes the demon away and walks further into the room. "You only assume the things you see. Her power and mine are the same, true, but where I was let to live, she will die." He clutches the air with his hand, and two makeshift figures appear before him—a replication of Jerrick and me. It's surreal to see myself standing there without care when Zier and Dureizen are in the same room. Additionally, I question if my physical appearance really looks so hideous.

"Look at me, Dureizen!" Zier yells and rips off Jerrick's hood to reveal a man in his forties. Despite my mentor being manhandled like this, he does not care and remains unmoving like a puppet.

I try to make out Jerrick's features and see that he has

black hair, a longer beard than I remember him to have, and bright, yellow eyes. Is this really what he looks like? There's only one other person I've heard about who has those eyes. A passerby mentioned it briefly, and I only remember because I thought it would be cool to have yellow eyes instead of my boring brown ones.

My thoughts are disrupted as Zier screams, "This man has no purpose!" He then pulls a black knife from thin air and stabs Jerrick. My heart weakens as he falls, and I cry a silent scream as he tumbles to the ground and lies motionless. "Look how fragile his life is with a dream that will never be fulfilled! You!" He rushes toward Dureizen, who rips off his humanoid skin and towers above Zier again in a blink of an eye. The shadow demon is daunting in this form, yet Zier doesn't care and points at him accusingly. "You really want Phoenix to suffer the same fate in your game? You're so bored, tired, you just want to have fun instead of thinking things through logically."

Dureizen chuckles and seeps into the center mound once again. "Then it's too bad you came to me first, Zayn," the creature speaks. "Found, stranded, alone. I saved you from a dull life and granted you a new one. Now you beg for more, silly one. Leave me in peace, and do not foil my plans."

"Wait, why did you call me Zayn? Dureizen!" Zier kicks the stone where his father disappeared into, and his black eyes turn toward me—the real me. I wonder again if he can see me. He walks toward me with vigorous haste and brandishes his knife. He's getting closer. In seconds, he will be reach me. I need to escape, but he's only a few steps away, and I still can't move. I close my eyes and feel a knife under my throat. It's cold. My body trembles and shakes. The smooth texture glides across my skin and slices into it, stinging my neck with a sickening wetness.

"I'm coming for you, Phoenix."

I gasp for air and clutch my throat as I find myself in my room. I'm still shaking. I'm thirsty. I'm afraid to leave my bed. Searching my surroundings, nobody is with me, and I'm safe. I'm safe. I let myself breathe deeply and relax as I stay in bed until my body calms.

What does Zier hope to gain from me? What does Dureizen want from me? Perhaps it was just a bad dream, but I will tell Jerrick everything when he wakes up.

15

This is when I found my journal and recalled my memories. The past few days have been insane, and I want to keep a record for those who may discover the life I led. Being hunted, using magic through blood—a concept that will always bother me—and training to kill a king. This assassination will fulfill my mentor's purpose.

Furthermore, there is something more significant at play here, something I do not understand. Next time I encounter Zier or Dureizen, I will interrogate them for the answers I require or die trying. This woman who has the power of death, one of two people in history to acquire such a gift, will utilize her potential to find her true purpose. I will give one hell of a fight to those death demons who wish to kill me first.

I place the leatherback journal on my desk alongside the other books. All the other books here are useless and are just previously tampered journals containing accounting and inventory notes—and one other regarding incidents in this bar. After scouring through about twenty of these, my newfound journal is the only one I can call my own. Still, I'm curious if Jerrick killed the previous owner or if they ran away.

Extinguishing my candle, I change into a new pair of clothes—a black short sleeve shirt and pants—and leave my room. I feel like I got no sleep last night. After my dream, I couldn't relax and decided to stay awake and write. I know today will be hell with Jerrick's training, but no matter how much I struggled to rest, my mind continuously drifted elsewhere. Ultimately, I have no answers to whether my dream was tied to actual events or just made-up hallucinations. No answers for who might've given it to me either. Maybe Zier is to blame? Perhaps it was some sort of premonition or warning from a greater force?

I notice Jerrick reading downstairs, seemingly wearing the same outfit as yesterday. Did he even change clothes, or is this an identical garment? Knowing his entire wardrobe is made of hoods, either option is likely.

Shrugging, I descend the stairs to join him. The shadowy surroundings still throw me off, but at least the candlelight helps ward away the immense darkness. I understand his shadow is necessary, for it protects against onlookers and demons who may be searching for us. Still, I wish to explore the world and be free. Living in a dank cave for sixteen years did enough for me.

Jerrick continues to read when I sit in front of him at the round table. It seems he lit all the candles before I left my room this morning, and I wonder how he snuck past me so early to do such a task. If I knew he was awake, I might've joined him earlier instead of sulking and reflecting.

The candlelight provides enough visibility to let me peer under his hood more than usual. Now I can make out features up to his nose. Matching them to my dream, his facial structure is identical. Nonetheless, I didn't have much time to examine him before he got killed . . . and I hope he does not die and leave me alone before I find my purpose. I don't think I can fight off Zier at my current state.

His beard is getting longer by the day, but is still not the length as the one in my dream. Will his facial hair help determine his time of death?

He slams his book on the table and watches at me. "What do you think you're playing at, foreigner? Maybe it was right of me to reread this book again."

Shifting my gaze to the book cover, I see two poorly drawn people and a title that reads, 'How to Live With My Out-Of-Control Partner.' I glare at him and say, "Once again, don't ever call me a foreigner, it makes no sense, and it's old. Also, maybe you're my out-of-control partner."

"Perhaps, but we can compete later. Why are you gawking at me?"

How do I approach the subject of my dream without making me look like a loon? On the other hand, there really is no way to sound logical, so I recall and explain everything from start to finish.

There's no movement or acknowledgment that he's listening to me when I tell him about my dream: how he died, how I was there, and how Zier and Dureizen seemed to know about my presence and knew of my purpose—despite me not having one yet. After telling my story, I ask him, "So, can I see what's under your hood to confirm if my dream was true? If you match the one in my vision, then . . ."

"Then it makes no difference in the end," Jerrick disrupts me.

"Can I see something new about you then? Or can you give me some indication on if the dream is anything to worry about?" I examine his clothes in detail and see he's wearing a long, brown jacket with a black undershirt. The coat provides a hood that, as always, covers up most of his face. Comparing this outfit to the one in my dream, I can't tell if it's the same, for I didn't pay much attention to his clothes, and everything looked hazy.

Jerrick responds, "You have told me enough to acknowledge we need to exercise caution. I already expect Zier to kill me after defeating Enzo, so you should consider what this hallucination means for you after my death."

"You think Zier will kill me afterward?" I ask. "What about now?"

He leans back in his chair and brushes his beard with his hand. "I cannot say about now, but he will target you after my death. If Dureizen has a purpose for you, changing it might be impossible. You can choose between defying fate or playing along with it, but it is ultimately up to you. That is, if your dream is real. I cannot make your choices after my death. I can only lead you to what I believe is right while I am alive."

"Then what about now? Knowing all this, do we change our goal to kill Enzo? Can we run away together and discover a new purpose for each of us?"

"Never. We have a little time to prepare, but Enzo will cause more harm than good if he is unchecked. He is my goal, and I can never sway from it. If you wish to live with Zier chasing you, you must stick with me until I defeat Enzo. Then, we can travel until you find your purpose and before Zier catches up with me."

"But what if I learn to manipulate my shadow, like you?" I ask. "We can avoid demons with this power since it helps us hide from prying eyes."

Jerrick shakes his head and explains, "They will still find us even with this magic. Surrounding ourselves in shadow can keep us secluded for a while, but never forever. Maybe it'll help us survive for a week or two, but there's a reason why there are no other magicians besides us. I can still teach you if you want, but not until you are ready. As of now, you need to learn how to control your link magic and how to heal. That is our lesson for today."

"Very well, teach me how to manipulate my link magic to where it's useful," I tell him. If my connection is with death, as mentioned in my dream, then controlling my spells can make me more powerful than Jerrick. Only two people in history—me being one of them—ever wielded death magic, so it must be formidable. That is if I can use it correctly.

Walking between the furniture, Jerrick proceeds to the center of the room. I follow him. I'm ready to prove my value and show my capability toward learning anything he throws at me. Yet, my nerves are taking control of my body. I must not make a fool of myself by accidentally bumping into anything.

When I approach him, he uses his nail to cut a small portion of his finger. A ball of electric energy emanates in his hand. He presents it to me, and I watch it spark and radiate in his palm. With this energy, the room glows brighter and darker at uneven intervals, depending on the wavering intensity of the chaotic power.

"Today," he begins, "I will teach you how to shift your link magic into a more concentrated form. A sphere like this holds an extreme amount of potential energy. Since it is connected to me, I can continue adding more power to it like so." The ball's electrical chaos grows more rampant from Jerrick's bleeding finger. Each static shock smashes into an invisible barrier that stops it from exploding out of his hand, so much so to where I can hear the crackling ringing in my ear.

He continues, "Now it is powerful enough to stop someone's heart. Before, it would have paralyzed if hit in the correct spot. I could keep strengthening it, but too much may cause it to become out of control and backfire. Only use as much power as you can handle." He turns and points at a chair in the corner. "Once you have this energy, the only way to release it is to throw it. You must sever yourself from the connection, feel the detachment in your mind, then launch."

He chucks the unstable ball toward the chair, and it obliterates into a million pieces in a blink of an eye. My ears ring from the blast, and wood scraps shower across the room—some shining with embers. Nobody can survive an attack like that. I can only imagine what I can do with mine.

"Now it is your turn, Phoenix. I will guide you through the process as much as I can."

Under his instruction, I slice my arm and let a small trickle of blood bleed onto the floor. I refuse to injure any other body part since I hate the idea of it. Many of them are fragile, and some I use too much. The arm is the only spot I can suffer a few scars. Afterward, I let the darkness seep out from my hand, and it drains toward the floor like honey. Jerrick explains how I must let the power flow through my palm and into my fingers, to tense them in order to have my link magic become a sphere in my hand. Instead, no matter what I do, the darkness refuses to obey and still trickles down. He tells me to cut myself more, and I shake from the pressure of trying to prove myself and slash a bit too much, but I will use this blood. I won't let my efforts go to waste. More darkness flows from my palm, and I put my knife away and try using both hands to force my magic to listen to me, yet nothing works! This spell never obeys! Something isn't right in what he tells me. Why can't I just prove to him that I—

"That's enough, Phoenix," Jerrick snatches my arm, and the darkness slows to a stop as I lose my concentration. "Try healing yourself now."

I shake my head and withhold the wetness behind my eyes. Another impossible task. He releases me, and I move my hand to my bleeding arm and take a deep breath. Thinking about my goal in life, traveling the world, and finding a purpose. Seeing my parents—Ashen and Flare. I've been alone most of my life, while everyone seems to have the freedom I desire. Now since I've left home, I find myself in another dank place with a man I just met. What am I really doing here? Do I really care about Enzo like Jerrick does?

"You know what," Jerrick disrupts my thoughts again, "I'll just heal you." I open my eyes as he puts a hand on my wound. It tingles, and in seconds, it is injury free. However, a scar rests in its place.

"I-I believed healing magic always cured completely," I falter, hoping I won't have a scar there forever.

"Most of the time, it does. Nonetheless, like everything in this world, it is imperfect. I have a few scars on my finger already, but luckily nowhere else yet."

I grind my teeth, knowing I will be a hideous freak by the end of training. So much for finding my reason to live. I will be a loner my entire life.

"Moving on, you will have time to practice alone," Jerrick continues his impossible lesson. "Next, we will learn how to cloak your body with magic."

"You want me to cover my entire body with darkness?" If I do this, I could die.

"Not at all. Let us say you lost your weapon and were stuck in close-range combat. Using ranged spells is a horrible idea, so you want to opt to melee." He penetrates further into the open wound on his finger, and his arms and hands disperse a reddish hell of unstable energy. Afterward, he grasps a surviving, larger chair piece from the initial demonstration, and it lights on fire. He crushes it in his hands moments later, not caring about the intense heat the flaming wood must produce. The power radiating on his body fades away, then he heals himself.

He turns to me, adding, "Every magic user's power is unique. Some people become stronger, others ignore injuries, and some people can change their shape entirely. It all depends on your link magic. Now, demonstrate yours."

Once again, he instructs me to cut myself, and I damage my other arm this time. If I get another scar, I might as well have it match the first one. My anger for being a failure pushes me through, and I let the magic trickle down my hands. Jerrick tells me to control its flow and have it climb up my arm. In order to achieve this, I clench my muscles to force the energy upward. I can slow the descent, and it looks like some of the darkness travels up my arm, but my excitement causes it all to fall apart and flow down faster, splattering on the floorboards. I take a few breaths and try again, but this time, the same thing occurs. We let this go on for a few more minutes until gallons of my link magic have spilled out of me. My arms shake, and my eyes darken. More blackness flows out of my palms, and I want to tear myself apart from all this.

"Stop," Jerrick commands, but I will not obey a horrible teacher. "I said stop, Phoenix." Not listening to him. I will do as I please and end my misery here.

A flash of steel slices through the air, causing my hands to bleed. The pain stings like needles penetrating the skin, and I stop the magic flow and stare at my palms and Jerrick. His sword is being put away. He cut me open. I was unprepared and unfocused. My hands bleed and drench my arms with red. I feel sick and dizzy.

"Heal yourself or die trying," Jerrick mocks me.

"I can't," I plea. "It's impossible no matter how much I try."

My vision blurs with tears. I know I will get no sympathy from him. Still, I lift my hands close to my face and try to offer them any healing power. I just feel so weak, and my focus falters. The blurriness fades to black, and my body tumbles to the ground. A girl with dreams of becoming more than misery and death; life is not meant for me.

16

My link magic is impossible to manipulate, apart from when my emotions go rampant. When I bleed a lot, I believe I can control my power better, but it's worthless to one who cannot heal themself. All I know is there's something wrong with me.

My body aches as I sit up on my bed. It's still bright outside, meaning I haven't been out for too long; nonetheless, my stomach growls, and my throat burns dry like it's been weeks since I've nourished myself.

Looking at my hands, one of them does has a scar from

where Jerrick cut me. I didn't just imagine it through my sobbing. At least he healed me before I died, even though death may relieve me from his torturous training.

My clothes are gross and sticky with dried blood, meaning my bed is no doubt disgusting too. Not like it makes a difference anyway. No matter how much I clean myself, the tangy sent of blood touches my nose in unpredictable intervals. Still, I'll wait to change my clothes in hopes Jerrick can see what he did to me and confess his cruelty.

Leaving my room, I see Jerrick sitting on his favorite chair—leaning back like he's about to fall—and I take a deep breath to rest my vengeful heart. I must eat before I confront him. I make my way down the stairs and stare at the wall instead of him. The shadow surrounding this building looks to be a consistent hue of darkness. Knowing this shadow belongs to Jerrick, I must take another deep breath in order to relax.

I arrive in the storage room, a smaller area with a decent selection of food and waterskins, and I grab some bread and eat and drink until I satisfy my stomach. This helps quell my threatening headache, and I can now swallow without my spit getting stuck halfway. All in all, I'm content staying in this room and not training today. Will Jerrick even care?

I close my eyes and relax, letting my mind go blank. All

my thinking has been stressing me out and provoking horrid thoughts, and I need a moment of rest. Then, I hear the front door open. An overbearing noise of a massive bear blundering inside piques my interest. The creature grunts as it enters, but I don't believe Jerrick cares, since his chair doesn't snap to the floor. The door clicks shut, and a man's voice accompanies the persistent shuffling.

Waiting until everything quiets down, I hear a continuous low murmur outside the storage room. An important visitor of Jerrick's? No doubt it's Rufus. I leave the room and confirm my suspicions. Rufus and Jerrick are sitting at the same table, discussing something important without me, I'm sure. They watch as I approach them with mild interest.

"Someone has finally woken up," Jerrick offers a fake smile.

Returning the expression, I reply, "It hasn't been that long. I've only been out for an hour or so."

"Make that an hour and a day," Rufus chimes in. "Jerrick told me all about your predicament yesterday. I wondered if you would wake up so we could all talk together."

"Well, I wouldn't have been asleep that long if Jerrick didn't cut me open and told me to heal when it's clear I can't do that!" I yell and point a finger at Jerrick. I wonder how he might react if I ripped off his hood like Zier did.

Jerrick turns to me, and his facial expression shares no pity. "You just need a new mindset," he dares to claim. "Something within you is stopping your magic from functioning. So, we will discover what's interrupting your flow another day. Now sit down so we can hear what Rufus has come to tell us."

I really want to pull off his hood, but I decide not to make a scene in front of Rufus—someone who understands me. Finding a chair, I move it closer to the knight and sit, never averting my gaze from Jerrick.

Rufus shifts his eyes toward his white helmet on the table and says, "Something's happening in Lirium. I can't put my finger on it, but the people are acting strange. Many of them refuse to leave their homes. Those who wander about behave like zombies. Those zombies are mumbling to themselves and aren't doing any of their regular activities as peasants: tending the fields, maintaining the streets, you name it. Instead, they just trudge around like a virus has taken hold of their body. In fact, their behavior is becoming worse by the day.

"They are not attacking others, or at least none of the knights moving in and out of the city. In fact, Enzo has released a royal decree forbidding interactions between us knights and those individuals, and to instead focus on our daily duties. Every one of us swore to keep our mouths shut regarding this situation, but personally, I don't like any of this. Here with you two is the first time I can discuss this phenomenon, and it's a huge weight off my chest. So I ask, what do you make of this?"

"Scare tactics, nothing more," Jerrick states, letting the rest of his chair hit the floor. He then stands. "Enzo is trying to lure us out by paying all our people to act strange and to weed out those who don't agree with his rule. The ones who refuse his money and disobey his command will soon be arrested and murdered. It is a clever strategy to force compliance."

I consider everything Rufus said along with Jerrick's prediction, then ask, "Is anybody going to the market for goods? People still need to eat. Are there any workers left to keep the city functional?"

"A few people, but not many," Rufus responds.

"Once again, paid off," Jerrick dismisses, walking to the shadow-protected door. "Enzo can just as easily send food to houses. All the supplies the knights take from other towns and villages must be used for something. Besides, those who are working must be essential for Lirium's economy. A crumbling kingdom punishes the king. The real question is, Rufus, as one of the knight commanders close to Enzo, have you witnessed any trickery?"

"None whatsoever. No food has been going to people's houses under my watch."

"And do you have any predictions on why these things are happening?"

"No, sir," Rufus says and puts on his white helmet like he's about to leave. "I'll investigate further. If I disappear, forget about me and continue your mission to end the new king. Every day he's gathering more supporters and seizing greater control, and if you wait too long . . ."

"We will be fine. I shall await your return in the next day or two."

Rufus nods and winks at me. "Don't train too hard, Phoenix. Jerrick can be a harsh man, but you got to know your limits."

I smile and thank him. Afterward, Jerrick moves his shadow from the door, and the knight leaves. When the shadow returns to its rightful role as sentry, Jerrick and I are left alone in a dark room full of persistent candles. Today marks our second day of training in this horrible place. I will keep Rufus' advice in mind, and I won't fail again and make a fool of myself.

"Phoenix. Yesterday you fell short of my expectations and ignored my instructions, so today, we will expand on a concept I know you understand: body manipulation. Two days ago, you displayed competence on allowing yourself to move faster than usual, as well as not breaking your bones from a large fall. I want to expand on these concepts, for your link magic is pathetic at a distance."

I nod and follow him to the center of the room where we trained yesterday. I get a slight sense of déjà vu, and a feeling of dread churns in my stomach.

He then continues, "Body manipulation can be used on yourself to make you stronger, or it can be used on an opponent to turn the tides of battle. Still, we will focus on personalized manipulation since using spells to modify another's body is too advanced, even for me."

"I already understand I can accomplish anything depending on how much I bleed. What more can I learn?" I'm a bit afraid of what he has in mind. His teaching methods haven't been ideal.

Jerrick walks away. I follow him, but he raises a hand for me to stop. He enters the bar area, where many bottles of various shapes and sizes rest upon three layers of shelving. Drinking has never been a hobby of mine, so I never cared to look over there before. However, Jerrick must have an interest in it. What's he going to do, drink to rid himself from me?

His hand grabs a bottle with a long neck and plump base. Moving it closer to his face, it seems like he is reading the label and deciding if it suits his fancy. I place my hand on my forehead and rub my eyes, wondering if we are actually going to learn something today.

On the table nearest to me, glass shatters, and a smelly liquid soils my bloodstained clothing further. I glare at Jerrick, who is already grabbing another bottle.

"What the hell was that for!" I yell at him.

I'm sure he's smiling under his hood when he says, "These are just as dangerous as arrows. If they break on someone, the individual will bleed and suffer from the alcohol staining their wounds. These bottles will be perfect for training today."

I grab a lit candlestick and throw it at him. He dodges to the side and feigns a yawn. I scowl and search for anything else I can throw.

Before I can retaliate further, he speaks loudly, like he is telling a story to a large group of people. "To defend yourself against these arrows, you must train your eyes to see things differently. Perhaps at a slower speed? You may also use magic to affect your body to grab objects which are moving too fast." I start to get the gist of what he's trying to teach me, then he adds, "Let's turn this into a test, my body manipulation against yours."

It seems like he cuts himself because before I can react, he snags another bottle at lightning speed and throws it. The glass crashes onto the same table as before, and again breaks and covers me with alcohol.

He's giving me no time to focus. I use my knife and slash my arm and concentrate on my eyes and body, shifting between the two to increase their effectiveness. Who knows when the next bottle will rush toward me, so I imagine my eyes becoming sharper than ever: to obtain a vision that can detect small and fast-moving objects. My thoughts shift, and I consider my arms and hands. These body parts will become invincible and capable of blocking anything. I switch back and forth between my eyes and my body every few seconds. When I notice Jerrick grabbing the next bottle, I breathe faster and hope I don't get splashed again.

"Phoenix, catch this one. It will be moving fast, so watch out."

He throws it, and I panic. All my focus returns to my eyes to try and decelerate the object, and it slows to a catchable speed. It moves directly toward me, and I grasp it with both hands. However, the bottle shatters and splits open my skin, and I cry out. Tiny glass shards are stuck in my palms and fingers, and the alcohol burns profusely. The pain is so agonizing. I want to blackout.

I falter and can only concentrate on my wounds, mumbling gibberish as I try not to cry. A hand enters my field of view. The shards of glass leave my body, the scratches disappear, and the pain diminishes. I look up and see Jerrick walking back behind the bar again and preparing to strike once more.

"Focus and relax," he remarks like I'm a child. "You need to expand your mind to focus on more than one thing. Imagine your eyes and body being as one."

I'm ready for him this time. I will do what it takes to not experience that pain again. Using blood magic is only as dangerous as I want it to be. Alcohol on open wounds is a whole other story.

I cut my arm and release a moderate amount of blood. Unlike before, I split my focus and enhance my eyes and hands together. I concentrate on the long bottle Jerrick holds and prepare my hands to catch it without it breaking. My eyes will see it coming, while my hands will provide enough cushion to slow it down safely so I can keep ahold of it. I can do this. I must do this.

Like before, the bottle flies in my direction, and I continue focusing on keeping my body in check. My breathing is steady, and I reach for the bottle like last time. The glass touches my hands. As a precaution, I keep it away from my body as I wrap my fingers around the fragile object. After a few moments, it's clear the glass won't shatter, and I place it down on the table and release a sigh.

Jerrick claps and says, "I'm impressed, to say the least. Succeeding on your second try is impressive for someone who knows so little about magic. Allow me to heal your wounds before our next lesson."

I widen my eyes and ask, "We're learning more today?"

He goes silent and approaches me. I wait for his response as his hands hover above my wound. Only after my cut transforms into a scar, he answers, "Yes. We are not learning one thing and calling it enough. There is one more body manipulation technique that you must learn as we prepare for our battle against Enzo. You demonstrated some of this in Zwelis, but I want to test you. Today, we will be learning how to speed your body up. Doing so will allow you to dodge arrows and incoming attacks and move around the battlefield without fear of anyone catching you. Observe."

He creates another small cut and leaps over me. The jump looks so unnatural. As he lands, I'm afraid he might crash into some tables and chairs, but instead, he places a hand on the table and somersaults into the air, even higher than before. The motion propels him across the room near the wall. This magic has a lot of potential.

"As you can see," Jerrick says as he regains his footing, "the tiniest amount of blood can enhance your speed and ignore the weight of your body. No need to focus on strength. Every movement you just witnessed is a product of those two factors. I did not have my weight slowing me down, and my speed gave me all the momentum I needed. It is a sensation you must try for yourself to understand."

"You want me to do what you did?" I ask. "I can always try something else. There seems to be many options in a place like this."

"Hmmm . . . alright. I want you to find a way to the second floor without using the stairs. Extra points for haste."

I look up at my destination and see only darkness. The candles on the first floor limit my vision and make it impossible to see anything on the second floor. Even the railing is difficult to see.

"You expect me to blindly make a jump up there and make it on my first attempt?" I challenge. "I'd rather not crash my head into the ceiling."

Jerrick smiles. "Wise. Body manipulation works on the eyes, you know. This same magic can modify your vision to see better in the dark. It may take practice since it is not an exact science, but I know you can achieve this."

"I'll try." I follow his example and nick my arm. Then, I train my eyes to see what lies within the shadows and awkward light. In seconds, the darkness of the second floor becomes a musty gray color, revealing the exact location of the railing.

Afterward, I imagine my body becoming lighter and swift as a bird. It works, and my legs feel more capable than ever, but I must scratch further along the incision to guarantee my desired goal. When my body is ready for this task, I risk mimicking Jerrick's somersault motion on a chair—instead of a massive table—and force my body to propel itself below the railing. This is exhilarating! When my feet land on solid footing, I find myself standing erect on a table. It does not wobble like it usually would with someone on it, and the candle stays in place. I smile and bend my legs and jump. My body overshoots past the second floor, and as I begin to fall, I grapple the railing and climb over it.

I feel a million times stronger with this skill. Nobody, not even Enzo's entire army, can hope to defeat me. It may even help me escape Zier as well. If this spell only needs a little blood, why not activate it whenever I please?

Jerrick walks up the stairs and places a hand on my shoulder. I'm sure I made him proud today despite failing countless other times.

He praises, "You seem to have a mastery over body manipulation. You have shown me that in Zwelis and now today." I take in all his words of encouragement. I need to hear this after dealing with nothing but my link magic's limitations. "Nonetheless, you cannot rely on this power alone in battle. Look at your arm."

I examine it, and it appears I'm still dripping blood, the red forming a sizable puddle on the wooden floor. I try to imagine my powers disappearing so the bleeding might stop, but it does not.

"You have pushed yourself a bit much," he explains. "You became lighter and improved your speed and vision simultaneously. Quite the strain on your body. As the blood will continue to flow during manipulation, it's possible the blood loss will flow until healed, a dangerous concept for someone like you. Be wary of pushing your body too hard."

"Additionally, if this was out on the battlefield, you might have died from blood loss. You must be wary. The constant flow of blood when using body manipulation makes it a risky choice. This is why link magic should usually be our go-to. Still, your case might be the opposite concerning your useless black waterfall magic. Nevertheless, I refrain from you using body manipulation unless I'm with you, so I can heal you."

He cures my wound, and I use my already-soiled shirt to wipe off the excess blood. "So, the one thing I'm good at, I'm not allowed to use unless in your presence?" I question him. "I disagree. I will do as I wish. If you want me to follow your command, you better not die anytime soon."

Jerrick turns away and returns to the first floor. He then adds, "Not until after Enzo dies. You have the rest of the day off. I don't want to push you after you fainted the other day. And besides, you look like you need a bath."

Relief spreads through my chest, and I waste no time grabbing new clothes and cleaning up. I change into my clean, black dress and leave the washroom. It appears that Jerrick will be spending the rest of the day reading in the main room. No surprise there. Unlike me, he does not need any tutelage on sorcery, for he learned everything through books in the castle.

When I reach my room, I examine my black steel knife—

a blade that has been bloodied countless times. Still, there's no rust or residue anywhere. It's surreal how I inherited this blade from my father. This is a knife of royal origin once owned by King Krolas Malfester himself. Although, how does Zier have an identical blade? Is it possible he forged a separate one? He is a blood demon after all. But Jerrick is confident about the origin of my knife, so there should only be one.

Perhaps Zier and I have more in common than I once thought. Death magic, black steel knife, killers . . . yet I have not killed anyone.

I squint my eyes and approach my window. Looking outside, I still see nobody like the other day. Rufus said there were people outside acting like zombies, but ever since entering this domain, there's not been a single soul outside. The streets are still perfectly maintained too, with no trash or heaps of dirt, and the buildings I can see are still standing. It's clear we have a few more days to prepare.

Nothing eventful occurs in the next fifteen minutes, so I sit on my bed and examine my new scars: two on my right arm, one on my left, and one on my left hand. I will be horrendous by the end of my life. Thank you, Jerrick.

I make a small incision on my right arm, careful to avoid the scars and getting more blood on my bed, and let my link magic flow out of my hand. I attempt to manipulate its flow again by imagining the darkness rolling into a sphere. No luck. I try to control its direction. Still no use, despite last time working a little bit—it must depend on the amount of blood I'm releasing. Nonetheless, I'm not going to cut more than necessary. I will use the rest of the day to practice.

I hover my hand over my arm and attempt to use a healing spell. The determination behind it is halfhearted because I know I will fail, but I might as well practice. Soon, my blood clots, and I reopen the wound. This is a process I will repeat until I get it right.

I continue this for hours, only pausing for occasional food breaks when my stomach growls. Jerrick's head is locked within his book whenever I leave the room. It does not seem he cares for what I'm doing. He must think I'm just relaxing in my room, writing notes and reading, then eating snacks to pass the time. If only he knew my mind. I want to be beneficial to him and strong enough to sustain myself. He won't be here forever, and I need to be ready to challenge Enzo and face this world alone.

17

Every day that passes is a step closer to our uncertain fate.

I wake up and prepare for my next day of training. I'm happy I had no dreams last night and, by extension, no nightmares. It makes me wonder if my previous vision was a coincidence. If it was, I'm relieved Zier hasn't found me, but I'm fearful my power isn't as potent as I desire.

According to Jerrick's prediction on when we will strike at Enzo, this makes day three of seven, and I can't help but feel unready. Yesterday, despite hours of practice, my link magic failed to follow my instructions. I used every mindset and thought of everything I could, but nothing worked. In the end, it appears my magic is impossible to manipulate. Perhaps my unique powers are limiting my potential to heal? Who knows.

What I do know is this place is starting to stink with rot. All the bloodstains are becoming more prevalent every day we train. There's some on my bed and floor. Many are around the furniture in the training area. There may even be some in Jerrick's room. I'm ready to get out of here and force Jerrick to begin the attack against Enzo early.

In the main room, next to Jerrick, Rufus is exiting the front door, and I rush down to greet him before he leaves.

"Good morning, Phoenix!" Rufus calls to me. "I arrived a bit earlier than usual because I have a meeting with Enzo very soon. From what I'm told, all the knights must report to him when the sun reaches its zenith, so do not worry. Your mentor will fill you in on the new information."

With that, Rufus leaves, and Jerrick slides his shadow over the door. I'm upset he has no time to talk, for he is one of the few people I have left. But duty calls, and Rufus can't break his cover. He will be back again soon.

When Jerrick returns to his chair, I ask him about their discussion while I was asleep.

"There is a new concern for us," Jerrick claims, leaning back and crossing his arms. "Lirium's knights are . . . becoming strange. Darkness is covering their armor like they are being controlled by demons."

"You think it's the work of Zier? It would make sense. Perhaps he can't find us and is receiving aid."

"Zier has never been known to stoop so low. From my knowledge, he always works alone and will lavish in the pride of dealing with us himself."

"Maybe he's changed?" I suggest.

"You are too skeptical of what is already understood. Still, there may be a different demon at play, one we do not know about. Beginning with the townspeople acting funny—which is still prevalent according to Rufus—and now the knights. I'm unsure what to make of it just yet."

"If we kill Enzo, do you think it might end all these strange events?"

"I doubt it, but it may give us an edge toward discovering what is happening." Jerrick rests a hand on his chin and adds, "There is one other thing. Rumors are floating around about Dalgin being targeted for an envision led by Enzo. Who knows what he hopes to gain."

"What! Why would he care about a place like that! We

have to stop him before he even thinks about going there!"

"No, Phoenix, I still need time."

"To reflect upon your life and wallow in your problems? People's lives are at stake, and the more time we waste, the more problems seem to follow us. Furthermore, Enzo might know about Dureizen and may try to meet him. Don't you see? We must stop him now. We are strong enough to end his reign!"

"You are flustered, and understandably so. I still need time to figure out a strategy and what may come after Enzo's death. Once we defeat him, this unknown power may come for us, and we must be ready for it. I am done *wallowing*, for your information. Now it's time for a plan, but it will not be ready today."

I shake my head and snap, "There's nothing to gain by waiting! If Enzo attacks Dalgin—"

"ENZO WILL NOT!" Jerrick speaks over me and stands. "Enzo is a fool, but he is not so crazy to attack a small town past a forest. He gains nothing from such an action, even if he does know about Dureizen. Additionally, what does he gain from blood magic? If he wanted it so bad, he would go alone without others trying to steal it and overtake him. Dureizen will not bless him either since it would directly conflict with my purpose."

I hold back my anger as he sits down again. Even though he wears a hood, he looks distressed and unpleasant. His body seems to shake on its own volition, and I worry about his health.

He then adds in a softer tone, "I don't even know if I can trust Rufus. He may be a spy, telling Enzo everything about us and our plan. Enzo may know about you too. Everything has been strange since we arrived, Phoenix." I keep my head down but try to make eye contact with his shrouded eyes. "I need time alone to devise a plan. We may attack tomorrow, so I want you to stay in your room, meditate, and discover what is blocking your magic. Without me today, I want you to prepare yourself in any way possible. Right now, there is no time for me to teach you more."

"I understand," I simply say and leave Jerrick be.

I clean myself up, eat, and return to my room. Concerning Rufus, he seems trustworthy, but Jerrick has a point about him. He's our spy, but he knows too much. If Enzo suspects him of treachery, there's a chance he will slip valuable information regarding us. Also, hopefully Jerrick is right about Enzo, but I will never forgive him if my home is destroyed when we could've prevented it.

Upon entering my room, I open my window to try and clear out the rancid smell of blood. It's impossible to focus with such a disgusting scent hitting my nose every time I breathe. I stand by the window for a few minutes and watch the day go by, and I wonder if anyone can see me, but I disregard the idea since there seems to be nobody on the streets. Today, the window will stay open. I've been cooped up here for far too long to not deserve a little freedom. The blood smell might eventually dissipate too while I allow airflow into this room.

I lie down and close my eyes. Considering Jerrick's recommendation to meditate and self-train, it's impossible to think of anything besides Dalgin being attacked, my mentor's questionable demeanor, and how the future will play out with this new, unknown force seeming to latch itself onto the knights and townspeople. It makes me wonder if Enzo is affected by these recent events and who is truly to blame.

Shifting around, I move my legs over my bed and sit up. I then pull out my knife and make a small scratch on my arm. It's too early to rest, and I want to be worthy of joining Jerrick's side by being competent on my own. If tomorrow is the day we prove ourselves and change the world, I want to be ready. It's time to show what I can achieve with all this hidden power within me.

The sensation of heat floods my hand as I imagine a fire materializing from thin air. Fire is an advanced skill that is impossible for someone like me to learn, but I'm ready to prove Jerrick wrong. If he can do it, so can I.

My mind remains calm as I solely focus on generating heat in my palm. The blood on my arm, the stench, my past, my future, nothing matters except for achieving this one thing. I keep my eyes shut while I concentrate, only opening them to check my progress since my hand is searing. Yet, there is no flame.

I cut deeper into my open wound since this spell must require a lot of blood for someone like me. The pain almost makes me black out, but my ambition keeps me focused and conscious. If I fail, Jerrick is just outside my room. My gash now runs from my elbow to my shoulder and is bleeding a healthy amount. This should give me the energy I require.

But it's still not enough. My hand continues to boil, so it must need a touch more blood to spark to life. I extend my wound to my forearm. I wince and feel lightheaded, but it is a sacrifice I will get used to. My upper arm no longer hurts as much when I damage it, so it's a matter of practice and determination.

Crawling dread tingles across the back of my skull. My efforts will end in disaster. There's still no fire. Despite my hand feeling like it's being plunged into lava, I am missing something. I'm bleeding heavily, and I consider calling for Jerrick. I'm afraid of what will happen if I stay in my room much longer. Still, I'm not a quitter, and I pour all of my internal hatred for being a failure into my magic. I will force this spell to obey me.

My vision fades in and out like a dream as a small flame illuminates the room around me. It's beautiful. Relief spreads through my body, and I let the flame die. I seem to be lying down, and I look over at my arm again and see a gallon of blood getting all over my bedsheets. I try and call for help, but I have no strength for words. The allure of sleep clouds over me.

Someone is standing near the door, and a spark of hope runs through my heart. Jerrick knew I would be reckless. He is here to save me.

18

The warmth of the rising sun within the vibrant blue sky wraps around my skin like a blanket. I bask in its glory and stretch, breathing in as much air as I can. A slight breeze gives a nice contrast to the heat. The birds chirp above and offer a living world full of happiness, where every creature can live carefree. No danger exists anywhere. Not anymore.

I sit up and examine the landscape. Lush hills of brilliant red, blue, green, and orange flowers expand across the horizon. They sway back and forth in the wind, and I am at peace.

What is a horrible person like me doing in a gorgeous place like this? My arms have more scars than usual, some larger than others. I'm hideous. So why was I transported here?

I stand up. The flowers go on forever, for this place has no discernable end. I guess if the world wants me here, I will happily abide.

The wind compels my dress to rustle and my hair sway, so I tuck my hair under my shirt collar and walk toward the sun. I've never been alone in such a grand landscape before, and this freedom feels great. I want to explore every aspect of my surroundings and uncover its secrets. Seeing this land's beauty in its entirety will make me happy and blissful—a strange feeling to me.

Ever since I was a child, my parents never acted like other parents. They kept me locked up at home and rarely let me outside. Despite my oath to secrecy, they feared what I may reveal to others. In fact, they treated me like an object who would take their place when they died. What kind of child would want their freedom stolen and told the meaning of their existence is for a worthless task and nothing more? My life has been for nothing, and despite my pleas to experience the outside world and discover my own desires, they never let me.

I only loved them because they were my parents. They taught me how to survive by using knives and how to interact with strangers who threatened my life. I guess they also fed and kept me safe, but they never respected who I wanted to be. A caged animal held by captors is all I was.

When they deserted me, I was afraid. I didn't know if they would ever return. They were the only people I knew. It felt wrong to leave. I believed I was going to be punished if I left home. Now that Jerrick gave me the courage to abandon that horrible place, I don't feel afraid anymore. The longer I was away, the lingering fear further dissipated into nothing. Now, there's no negativity left. I want to embrace my life and experience everything I never got to as a child.

"Phoenix? What are you doing here?" a strange voice provokes confusing emotions within me. I turn around to find where the voice came from and see a woman and a man sitting together with bread, fruits, and vegetables—almost like they are picnicking. They aren't looking at me, so how do they know me?

I approach them with caution. They are eating and laughing together, stuck in some intriguing conversation. I'm curious who they are and if the voice I heard really came from them.

I rest a hand on the woman's shoulder when I get close. From this distance they're familiar, but I can't put my finger on who they are. Why are they here with me?

They turn around from my touch, and two familiar faces stare back at me. Ashen and Flare, my parents.

They look different from what I remember. Still, they are in a better place where they can care for their looks easier. Ashen has his usual dirty blonde hair, but it's now smooth over his head and not curly and crazy. His green eyes are the same as they always are, piercing but caring, and his beard is now short and maintained.

My mother, Flare, has long blonde hair like mine, except hers doesn't have tangles. Her once soulless blue eyes now resemble joy as they shine in the sunlight. She never smiled in my life, but here, she is happy as can be.

"What are you two doing here?" I ask and retract my hand. "What happened to you?"

Ashen and Flare prolong their smiles, and Ashen replies, "Just in a better place. We hated that cave as much as you, protecting a worthless demon who didn't care about his son's desires. No, once we died, we came here."

"Died!?" I yell. So it's true . . .

"Yes, honey," this time Flare speaks. "You have grown to be a fine woman. Ever since I've taught you to use knives, you have never disappointed me. Now look at you! You are traveling the world and beginning your own journey, right?"

I shake my head, thinking about my time with Jerrick. "Not yet, but maybe later. But how did you two die? Does that mean I'm dead too?"

Ashen responds this time, saying, "I left home to grab some goods, but a strange woman killed me. I have no idea who she was or what she knew, but after I noticed her, she stabbed me."

"Likewise," Flare adds. "She killed me while searching for my husband. We are sorry to have left you all alone. Even so, thanks to that man over there, you are still alive and well." She points toward the horizon, and I see a figure sitting away from us. He's hunched over and wears a brown cloak. All alone.

"He's the one who saved you from dying," she continues. "Why don't you meet him?"

My parents return to their idle, indistinguishable chatter. Then, my body starts stumbling toward this newcomer. Who has the power to save me from death? Is this a new ally aside from Jerrick who can lead me to a better future than the dark one I'm charging headfirst into?

Goosebumps rise on my skin as the air becomes colder with every step I take. The sun tries to warm me up, but there's a forcefield here which must block its radiance. I shiver and wrap my arms close but continue to walk toward him. He pays no mind to me.

I touch his back, and my hand becomes numb from his resonating chill. I expect him to acknowledge me like my parents did. Instead, he refuses to move. He is an icicle which needs to be warmed up to budge, so I wrap my arms around him.

The temperature rises between us. My touch is working, and he is no longer frozen in place. His warmth is helping me become warmer too. If he was the one who helped me, now I have returned the favor.

"Thank you, Phoenix," the man's voice is raspy but grateful.

"It's the least I could do. You were cold. I was worried you might've died."

"Perhaps another time. As for now, I'm stuck wondering what to do about the future. My purpose has run dry."

"Sounds a lot like me." I let go of him and sit beside him. I only see darkness under his hood, but I'm used to people who refuse to reveal their faces. "I'm searching for a new purpose too."

"Oh?" The man sounds interested and leans a bit closer to me. "Please, tell me more. Does it have something to do with your parents?"

"That obvious? It has everything to do with them. They kept me locked away for most of my life, aside from going out here and there to wash or whatever, and my only purpose was to keep a door with a demon inside safe. Never asked for this sort of life. I want an adventure where I feel like I belong. A place where I feel safe. Strangely, my parents over there don't care about me protecting the door anymore. Now they finally act human."

"I completely understand, Phoenix. Talking to you, I realize how similar we are. My parent kept me tied to a purpose I no longer wish to live by. I desire a livable life instead of the one I'm chained to, but it appears you are already receiving what I crave."

I look down and consider my life with Jerrick. "Not at all. I'm free, but I'm also trapped. Still, tell me about your situation. Maybe talking about it might help you feel better?"

"I found that I was adopted," the man speaks without hesitation. "My parents were killed, and I was taken in by a new parent, a parent which I can no longer support."

"Is there something I can do to help?" I place my hand on his back again. It's warm.

"For now, nothing at all. But I can help you. Look at your

arms.”

Following his instruction, my eyes widen as I see what he must've wanted me to notice. No more scars. The large one across my arm, gone. The one on my hand, just like it was before Jerrick cut it. The sporadic slashes across the length of my arms are no more. My body is flawless once again, perhaps even better than before. I'm uncertain if I want to use blood magic anymore and destroy my body. Unfortunately, this is not an option for my predicament. At least I have a fresh start.

“How did you . . .” my happiness causes me to choke up on my words.

“You're welcome. I know your skin has been disturbing you, so I needed to help you. This is a small example of the magic I possess; magic I can teach you.”

My gut becomes queasy with distrust. How does this man know me so well, and what sort of magic is he referring to? This power is far from Jerrick's capabilities, and he's a master who knows all. Healing scars is near impossible.

I peer under his hood and ask, “Who are you?”

He grasps the front of his cowl and slides it back. I recognize the wicked smile, malicious eyes, and the demon who's ready to kill. Zier.

My body jolts like it's been brought back from death, and

I'm in my room again. I instinctively check my arms and feel a cold chill, realizing my experience was not only a dream. My body has no scars.

I'm grateful, but I cannot shake the feeling of someone stalking me. Is Zier inside this bar? Did he find us? I scan my room and see nothing amiss, yet, the figure who was by my door . . .

I close the window and leave my room. There's no time left to spare. We must strike Enzo today and escape from this place.

19

My dream must've been a make-believe world Zier concocted to mess with me. My parents would never be so careless and warm with their words. Them telling me that Zier saved me from death? Ridiculous.

However, they told me that a strange woman killed them, and if that's true, Zier must know what happened to them. I should not reflect on this subject much, for it could be a trap. Instead, next time I confront Zier, even if it's on my deathbed, I will pry the truth out of him.

What does Zier even accomplish by tormenting me? What does he want from me that he can't obtain himself? If he and I are the only ones with death magic, why should my existence bother a demon like him? I need all these questions answered.

Jerrick does not need to know about my dreams anymore. The last time I told him about this situation, he had nothing much to add. Furthermore, my latest nightmare had nothing to do with him. My future involves Zier. He is destined to kill those with magic, and his next target is me.

Perhaps my magic can end his life, which may be why he's after me. He's afraid of me. He's trying to scare me into submission by worming into my dreams. Even though my magic isn't strong enough yet, all I can do is hold my ground and hope for luck to be on my side when that fated day comes.

"How do you not have scars?" Jerrick asks as he grabs me. "How the hell did you achieve this, foreigner?"

"I don't know," I half-lie. "I woke up and found my arms to be scarless."

"Stop playing around! If you discovered a way to perfectly heal yourself, something nobody in the history of sorcery ever knew, you need to tell me."

"So, it's true you don't understand everything about magic."

"What!?" he growls and shoves me away. "I don't know why you're trying to hide this from me, a revolutionary spell beneficial to both of us. Nobody has discovered how to fully cure themselves, and you want me to believe that you—someone who cannot heal—came up with a way to achieve this? You must know how you did it, so tell me!"

"Power hungry much?" I mutter under my breath and walk away from him. I can feel my arms shaking from anger, and I'm not in the mood to argue this early in the morning.

"Phoenix, get back here you insolent—"

The door knocks three times, and Jerrick grumbles as he lets Rufus in. Jerrick pursues his meaningless anger and pushes the knight into a chair. "And I bet you're going to tell me that you killed Enzo yourself, Rufus," my mentor goes off on him. "Or maybe he has taken over the world, and our plight is now pointless."

Rufus removes his helmet and appears calm, almost like he's used to this behavior, then he brushes off the shoulder Jerrick touched. The knight then explains, "About that, I've confirmed Enzo's plans. He will destroy Dalgin tonight. As we speak, he is gathering a capable force to do his bidding."

"Do you know what he hopes to gain from destroying my hometown?" I chime in. Here is another reason why we must liberate Lirium today.

Rufus frowns and explains, "He's using the town as a demonstration of control. Despite Dalgin being a weak territory unable to defend itself, a successful raid will show how the kingdom is unafraid to take what it desires and kill for pleasure. It's a bold tactic and may even be used to lure you out of your hiding place, Jerrick. He knows you are still alive."

Jerrick responds, "How could he not? I will not die from his pathetic hands or a lowly knight. His priority when he took over the kingdom should have been killing me."

"Why would Enzo care about you?" I ask with a touch of haughtiness in my throat. It's nice pushing him down from his high and mighty throne. At times he treats me well, but many other times, he treats me like worthless trash.

"Phoenix, I protected King Krolas when Enzo took over the castle. Though the king was wise, I knew all the hidden passages and where the most trustworthy guards were patrolling to form an escape plan. We avoided all the bloodshed and chaos as Enzo slaughtered everyone, but he never did find us. We escaped without a scratch. Nonetheless, it seemed Enzo did not care about us after all. Krolas was poisoned. He died in my arms, and as I stayed during his final breath, he entrusted me with one final task. I must be the one to avenge him. I must kill Enzo."

"I still don't see why Enzo should've paid any mind to you," I say as I consider Jerrick's story.

"Well, Enzo's mistake was clear. Ignoring the ones who helped Krolas escape will be his downfall. For today, we will strike Lirium's castle and cleanse the throne."

"About time." I smile and happily grab my knife. "Kill him before he sets foot in Dalgin, and we can get out of this dump."

"Exactly," Jerrick agrees. "We are out of time anyway. Considering your dream from the other day, Phoenix, and the recent events surrounding Lirium, we are no longer gaining anything by lounging around. At this point, Enzo is just getting stronger as his confidence grows. We need to stop him before his reign lasts too long so we can snuff him out like he never existed."

Rufus raises a hand and adds, "That would be wise. He is focused on other matters and will be open to a surprise attack. Though he expects to lure you out, I believe he thinks you'll attack him after Dalgin's destruction. Little does he know I'm working with you two and spreading all the inside information."

"Do you know what Enzo might be doing now?" Jerrick asks.

"Likely in his chamber going through the final details of his plan. I've noticed he's in there alone quite often. I'm called to join him in the next hour when we plan to advance toward Dalgin. So, I suggest attacking him when I leave, so I can provide backup if needed."

"Won't there be other knights we must fight then?" I ask. "If we attack now, he is all alone, and we can make this a personal matter."

"For once, Phoenix is right." Jerrick agrees.

"But sir, don't you need time to prepare for an attack?" Rufus stammers. "Besides, if we wait, there will be less knights patrolling the castle, as most will be gathered in one area."

"No. Phoenix and I are as ready as we will ever be. We don't need armor, don't need to prep our weapons, or partake in any final training. Our capabilities with magic are suitable enough to kill Enzo with a flick of a finger. Enter his domain undetected and reveal ourselves as he draws his final breath. This is the perfect time to strike."

"But sir, I really think—"

"Enough, Rufus!" Jerrick yells and points his finger at the knight sitting straight in his chair. "Is there a reason why you are so reluctant about ending this now? Speak!"

"I . . . uh." He fails forming any words, stands from his seat, and steps away from Jerrick. I don't understand why he's acting so strange. This isn't the Rufus I used to know. He's too fidgety and afraid, like an abused dog. If Enzo threatened his life, we could always protect him.

"Enzo was right," Rufus snarls and replaces the helmet on his head, completing the shining knight armor he wears. He then releases his blade from his scabbard and brandishes it toward us. "My king said you weren't going to follow my direction. No, he expected you to march toward the castle and ignore my pleas to let you prepare. At least he foreseen this predicament, despite my misguided confidence. I just need to hold you off until he arrives, for he is ready for you. He will kill you here in this bloodstained grave."

20

A man I once called a friend . . .

Rufus' armor drains pale before my eyes, and a dark aura surrounds him. His steel blade exhibits broken streaks of darkness, displaying an appearance of devilish horror. The only person I knew who treated me well is now someone I disgust—someone who believes they can kill me.

However, this is the affliction Rufus mentioned during his last visit. Lirium's knights have been transforming into dark creatures with the aid of an unknown force. Perhaps Enzo is to blame. Or it's a demon. Still, Rufus' personality is no longer the man I knew. From this moment on, he's my enemy who betrayed us, swearing his fealty to a false king.

"I was correct not to trust you then," Jerrick breaks the silence. "How can I expect loyalty from someone so close to the one I hate most. I will spare you no more words. You will die today."

"And what about you, Phoenix, friend?" Rufus offers me a hand, assuming I will take it. "You can join Enzo and I. Don't think I don't know about your plight. If you stand by us, we promise you a new purpose. You can be free from Jerrick, the man who abuses you, and you will have endless opportunities to explore the world. As someone who can't heal, Enzo has the power to protect you. His abilities can affect every townsperson and knight within the kingdom, and soon his reach will spread across this earth! We will all be safe from misgivings, fear, and even demons."

I mutter, "So all these wicked deeds came from him? I think I'll pass joining someone like that. Had my fair share of demons in my life already. Instead, I'll have more fun ridding you from my life."

I swipe my knife across my arm—my flawless skin isn't going to last anyway. Readying my blade, I push past Jerrick and dash toward Rufus. I slash at his neck, but he blocks it with his sword. The screech of metal-on-metal rings in my ears, but I refuse to let up. I slash at the betrayer with various strikes, every angle imaginable to discern a blind spot, to break his defense and confuse him. My magic increases my speed with every blow, so I must press on and never allow him to retaliate.

Still, nothing seems to get through. Every attack is blocked at the perfect moment. Rufus doesn't even seem to be struggling under his heavy armor.

"Phoenix, duck," Jerrick commands. I do as he says. A harsh, reddish light above me causes me to squint. It crackles above, and a crash echoes from where Rufus stands. The magic connects with the knight, and he staggers backward. Nonetheless, Rufus somehow stands as the illumination dims. He then rushes at me without hesitation.

I cut my other arm. Rufus' sword slices down with insane speed, and I grab it with my free hand. The blade is sharp, and I must focus my magic on holding off the sword's weight without being sliced open. Still, the sword manages to penetrate my skin. I wish to retract my hand, but Rufus continues to apply downward pressure to make it impossible to escape. It's becoming painful, and I'm afraid he might cut through it entirely if my magic flickers for even a second. I bend my knees to adjust to the force of the blow, but it only hampers my predicament.

This is hopeless, and my only viable option is to fight back against the pressure. Blood rushes to my cheeks as I grip his dark blade with all the force I can muster. He attempts to yank it free as he looks toward Jerrick, but I refuse to let go. There's no escape from whatever he's afraid of.

Then, two orbs of purple lightning smash into Rufus' side, and he is blown away from me. I continue to hold his sword as he crashes into the wall and struggles to stand back up, defenseless. This battle is over.

I throw his sword behind me and chuckle. "Just stay down," I tell him. "You're weak. Did you really think a normal human like you could defeat us? We are gods compared to you."

Jerrick walks over to me and heals my wounds. I thank him and move toward the pathetic scene before us.

I spare no words as I tear off Rufus' pale helmet and view his smug face. It pisses me off, and I slice his neck open. He falls over with a satisfying thump. His death reaches my lips as they widen. That's what happens when people mess with my feelings.

"You didn't think I'd die that easily." Rufus' voice gurgles. There must be so much blood in his throat. My eyes widen with horror as he bleeds everywhere, yet he reclaims his helmet from my hand, puts it back on, and stands like nothing happened. My mouth opens and closes several times as I try and process what's going on.

"How?" Jerrick asks the betrayer who should be dead.

"This armor gives me power, *Jerrick*." Rufus' voice sounds normal again, somehow. "Blessed by Enzo himself, it has regenerative abilities to keep me alive. Fatal injuries are only inconveniences. You will have to chop me into bits to rid of me. But you won't have time for such a task. Please welcome our star guest!"

21

Enzo and Krolas must have a history together. They crave to kill each other with every bone in their bodies. This kind of mutual hate only comes from a lifetime of understanding one another, something I am unfamiliar with.

Nothing happens. I lock my gaze on Rufus to test his bluff, for if I reveal any weakness, or even turn away, I might fall into a trap. Perhaps Enzo isn't planning to show up, and Rufus has just gone insane? It's possible with how he's been acting. No matter the reason, I will forever be angry with how he betrayed our trust.

"Phoenix, come to me," Jerrick speaks in a low voice.

His shadow stirs on the walls. I'm assuming Jerrick is planning an attack with his shadow, so I back up toward my mentor. Every ounce of darkness relocates somewhere behind us, and even though I want to see what Jerrick's doing, Rufus is staring right at us.

"Enzo's approaching, Phoenix," Jerrick mutters under his breath. "Be prepared to fight like your life depends on it."

I tense up. Sure, I had plenty of time to mentally prepare myself for this moment, but I never expected to encounter our target here.

"So, what's our plan?" I whisper back.

"Stick close to me. I can heal you while you focus on body manipulation. Worry about killing Rufus, and I will deal with Enzo. Be wary. We don't know what to expect."

Rufus steps forward, and I harm myself on instinct. I become lighter on my toes and focus on striking speed to pierce any weak points in Rufus' armor. The knight notices my preparation and pauses. I snicker at him and yell, "Just try it and see where it gets you!"

"Oh, I think we will," a familiar voice halts my breathing. "Phoenix, Krolas, the pleasure is all mine."

"Krolas?" I question and look behind me. A lone figure is standing behind us, and I must blink a few times to confirm

I'm not seeing a phantom's silhouette in the darkness. No. Enzo's standing in the middle of the room. A dark glob, what must be left of Jerrick's shadow, surrounds Enzo's feet as he stands defiant with his arms stretched. His blood-red, regal jacket makes him appear bulkier than what he actually is, and he's wearing dark brown pants and black boots with gold accents. A pitch-black sword resides in his hand. His black hair seems to go back into a ponytail, and his devious brown eyes stare at us with unrelenting amusement. This man looks like a king, even though he's not. But where is Krolas? Doubtless he believes Jerrick is the lost king.

I turn to Rufus again. He's the one I will be focusing on. Jerrick trusts me with this task.

"Rufus," Enzo starts again, "come over to me so Phoenix isn't distracted."

"Yes, my lord," Rufus acknowledges, and I watch him hustle to his side. Now that they are standing together, Jerrick's focus and mine will no longer be split.

My mentor places a hand on my back and exclaims, "Enzo, you're here for me, so let's just settle this together. Phoenix should be let free, for she has no part to play in this. Besides, I can end our predicament myself."

Enzo laughs. "Why would I allow such a thing? To have

more than one blood magic wielder is too much. Only one can rule this world with power; leaving someone alive who can rival the king's strength is out of the question. You both must die. And I want to make a mockery of your name, Krolas."

Enzo looks at me and adds, "Phoenix, my purposeless friend who cannot heal, Jerrick is Krolas. Go ahead and show her the truth, brother. There's nothing left to hide."

My mouth is agape as Jerrick removes his hood and reveals a similar face from the one in my dream. His yellow eyes stare at me. He is a pale man with black hair running down to his shoulders. The stubble on his face is still a bit short when comparing it to my dream. But overall, it's clear he's the same man.

"You deserve to know," Jerrick tells me. He then returns his gaze to Enzo, who is just standing there and presenting a disgusting smile I wish to rip off. "Enzo, I assume you have acquired Dureizen's blessing then? If I die fighting you, Phoenix deserves to know the truth about me. Everyone deserves to know who I was, the seventh king of Lirium who fought the corruption overtaking his kingdom."

Enzo responds, "You're too kind, Krolas. I'll tell you what, we can have our one-on-one battle to end our rivalry forever. If you kill me, Rufus' fate will be in your hands, you become king once more, and so on. If I kill you, Phoenix will also die, and I will live forever and rule, for it's my purpose given to me by Dureizen himself!"

"Why would Dureizen care about you?" I yell at him. I step forward, but Jerrick tugs my shirt.

Enzo snickers. "Bold of you to speak to your king that way. Still, I guess I should thank you for leaving Dureizen's cave defenseless for me, not that someone like you could stop me anyway."

"You're wrong!" I retaliate. "I could kill you with my eyes closed."

"A threat? Perhaps I should—"

"Enough!" Jerrick, I mean, Krolas, interrupts our dispute, despite me waiting to hear whatever bold words this *king* had for me. "Enzo, a fight between us for the throne. Phoenix, stay back and watch how the true king of Lirium avenges his kingdom."

Enzo raises his hands in a hopeless gesture. "Whatever you say, ex-king Krolas. Very well, I was getting bored of our idle chit-chat anyway. Rufus, stay back as well. I'll have this over in a moment."

Rufus and I leave our kings and wait at opposite sides. Though I am confident Krolas can kill Enzo with his mass array of spells and skills, my heart sinks into a bottomless pit of despair. Am I really not able to assist him in this fight? Furthermore, if his face was the one from my dream, does it mean Zier's words about his death will come to pass? Is my master's purpose going to lead him to death?

Dureizen is a demon who I now know does not choose sides. Why grant Krolas sorcery to kill Enzo? Why did Enzo receive the demon's blessing days later to live forever and rule? Enzo's purpose may be metaphoric. What if Krolas defeats Enzo, and the false king's renown is too high to where Krolas can never return to the throne?

Interrupting my thoughts, Enzo and Krolas brandish their blades and cut themselves—Krolas on the arm where I usually do it, while Enzo on his hand. Blood oozes down Krolas' blade, but on Enzo's sword, the liquid is repelled and slides down without any residue. Black steel, no doubt.

My king charges with blinding speed and yells at Enzo, striking him numerous times. Our enemy has difficulty keeping up, barely blocking the strikes in time. Enzo's face snarls, and his eyes become glossy with fear. The strikes never relent, forcing our enemy to back up until he reaches the wall near Rufus.

Their blades clash and maintain their position, the metal

screeching as they grind upon each other. Enzo pushes Krolas back with his sword and creates another slice on his hand. Krolas makes the familiar cut with his nail and blasts purple lightning at Enzo. The building shakes as the spell explodes upon impact. Enzo cannot survive this.

The smoke fades away, and somehow the false king is still standing. Then I see a sheen of blue magic covering the front of Enzo's body. It shatters like glass. Enzo cuts his other hand open, leaving a nasty gash. He's grimacing, he looks determined, but no matter how many defenses he puts up, Krolas will always break them down.

"This blade is destined to make me succeed," Enzo taunts. "It is a sign of the bleak future for my enemies. Blood will never stain it and instead will always drip from it. Blood that grants me magic and will make my enemies bleed." Enzo seems to talk to himself. Krolas is done listening to his nonsense and makes another cut on his arm and responds:

"A blade that was passed down to you from our family. A blade used as a symbol of power and, now, magic. Just having it doesn't make you stronger or better than anyone else, for you must prove you are worthy of taking on the hardships clouding the path to your purpose. Hence why I don't require my black steel knife to defeat you. I already know where I belong. I already know what I need to do for my people. My blade is better off in another's hands. She is a worthy successor in Lirium's future, and the knife will guide her toward a brighter horizon."

My heart feels like it's lifting toward the heavens with his words. My knife belonged to him all along. I examine it and see the same blackness as Enzo's larger counterpart, yet, I understand what Krolas is telling me. As its wielder, I can pave whatever path I desire, and Krolas trusts my future will be beneficial to others and myself. Enzo's path is nothing more than a power-hungry, darkness-filled hole.

Enzo shrugs. "What weak words for a king who was never meant to rule. You were born first, yes, but our parents knew I was the worthier candidate. No matter, you and that girl will . . ."

Fire sprays out of Krolas' palm and forms a massive flame above us, swirling and winding as it expands. The heat makes me sticky and sweat. My eyes burn with tunnel vision, but I can't look away.

"I have heard enough out of you, Enzo," Krolas yells above the hissing flames. "You are nothing more than a fool who hated his brother since the beginning. For what? It was all a rivalry to you. You will no longer receive any sympathy, for you are nothing to me. Not anymore."

Enzo shoots his blue link magic at the fire to try and prevent his inevitable demise, but his spell wisps through it harmlessly. The false king looks desperate. Still, there's nothing he can do now. Krolas is ready to kill him and fulfill his purpose.

The magnificent blaze shapes into the likeness of a creature, almost like a great, majestic bird. Its makeshift feathers radiate heat gusts with every flap to keep itself midair. Krolas breaks the connection between him and the bird, and the animal no longer expands or changes shape. It is a phoenix.

Wasting no time to allow Enzo to react, it charges toward him like a meteor and splashes directly into him. The flames swirl and engulf the false king. There are no screams, for the death must've been instant.

The fire dissipates into the air with every rotation around Enzo. Parts of his body begin to show between the flames, and I wait to see the standing corpse of ash. However, instead of a dead body left in the wake of the attack, I see desperate, unwavering brown eyes staring at Krolas. The false king's face is red, but he is still alive. The flames become no more, and I wonder how Krolas can kill his brother at this rate. Magic like this should destroy anything it touches.

Still, Krolas just stands there, unmoving and soundless, seeming to face off against Enzo. I wonder if he's given up, but that's not the man I know. I run up to him. Who cares if this battle is only between them? I can't leave Krolas with this monster.

Continuing to stare at Krolas, Enzo doesn't seem to acknowledge my intrusion. I touch my mentor's bloody arm, and he makes an agonizing squeak from the deepest part of his lungs. He doesn't turn to me. He doesn't say anything to inform me he's alright. Instead, his face and hands change colors at a dangerous rate. His skin is becoming a deep red . . .

"Hey! Do something! Heal yourself and fight!" I scream and shake Krolas with all my might to try and break his trance, but he refuses to budge or even look at my direction.

"A delayed reversal," Enzo says while walking toward us. "Been wanting to try it, and it seems to have worked wonders. However, perhaps I overdone it. He will soon die from the inside out. Oh well. This is what happens when someone says I mean nothing to them."

"You monster!" I scream at him before he gets too close and cut my arm open and focus all my energy into one attack.

Darkness erupts from my hand and splatters in front of me in an explosion of mist. Enzo holds up a magic blue shield to block my attempt to kill him.

"Being called a monster means I am important to you," Enzo claims. "I have a role in your life, and I have just the game we can play to determine the future." I cut myself again on the same arm, but Enzo puts up a finger just in time to stop his inevitable demise. "Save your strength, girl, and save my brother."

"Why?"

"Well, I mean nothing to him, so I cannot save him. Mostly because I don't want to. But you care for him, and with those engrossed emotions, I want you to cure him. A wielder is useless without healing, after all. So I ask, are you worthless?"

He's right. I'm running out of time to save him. His skin is turning darker by the second, his eyes are swollen red, and if I wait much longer, he and I will die.

I dedicate my magic to any pleasant thoughts I can grasp in this horrific time. Enzo is staring at me, forcing me to lose total focus, and I know it is impossible for me to heal, but I must try! My hand touches Krolas—his body is hot and burns— and I relish memories of my family in my dream and Krolas forcing me out of my dark life. It can't end here; I will not allow this to be our demise.

A flow of energy comes from my mind toward my hand, and I feel a strange sense of happiness corroding my magic. It's unnatural. It may be right? Is this just my imagination, or is Krolas cooling down a bit from my touch?

Enzo clears his throat and adds, "By the way, I'm responsible for your parents' deaths, Phoenix."

His words grasp my heart and crush it. I turn away from Krolas and stare at Enzo's cold face, dead in the eyes. My mouth twitches. "A woman didn't kill them? You did?"

"Hm? Yes, Agnes did the job. Yet, she wouldn't have done so without my command. I needed your parents out of the way so I could meet Dureizen. Furthermore, their dying words gave me all the information I needed concerning the exact whereabouts of Dalgin's cave and how to get inside. You can only imagine my surprise when I didn't see you guarding that bloody door, and so I knew my brother had gotten to you first."

I cry out and make multiple cuts on each of my arms in seconds. They sting, and some are deep, but I do not care. I put my knife in my pocket, and darkness spews from my hands. I will kill him and die in peace, soaking in his blood.

Enzo injures his body just before I reach him, and I claw at him with the intensity of a starving lion. He tries to block with his sword, but I grab it and knock it away, making him lose balance. The maneuver causes my hands to bleed, giving me more power. I cut through his clothes and rip his skin open. His ribs expose themselves to me. I'm happy to see him bleeding out. I slash more. His legs, arms, face. He tries to escape, so I claw his back. Who needs healing when I can make those who do me wrong suffer. He will die.

My vision goes hazy momentarily, and then my shoulder becomes numb like my nerves are no longer there. The feeling spreads to my chest and arm. It's cold. Then I notice Enzo's hand is on my shoulder. He's bloody. He should die from his injuries, but I need to do more so he can't heal himself. I grasp his arm and scratch his skin. He bleeds as he pulls away in fear. Still, the numbing sensation of death is pumping through my body, crawling upon my arms and face. I drop down. I feel frozen. Exhaustion is taking over, and the lack of blood in my body leaves me weak. But I will continue to watch him until my dying breath. I will see him die.

"Foolish child. Foolish brother! Why did it have to come to this . . ." Enzo monologues in his own imagination. I laugh in my head as my magic takes effect, forcing others to reexperience painful memories. He should bleed out before he comes to his senses. As of now, I get to see his misery in full detail.

"Phoenix, you are a product of death that Dureizen warned me about. He said you would be my downfall, but I will not allow it. No, Krolas will die instead. You will die instead! And I will live."

Rufus runs up to the false king, but he pushes him away. Enzo then heals the wounds across his body, and I try to curse through my numb mouth as I see his injuries fade away like they were never there. Still, he will need a new pair of clothes.

Enzo approaches and stares at me like I'm a nobody. It makes me so angry. I just needed to finish him off. He was within my grasp!

"Behold," Enzo monologues some more. "My power turns those I connect to cold and numb. Unlike you, my link magic can end lives, for stabbing you now would be so easy. But why would I do that? How tragic would it be for poor little Phoenix to kill herself because she didn't heal? Perhaps the magic has abandoned you because you're so sad about my brother's death? Maybe your parents' departure from this world traumatized you too much? Nobody will care or even know who you are, but it makes me happy to see you dying from your own stupidity."

My vision fades in and out, but I grasp onto consciousness. I must have a bit of blood left in me. Death isn't supposed to fade.

"Just know," he continues his ignorant speech, "it was an honor finishing the feud with my brother. Now I will be king forever. Nobody will ever stand up to me again, and I can go to Dureizen and receive more strength whenever I please. Your magic is strong and can cause negative emotions in others, but Dureizen should've never underestimated me. How can a weakling like you kill a seasoned king like me? Anyway . . ."

Enzo turns and exclaims, "Rufus, let's go. I'm sick of the smell of death. It's found its way on me, and I want to scrape it off before my speech later today."

Rufus enters my vision, the betrayer not sparring me a single glance, and they walk away. I'm left staring at a few candles, chairs, tables, and a bloody wooden floor. I feel sick. Colors swirl and I feel my mind slipping away with nothing to hold my focus. The candles go out, and everything fades to black. I can't feel my body. I can barely think. What was my purpose in the end? Revenge? Did I fail it? Life is nothing but death.

22

Death. One must experience it to become it. Rage will start your journey, sadness will carry you the mile, but what does the ending offer?

"One could've told you this would happen."

My head stings. I feel like I'm floating. However, my vision is blurry, and the world spins.

"And I did, but you insisted on caring for his meaningless cause. Your purpose does not lie with him, at least from what he tells me."

I try to move my hands, arms, legs, and feet but cannot tell if they obey me. Everything still feels numb, so much so like my body doesn't exist. Enzo's to blame for that.

"Perhaps it's for the best. Having someone close to you die can fuel your emotions to even greater heights."

My vision bursts into reality like dunking my head in a bucket of ice water. All sensation returns to me. Every heartbeat pumps vigor of a newfound passion into my veins. Enzo's demise. Revenge. Death to those who did me wrong. I jump out of bed, pull out my knife, and stop dead in my tracks. A boy is lounging at my doorway.

"You and I are the same. We want revenge, and our power is identical. Allow me to train you so you can receive all you desire."

I blink. Where I would usually be afraid, a lust for death is all I have. If I die, so be it. There's nothing left for me anyway.

"Zier," I acknowledge his presence.

He walks toward me, and I strike his chest like a cobra. My blade punctures a hole in his black and red armor and into his body, creating a fresh crimson flow like a faucet. I smile and brush away my weak nerves. He smiles back at me, and I stab him repeatedly, forming numerous holes pouring an insane amount of blood. I keep going, and Zier's smile widens evermore. There must be twenty holes in him by now! Still, I return the smile and never let it fade. I'm not one to back down from a challenge.

Then my hand jerks still, and I wince as he pierces his nails into my arm. He steals my knife and angles it above us, where blood drips off the black blade. We watch as every drop splats onto the floor, and when the last bit is about to spill, Zier lets the red liquid fall into his mouth.

"What are you?" I ask. Every second I observe him causes my insides to twist more and more.

Zier waves his arm over his torso, and all the blood pouring out of his body freezes, and the holes become filled, and his armor mends in seconds. Then he answers, "A demon. One meant to slay the all-powerful. Still . . ."

He drops my knife and lets me go. I grab it and prepare to stab him once more. He's here to kill me. I'm not ready to die. It gives me aspiration when I draw blood from him. I have yet to end a life when it seems everyone around me has already done so—so many times. Killing a demon would be an impressive first victim.

A purple-black flame radiates from his arms, shoulders, and head. He looks down at me, almost like he's challenging me to strike again.

"I have the power of death, too," he confirms. "The

difference between us is that I have trained with the most powerful demon in the world. Aside from this fact, you have the potential to grow. We have both lost everything we love. There's nothing left for us anymore. Our purpose is to kill those who we deem as evil."

"What do you know about my ambition?" I grab my knife and stand before him. It doesn't seem like he's here to kill me. Instead, it appears he's making some sort of proposition. "Why do you want me?"

"Your voice is lacking passion, Phoenix. You already seem to be one with death. No, your purpose is up for you to decide. Dureizen longs for you to waste your life away, but I require a more promising outcome."

"And my dreams?"

Zier shrugs. "Just part of the fun."

"And what about your identical knife?" I ask.

"A gift from one who I once trusted."

"How specific."

"I know," Zier states, dodging the implication to elaborate further. "Now, enough chit-chat. We need to get you stronger."

"Strong enough to kill Enzo," the words burn hot on my tongue. What a disgusting name. "I'm ready to kill him now."

Zier turns away and softly says, "Not yet. I'm sure you feel it in your body, for death magic becomes potent with anger, but there are things we must do first." He takes my hand. "We're going to weaken Enzo; force him to suffer. It's time to teleport to Sivertin."

I feel my body become lighter, and I pull away from him and leave the room. It's dark, yet I've lived here long enough to know my way. Zier chuckles for whatever reason as I descend the stairs. When I reach the first floor, the large, open room brightens with an unnatural yellow, and I look back. Zier stands prominently behind the railing upstairs. He nudges his head forward and smiles as if he wishes me to continue.

There's no sign of Krolas, but as I walk farther into the room, there is a deepening rancid smell. The scent is different from the bloody odor of death. I cover my nose and breathe as little as possible. My chest tightens as I cough and choke on my own vomit, but I must find my answers.

I walk around the fallen furniture to get to where Krolas was standing before I passed out. The stench worsens. Then I see it: gray-black ashes with a tiny ember still lit. Krolas, the man I once knew, my mentor who offered me a much brighter future than my parents ever promised, burned inside out in his entirety from the heinous acts of his brother. Tears well up in the back of my eyes as I stare at the death. What am I supposed to do without you?

Dropping to the floor, I touch the ember and burn my hand. It sears my flesh, but I don't care. Krolas hurt me before, and this is no different.

When I pull away, my hand bears a swollen red wound on its palm. "Rest in peace, friend. You were the closest thing I had to a father, and it pains me to have never told you that." Tears drip down and soil the ash, and my lips quiver. "You've done more for me than what I've ever deserved," I blurt out. "Despite my aggression toward you in the first couple of days, you stuck with me, cared for my emotions and needs, and never lost sight of your goals. I can see why you wanted to kill Enzo, and I hate you for protecting me from him. We could've killed him together and traveled the world until your last breath as a magic user. I would've been happy to comfort you in your final moments. I would've been fine dying by your side."

"And yet," Zier butts in and stands behind me, "I could not allow that to happen. He's a nobody whose only purpose was to make you stronger. Make you hate. He was destined to die."

"Shut up!" I yell at him. "This is all your fault, isn't it! If you saved me, why couldn't you save him! You want me to suffer! WHY?"

I burst into tears, and Zier covers my mouth, making it impossible to breathe. I try to bite him, but his palm is just out of reach.

"Come with me. It's time to move on and get revenge."

My body floats once more, and the last thing I see of this bloodstained house of horror is Krolas' ashes. I will miss you. I will obtain the vengeance you've never acquired. I swear it upon my life.

23

Is killing Enzo my destiny? Yes. Before, I hardly understood what I wanted. Before, I just followed Krolas and dreamed of some magnificent life afterward—who knows what that could've been. Now, revenge is the only thing left in my mind. Is this how my mentor felt?

The world shifts and bends, and I find myself on my knees. Cold, crisp grass crinkles under my legs. Beside my sorry stature, Zier stands and pays no mind to me. I brush away my tears and see single-story houses and shops bunching together in a sizable area. I believe we are still in Lirium, considering how most of the buildings are made of stone. The only difference these residences have are the thatch roofs complementing the rock walls. Otherwise, there's an occasional wood cabin which must exist for the wealthier individuals. There's also a smithy, with a burly man hacking away at a weapon, and there's a butchery, where two times the population of Dalgin crowds the entrance while shouting out numbers.

Nobody cares about us. The butchery seems to hold everyone's attention, including mine. Buckets and handheld wagons of fish—varying in size and shape—are taken to the back of the shop. The people in dirty rags—male, female, child—lunge at the meat within the containers. A couple of them succeed and escape before anyone can catch them. Others are not so fortunate. Lirium knights serve as escorts to notice and prevent many thieving attempts. Aside from the lawless bunch, most others ignore the incoming fish and do business with the two salesmen in front.

I wonder where the fish are coming from because Lirium is far from the ocean, from what Krolas explained in his geography lesson. I gloss over the line of fishermen and pinpoint the location where they're coming from. A large boat bobbles up and down next to a three-story stone structure past all the houses. This is not Lirium. This is Sivertin! Perhaps Zier mentioned this, but why are we here and not near the castle!

"Explain to me what we're doing here," I command and stare at Zier, who is paying greater attention to the butchery than me.

"I'm looking to buy some fish, why else?" My cheeks burn, and he must've seen it because he raises his hands and laughs. "Just kidding. Welcome to Sivertin, the most important and only trade port near Lirium. Here is our first step toward demoralizing your enemy."

"And why should I care about demoralizing when I can torture Enzo myself?"

"Because you're weak," his cold words bite my soul.

I shake my head at the harsh reality. Comparing myself to Enzo or Krolas, I'm nothing.

"Didn't you say anger makes us stronger?" I ask. "If I'm still not strong enough, you can pin him down while I tear up his flesh."

"Not my job. Honestly, I could care less about you killing Enzo or not. What I need from you is your life. I'm left with nothing if you die because of your lack of skill."

"And what do you want from me?" I push while he is on the subject. I understand he's still a demon who hunts those with magic, but I sense I'm too important to him. He refuses to cause me harm, but I need to know why.

Instead of answering my question, he strolls away and heads toward the boat. He sticks out like a sore thumb, and I wait for the locals to turn and stare at this cocky man wearing black and red armor—unlike the knight's silver—but nobody bats an eye. He passes a couple of knights, but they pretend he's not there. My confusion must be evident because Zier gestures for me to follow. He doesn't stop walking, so I must run to catch up to him.

When I reach the demon, I ask, "Aren't you going to answer my question? This is the second time I asked you, and yet, you don't provide me with an answer. How can I trust you when—"

"Stop talking, or I will shut your mouth myself." A sense of fear washes over me, and I shove the rest of my words out of my mind. "Just appreciate what these humans have worked so hard to create. This is a community they believe to be unshaken and protected. It is also the only trading port within miles. So confident. Too confident."

I consider his implications and examine the boat becoming more massive with every step we take. It has a black sail with white, sporadic lines across it—who knows what the symbol means. There's also a large mass of people on board hauling crates around, which makes sense, assuming they caught a bunch of fish. Although, is this the only thing a trading port is good for?

Zier looks at me and grimly says, "No. Right now is the time for fish. Early mornings or late afternoons are when trade comes in. It's supposed to make it easier to rally people and get things done without intruding on daily activities. Just my understanding."

"So even my thoughts aren't safe from you, demon?" I confirm.

"Nothing's safe from my eyes, or else this world would have been decimated three-hundred times in the last one-hundred years."

I nod and let the conversation die. However, I'm curious how a boy who looks to be about my age claims to be over a hundred years old.

We then walk toward the large, three-story building near the port. A flag on top bears the same sigil as the ship's sail. Guards, each wielding spears or swords, patrol the balconies surrounding each floor. A large courtyard with a black metal gate surrounds this place. It seems unlikely we'll get in without a fight since two knights restrict entry at the gate.

"That's our destination," Zier explains, interfering my

thoughts again and causing my eyes to widen. I'm not used to this sort of communication.

"What is it?"

"Some say a watchtower. Nonetheless, it's where the officials determine where stock goes. On another note, the guards here protect this place from possible invasions, which never happen, and regulate access to the river. And . . . speak of my father."

The two guards at the gate of the watchtower spot us and walk our way. I think about running, but Zier glares at me, giving me the impression to not give in to that temptation.

He tells me, "Pay close attention. Death does not care for those who notice it. It does not stop it."

"You two!" one of the knights with a gruff voice exclaims and raises his weapon. "You are not from around here. Unless you're on official business, begone at once. We will not tolerate misdemeanors of any kind."

The other knight follows suit and adds, "This is a peaceful place. I will protect my home from those who wish to harm it."

"Why do they act like we're planning on destroying . . ." I stop mid-sentence as I look at Zier. My heart skips a beat from a familiar image burned in my mind from days past. His black eyes gleam with a glossy blackness—much darker than before, and his smile exposes a few sharp fangs jutting out of his mouth. It's disgusting. The guards pause before us, and I want to leave this uncomfortable situation, but my legs refuse to obey.

Zier brushes back his hair and stares into my eyes and soul. "It's funny because . . . we're on official business," he remarks.

I blink. Zier has his hands on the knights' shoulders and stares at me with his gleeful expression. The interrogators freeze, and Zier whispers, "Death can touch you, but if it wills it so, you will die. Behold!"

The knights crumble to the ground in an awkward position that shouldn't be possible. Then I realize their bodies are no more. What's left of them is a pile of armor. There was no scream of agony or fear. I stare at the dead knights and try to comprehend what just happened as their armor sets bleed a puddle of blood and gore.

Some onlookers notice us, screaming and running away, and I chuckle out of dismay. Then, Zier looks toward the watchtower.

He claims, "Don't worry about those who cower. We are hidden from everyone once again. Now, behold what death magic can become, Phoenix. This is the power I will train you for." He raises his hand toward the sky and clenches it abruptly. A purple orb engulfs the tall building and disappears in a flash. Those not searching for the unordinary might've mistaken it as a problem with their eyesight. Despite this, screams erupt from the watchtower as all the knights clutch their heads and fall from the balconies to their deaths. Others who are already on ground level crumble to their knees. Their terrified voices die out one-by-one as their bodies give up from what must be internal torture.

I feel bad for these people, but then again, not so horrible to mourn for them. They're knights who work under Enzo, and judging from Rufus' example, there are no good ones. This is payback.

Zier extends his hand out to me and explains, "Though you're not a demon, you can be one in another's eyes. I can transform your power to be closer to mine than that fool Krolas, for I understand how your magic functions."

"Don't you dare insult my mentor."

"Suit yourself. So will you take my hand or not. Partners in death?"

I glance at the stagnant pool of blood near our feet, then once more at the many guards who died. No survivors. Not a scratch on Zier. He didn't even cut himself to achieve this, which might be a demonic trait. Who knows what else he's capable of.

"Did they all have to die?" I ask monotonously.

"They fell into my trap. People only see me when I let them, and they targeted me after I revealed myself. If they had ignored the approaching danger, perhaps I would have been impressed and spared their lives. Oh wait, I wouldn't have."

I blink, and his face returns to normal—a teenager with dark eyes and a slim, strong face.

He still holds out his hand for me to take, but knowing what he did to those who touched it, I'd rather not take my chances. Instead, I walk past him. I can feel his eyes follow me as I walk toward the watchtower. After a few steps, I stop and look toward the sky.

"If revenge means working with you, then I accept," I tell him. "But I won't shake your hand after what you just did. We can be partners, we can torture Enzo and Rufus for a lifetime, and you can teach me the ways of death. But as for your desire with me, about what purpose you have in store, know that I will always follow a path I see fit. If our goals align, then so be it."

"Very well. Still, I assume your goals will align with mine.

Now, will you follow me to the ocean? The watchtower will serve as our living quarters later."

"Won't more guards reclaim their positions? There are still those who are patrolling Sivertin."

He shrugs and says, "I'll kill them to keep you safe. What we need to focus on is the large party heading our way once word and supplies fail to reach Lirium. I'd say we have two days before we're attacked. In turn, we will test your newfound strength."

"Then we kill Enzo."

"Perhaps. First, we focus on our current predicament. Follow me."

Accompanying Zier, we depart from the watchtower and head toward the ship. A couple of knights arrive and notice the armor sets lying in blood, and when they touch them, their bodies collapse and bleed out like those before. It's sickening, but I'm glad Zier can keep us hidden.

All the unloading on the ship must be complete because it's sailing away and heading toward open water by the time we approach. I didn't want Zier to kill those fishermen, for they have little to do with Enzo, so I'm happy they escaped when they had the chance.

We continue walking until we reach the ocean, where we

stand and watch the waves crash into shore. Where we are, it's a reasonable distance away from onlookers, which makes me feel comfortable. Although nobody could see us throughout all of Sivertin, except for the first two knights at the entrance of the watchtower, being alone with Zier is ideal for me. Whatever he has in mind, I like not being around others. Despite this, I feel wrong to be standing beside one who makes a scene through death, especially when I've killed nobody.

Still, no matter what Zier means to me, the ocean before me offers peace. The water is beautiful, a fish fin rises above the water here and there, and I wonder what adventures might await beyond the open water. It's amazing something like this can exist in the world. I envy those who experience this brilliant blue and the sunlight reflecting off of it every day. It makes me wonder what the life of a fisherman might be like. To ride one of those ships and travel anywhere I want to go. Quite the rewarding occupation, I'm sure.

"Don't get distracted by this beauty, Phoenix. Though it's important to acknowledge the potential of this world, we mustn't deter from your goal."

"And what about your goal?" I ask him again.

He goes silent. I stare at the waves. It annoys me that he never answers my one question.

"You know Dureizen is the one who blessed Enzo, right?" he asks.

"I figured."

"And do you understand why?"

"No," I state. "My best guess was a cruel attempt to defy Krolas, but it makes no sense. Dureizen understood Krolas' purpose was to defeat Enzo and take back the crown. So why conflict with fate?"

Zier's face turns grim. "Dureizen doesn't really care about whose purpose is whose. He grants magic to those he believes would entertain him the most. Why give magic to someone who desires to be wealthy when you can offer it to someone who wants to destroy civilization? Dureizen is old, so I believe he solely wishes to entertain himself and not care about society's longevity. You can only imagine his joy when Enzo arrived after Krolas, and the two kings' interests conflicted."

"That's horrible."

"I know."

"Are you suggesting you'd not follow in Dureizen's footsteps?" I ask Zier. They're both demons, so what can he gain from others?

"If I was in my father's spot, I would only grant it to those who deem to do the world good. Only a few people per hundred years, of course. Good people seldom exist. Still, once they become power-hungry and use their abilities for evil, I would take it away because they betrayed my trust. Dureizen offering power to all these unworthy fools makes me sick, so I kill them all once their *purpose* is complete so I don't upset my father too much. Nonetheless, I'm tired of playing this game, and since Enzo's *purpose* is to rule, it will last a lifetime. He will die an early death. It will serve as my resignation."

"Won't Dureizen go after me, though?" I ask. The image of that creature hunting me is somehow more terrifying than Zier.

Zier shakes his head. "No. I won't let him capture you as long as you stand by me. Dureizen has a purpose for you, but I do not wish to share it. For now, I need you to understand your personal goal is to kill Enzo. Afterward, you can experience your life as you see fit." He gives me a wry smile.

I turn away and see a new ship in the far-off distance. It's difficult to tell if it is heading this way or not. I think it may be moving left from us? Are there other lands worth exploring besides ours?

Aside from that, I'm curious about Zier's philosophy of who deserves blood magic. What defines good and evil in his eyes? I just saw him murder many people only because they were under the banner of Enzo and we needed a place to stay. Could all of this be to defy Dureizen?

I can't help but wonder what Zier plans to do with me. His goal must be better than Dureizen's, judging from Zier's harsh words about him. So, I blurt out a growing question on my mind. "Would I deserve magic if you made the choice?"

"Someone who is lost and spent all her life protecting a door with a demon? Sounds like a hard pass." I feel let down, but Zier turns away and adds, "Knowing your personality, however, I would grant blood magic to you. You have a strong sense of what's good and evil. When someone does you wrong, you bite back. You wish to explore a life that was robbed from you, and nobody could ever return those lost years. In fact, I may even turn you into a demon—to live forever—if only I knew how."

"Is this possible?"

Zier nods and explains, "I have a strong suspicion. But enough of this. If I recall, Krolas mentioned something about Rachel Kuemarin, the woman who used to live here with her husband before moving away."

"Yes. It's a tragic story. After seeing the ocean for myself, I understand what she gave up. This place is beautiful."

"And once something beautiful destroys the thing you love most, you can never trust it again."

Before I can contemplate his words, Zier steps onto the ocean's surface like it's made of ice. It makes no sense at all since ice only forms when it's freezing. Unless, this is a hidden property of the ocean.

"This is my doing, Phoenix. Now, follow me. Out here is the perfect spot to train. As a user of death, the fear and uncertainty of sinking into the water where strange creatures lurk is the perfect tool for us."

I follow his example and step onto the ocean. Cold water brushes over my shoes and leaks into them, causing my feet to become soggy and gross. Yet, I do not complain since I see no reason to. Zier is in the same predicament as me.

We walk out about one-hundred feet from the shore. Here, I can't see the ocean floor. A large fin near me comes out of the water and sinks back below, and I feel afraid of what might lie beneath. Nonetheless, my heart pounding with fear makes me feel alive and strong.

Zier has me stay put, then moves away about twenty feet. Being alone without his immediate support makes my legs wobble, but I'm sure I'll feel more confident the longer I'm alone. I must do this to destroy those who did me wrong. This is just a small hurdle I must cross to enact revenge. Now is the time I live in death.

24

Perhaps Zier isn't a horrible guy. Maybe I was just afraid of him because I never understood him. We share the same magic, so there's a bond here. I don't wish to kill him; he must feel the same for me.

I check the water once more after drawing my blade. Below, I can see a large gray fish swimming past me. There are a few smaller fish as well. Deeper down, I see nothing but blackness, and I wonder what creatures may exist in such waters. Perhaps nothing since it's too dark to see, but maybe some nocturnal, colossal monsters rise to the surface at night, anticipating their next meal. The idea of something swallowing me whole leaves me uneasy.

Nonetheless, it's no use staring into the water, all it's doing is bothering me with the terrifying possibilities of an unknown world. If something comes up and tries to eat me, Zier will not let that happen. At least, I hope he won't. I lock eyes with him once again.

"It's good to be afraid, Phoenix. Even I have my fears, and I'm glad you share the same one. Now, use it to your advantage and show me your strength. Don't you dare hold back the amount of blood you spill!"

I use my blade to cut a large portion of my limb, ranging from my shoulder to my forearm. The action causes my body to bleed progressively with every pulse from my heart. It's a nauseating feeling, and looking at it makes me queasy, and it doesn't help that my clothes are stained brown because of it all. Still, I must show what I can do for Zier. I'm not useless, not anymore.

He snaps me to my senses by saying, "I'll get you a new pair of clothes after our training today, my treat. Now stop standing there and strike me!"

I nod. Pouring all my fear into one attack, my hands radiate immense darkness. It feels more potent than ever, and the confidence it offers pressures me to lurch forward with my hands and release the death toward Zier. The power leaves me and rushes on. I close my eyes and don't let up. I'm here to reveal my true potential.

"Is that really it?" Zier mocks me. "After all the fear swelling within you?"

I open my eyes but refuse to extinguish my magic flow. Darkness seeps from my hands and juts out toward him, but only by a little bit. This letdown causes my heart to sink.

"I'm trying my best!" I plead and pause my spell. "I don't understand why it's not working!"

"And what's the best you've ever done?"

"Well, when I fought against Jerr—I mean, Krolas, in Zwelis, I released a powdery explosion. It didn't do much, but it stirred strange emotions within him which gave me an advantage."

"I know all about it. You felt determined to show Krolas your worth only when you were shoved into a corner. But as you know, I can't always offer these life-or-death situations to bulk you up. Now, patch yourself up." He looks at me expectantly like I can heal myself. If he really was watching me beforehand, he should know this action is impossible. "Well, what are you waiting for? Don't die on me now."

"I can't." I point out to him and raise my arm to slow the

blood flow. There's no use in me trying. If I can't do it to save the life of a man who gave me purpose, I can't use it to cure myself. "Can you heal me instead?"

From this distance, he reaches out a hand, and my wounds seam together like nothing was cut. It reminds me of my dream, where he healed every scar exposed on my body. I believe he can also replenish all my lost blood, for my arm feels as good as new again. Checking my palm, he has left my burn untouched. Zier's healing capabilities are relentless, so I'm glad he did not take it too far this time.

"You are wise, Phoenix. From your consistent failures to do something so simple, you finally acknowledged the fact that you can't heal yourself. Fools like us who are blessed with death cannot heal—the one drawback to such power. Still, know if I'm not here to save you, you are one with death. Therefore, you can manipulate yourself and freeze the loss of blood. It will be like your body is in stasis, and it's a spell you must figure out alone when the time comes."

"If we can't use healing magic, what did you just do?" I call him out on his bluff.

"Healing magic. A special kind only demons can use. Once again, if I could turn you into one, I would. Then you would be unstoppable, won't have to injure yourself, and can heal with your type of magic."

I give a slight smile. "I wouldn't be against it if you discovered how to transform me." Looking down, the same overgrown gray fish swims by me. Its size rattles my nerves as it's big enough to devour me.

"This creature may want to eat you," Zier confirms. "But don't let it distract you from me. Do you know why you can manipulate your body so well when you fail at everything else?"

I consider his question and realize I always wondered the same thing. Then, I say plainly, "No, I don't understand why."

"That's because you are dying. You are closer to meeting your destined fate every day you grow older. You can also manipulate other people's bodies to some extent. You can even modify the properties of plants and make them die faster. Fire, like Krolas could use, can also be modified by you. You can technically create it with practice, but changing the property of fire with your spells can create some fascinating effects. If you knew this, you may have been able to freeze the burning inside Krolas and even prolong his life, but Enzo might have killed you for succeeding."

"And he would've died trying. When I get my hands on him, I will shred him to pieces and mock him until his last dying breath. The only one stopping me is you, Zier."

"And yourself. Hold onto that anger and show me you're strong enough to follow through with your words."

Zier sparks a flame in his palm, mimicking Krolas no doubt, and walks toward me. I wonder if there's something he wants me to do, and in return, he shakes his head and stares at the flame. When he's an arm's length away, he presents his palm.

He then commands, "Use your magic to modify its properties into something hazardous. A fire can only burn the body; magic can sear the soul."

I consider his previous words about how I'm able to modify fire. Although, this lesson focuses on our unique magic rather than body manipulation. He wants to test and help me enhance my link magic into something more formidable, not to make a fire burn brighter.

He watches me with those cold, dead eyes. The length I will go to kill Enzo brings me to this demon, one of the most powerful beings in the world. An itch in my body has grown ever since my encounter with the false king. His sardonic words while killing Krolas, his role in murdering my parents, influencing Rufus to betray us, invading my home to receive a blessing he didn't deserve, how he let me bleed out because I wasn't enough of a threat.

Slicing my arm, my hands turn a blackish-purple, and I strain my eyes on the chaotic waves crackling in Zier's hand. The source of this power comes from his palm, for the flames higher up die into the air. So, I focus all my energy on the base, raise my hands above it, and clutch the air so tight to where my nails pierce my palm.

As I expect, the fire poofs out like it's awoken from a steady slumber and burns purple. The color is frightening. Knowing I caused this widens my lips into a sinister smile. Imagine if I kill Enzo with this.

Still, my heart feels like it's received an injection of negativity. The sensation floods my body and pulses through my veins. Though I'm happy to achieve this feat, I want to give up and lie down forever, plotting revenge but never able to achieve it because I'm too weak.

"Congrats," Zier appraises and smiles. "Now this flame will burden those it burns. Negative emotions will flow through those who touch it. As for that feeling inside of you, it's a confirmation of your actions. Whenever you use your link magic correctly on an outside source, your body will inhibit the strain and advance closer to nothingness. It's not too dangerous, but you must keep yourself in check by not overexerting your spirit. One fire is fine, but multiple fires at once will destroy your well-being. Now ignite this one!"

Another flame shoots into the air and holds its shape. I reach out and clutch again despite the strange sensation it brings. Afterward, the fire bursts into a purple hue, and I bend my knees and try to relax my heart. I feel horrible, yet I refuse to fall for I'm afraid I will no longer be supported by Zier's magic and will sink into the ocean.

"Now, how do I rid myself of this emotion?" I beg him. "There must be a way. Tell me!"

The fire in his palm and the one above dissipates simultaneously, and my body's burden is lifted like millions of leeches releasing their bites at once.

"Notice how you achieved this without much issue." Zier lectures me and ignores my agony. "The benefits and drawbacks of death magic are noteworthy. The more your spell influences the world around you at a given time, the easier it is to do so again. Nonetheless, since the fires are put out, starting from scratch will take a bit more concentration, but you will feel normal again. This is the balance you need to consider.

"Since you weren't the one who created the flames, and you can't heal yourself to stop the blood flow and end your magic's influence, you must be cautious when alone. Just know you will be safe as long as you're with me, for even if you push yourself too hard, I can alleviate any burden dragging you down and will keep you safe. At least safe enough."

"I understand." I stand erect and confirm the fires are truly gone. "So, I can use this on anything living or semi-alive?"

"Yes. Just acknowledge your limits, and don't go influencing another person and killing yourself from it. It's better to manipulate other sources with your skills, which leads us to the concept of link magic spells originating from traditional users like Krolas and Enzo."

"I'm listening. Anything to boost the usefulness of my spells. Although I was wondering, how much longer are we training for? I'm getting sick of this disgusting outfit. It doesn't smell great either."

"Understandable," Zier recognizes and glances over my clothes. "This will be our last lesson for the day. I want to confirm you understand all the basics before tomorrow."

"Fine." It's annoying how I'm being forced to wait. I'm anxious to leave this water and return to solid ground where nothing's lurking under me.

Zier explains, "Follow my example: think about your hatred toward Enzo and force all those emotions into a small shard of energy, do not allow any positive thoughts to cloud your mind, and once you shoot one spell, allow another to follow. Do this as many times as you wish, like so."

He produces the mimic to my blade from thin air and pretends to form a small incision on his arm. Afterward, he exaggerates, "Oh, I hate Enzo so much. He's such a bad person. Oh no, he's not allowed to live." My cheeks turn red, but before I can comment, small, dark, sharp objects penetrate the sky from Zier's hands at lightning speed. One after another, they zoom and disappear into the blue sky.

After about fifty of them leave his body, he joyfully exclaims, "Your turn!"

"Will I feel horrible like before?" I ask. "With so much darkness leaving my body?"

"You will feel death's pull, yes, but the shards dissipate after traveling so far. Since they are moving so quickly, the first spell will be long gone by the time you shoot a third shard."

I nod, follow his example, and steadily release shard after shard. The negative strain invades my heart with sorrow. Krolas and my parents dying at the hands of my mortal enemy, in addition to everything that weighs me down as someone with an inferior life, but the anguish never exceeds my body's limitations.

Like Zier, I release the same number of magic shards from my body, look at him, and smile. This beats my stupid waterfall trick.

Zier returns my expression and praises, "Good! A simple spell that will enact suffering to those they hit. It won't kill, but the impact will torture the victim's emotions. You will be using this quite often, Phoenix. It will allow you to kill others while they're occupied with their wellbeing."

I remind him, "So what about the outfit you promised? Let's go to town and—"

He snaps his fingers, and my clothes feel tighter somehow. I look down and no longer see the gross, bloodstained outfit I had on before. Now, a black, skin-tight short-sleeve shirt is in its place. Another black short-sleeve jacket hangs loose around my body down to my hips, and it has a hood too! Concerning my pants, it has the same color as my top, but exhibits tears in the fabric, but not enough to reveal skin which I appreciate. My knife has a leather sheath, so it no longer has to dangle in my pocket. Lastly, comfortable shoes—water still soaks through them, but I expect as much—match the outfit and complete my look.

"Th-thank you!" I briefly hug Zier out of happiness but

don't overstay my welcome. I'm not used to getting new clothes, especially ones of this stature, and this outfit is perfect after the past week of trudging around in bloody garments. I can only imagine Enzo's shocked expression when I arrive out of nowhere with this attire and kill him.

"This special outfit will never dirty, stain, or wear. No need to thank me. These can be your lifetime clothes, but if you don't like it or fancy a change, I can—"

"NO!" I cover my mouth, afraid the abrupt sound might ruin the moment, but I see Zier still smiling. "Thank you again. It's perfect."

"I'm glad. You're working with a demon now, so you must look the part. Besides, I'm sure you'd appreciate people being cautious around you."

"I agree. Although, can we get back to solid land? This creature below me is relentless."

Zier accepts my request, and we walk together back to shore. When we step onto the sand, I fall to my shaking knees and grasp the loose ground. I didn't know I was that nervous out there.

After a moment, when my body relaxes, Zier offers a hand to help me up. I refuse to take it and stand on my own.

"You are free to explore the town if you'd like," Zier offers. "Or you can return to your lodging at the watchtower inn."

In the distance, the building is now bordered by even more armor sets which bloody the area. Furthermore, there are no more people out and about, yet I hear the chatter of locals somewhere in town. Understandably, people are afraid of this place.

Staring straight into his eyes, I ask, "You mean the building full of dead people? I expect the fee will be waived."

"Oh, it will be. In fact, it's almost like I'm paying you to live there, knowing those are Lirium soldiers."

I chuckle and head to the tower. However, quiet footsteps no longer follow me. I turn around and see Zier still standing where we were, looking away toward the town.

I frown and ask, "Aren't you coming?"

He jumps like he wasn't expecting me to say anything, then he explains, "I have important business to attend to, alone. I'll join up with you later tonight. As for now, you will be safe at the watchtower. Are you sure you don't want to explore the town and see more of the world? You've been stuck indoors most your life, and I thought you'd want to get out more."

I shrug and suggest, "Perhaps I just got used to it. Nonetheless, I had my fair share of adventure today and am ready to be alone for a while. Besides, I'm curious as to what books might be at this inn, and if I can claim one as mine."

Nodding, he disappears in seconds, and I depart toward the watchtower. All the death I walk by doesn't bother me, it's as silent as I remember back home when my parents left. Blissful and peaceful.

25

I find myself in an all too familiar place: a room leaving me with chills and delivering dread to the root of my soul. A black shadow with no distinct shape rises from the dirt mound until it represents the size of a human. It exhibits spines across its body, long arms, and fingers. Approaching it, Zier brandishes his blade and focuses on the newcomer. The black shadow opens its see-through eyes and sharp-tooth smile. Dureizen.

"So," the taunting voice of Dureizen begins, "my son returns to me. Or should I say, my adoptive son, Zayn."

"Tell me what happened that night! I demand to know!"

"Well . . ." The black demon hovers behind Zier and clenches the man's shoulders. "I suppose it wouldn't hurt."

Zier yanks away from him and brandishes his black steel knife. "Tell me, demon, and keep your distance."

"You are too kind. I deserve to stand alone on my pedestal when telling this old, tragic story." Dureizen fades away into naught and consecutively reappears upon the stone mound with four surrounding pillars. He's right to call this a pedestal, for how strange and ugly the design is, he seems to admire it so much.

Dureizen cocks his head toward me in a sudden motion, then turns back to his son. He might've just been stretching his neck—if he even needs to do that—but I'm sure Zier is keeping me safe and hidden . . .

Pointing his knife toward Dureizen as a threat, Zier causes the demon to smile even more unnaturally. Then, the pitch-black nightmare begins his tale:

"Long ago, back in my glorious days, I met a baby boy. This human was you. Within you, there existed potential for a newfound power this world has never seen before. I could see it in those eyes of yours. Black and soulless but fresh. You screamed and cried for nonstop food and drink, but when I found my chance to visit you alone, you became silent and smiled a devilish smile. It was fate that you and I were meant to be together. I also wished to see what this hidden power within you might've been.

"But stealing a newborn baby from the king and queen of Lirium is enough for a nationwide uproar. As I snatched you without any selfish intent, for you deserved much more than a plain existence, your father, with his shining, yellow eyes, came bursting into the room. He pronounced himself as Hythem Malfestor, third king of Lirium. He was a silly fellow, trying to grow a beard but could only manage out-of-control curls. Furthermore, he rushed at me with blade in hand! The nerve.

"His sword, might I add, and as you know, comes from black steel ore. This ore is one of the few things I offered Lirium to push the kingdom into peace and prosperity. I promised to never go too far with my shenanigans and experimentation, for if I did, the royals would be permitted to strike me down. Still, the baby became far more precious and rubbed my curiosity raw. I disappeared with you in hand before Hythem could strike.

"I understood your name was Zayn at the time, but that is unsuitable for a son of a demon. Zayn is a name given to you by a king, so I renamed you Zier. You smiled when I granted you this title, so I knew our relationship was destiny.

"As you grew older, I still failed to find the hidden power within you, so I presented you two gifts when you turned sixteen. You might recall me giving you blood magic, but I also gifted you a black steel knife meant for the new prince of Lirium. What better weapon than the one created by your original father?

"Your blood magic became exactly what I anticipated. The moment I gave you my blessing, I summoned three sorcerers to test your skills. Soon after, you discovered a hatred within you and caused them suffering, beautiful misery and despair, for all the sins they've ever committed. The anguish was profound! Your hidden power was none other than death! I had the perfect job for you, which you followed through without folly.

"There was one downside to this power, for you surely remember. You continued to return to me time and time again with many wounds on your body. You were a cripple! Death eats others and yourself, for you could never heal and were abused by your thoughts. This is why I transformed you into a demon in the middle of your dreaming. I didn't know if you would survive the transformation since I had never done it to another, but you lived! When you awoke, you felt so strange, and I taught you my tricks and skills so you would never torture yourself again. But despite being a demon, shapeshifting was never a skill you could manage, yet you have death to make up for this shortcoming."

"And how did you turn me into a demon?" Zier asks, likely for my benefit.

"Is that all you desire to know? No care about your parents or what Lirium was like back in the day? I expected my son to be surprised about his royal origin."

"I am, except this concept intrigues me. The process of becoming a demon is strange and must be seldom understood."

I need Dureizen to tell him so I can no longer be human. I'd prefer to use magic without harming myself in the process. Hearing about Zier returning home in a sorry state, I can relate to that now, for being dragged down by emotions and injuries is eternally miserable.

Dureizen faces me again. Although unlike before, he doesn't look away. He just watches me, and his smile shifts into a frown.

"Son," the shadow demon says, "I always taught you to place yourself first. Your needless meddling into my affairs is doing nothing but bringing you harm."

"From you?" Zier snaps.

"Perhaps. Nothing you do will stop me from getting what I want. You tell him that, Phoenix. He only cares about you because you are somewhat like him. So childish for one his age."

"Who are you talking to?" Zier tries playing dumb, but I realize just how bad of a liar he is.

"Zier!" Dureizen grows and grabs his son with one fell swoop. "Do not attempt to thwart my plans by turning her into a demon. You are a product of mine who should follow orders. I don't truly understand what you are planning with that girl, but just know you will always fail when you oppose me."

Zier squirms in Dureizen's grasp. The colossal demon then reaches for me. I shake my head and try to escape. Anything I can do to get my body away, but it's of little use, for all I can do is watch the darkness overtake me.

I'm afraid. The blackness numbs my senses.

Dureizen chuckles and states, "You deserve more, girl. What this fool and you have in common is nothing. Only I can grant you freedom, for if you fail to heed my warning . . ."

My body's insides snap. Groaning from the terrible agony, I try to apply pressure to my stomach as I feel someone attempting to pull out my entrails. My veins split open and drench me in vile wetness. I scream for help but no sound resonates, but instead, the deafening noise of my heart bursting through my chest ends my struggle.

26

I'm beginning to feel used. People are fighting over my destiny, but why am I so important to them? Would it have made a difference if I never met Dureizen, or would he seek me out when I least expected it? Imagine how horrified I would've been if he manifested before me while shopping for supplies. I'd probably die of fright before he could use me for his own devices.

But reality had different plans for me. My only option is to live the life I wish until Dureizen hunts me down. Still, I can always fight destiny and die trying. If his goals are against mine, who cares what he wants from me.

I wake up sweating in my sheets. My breaths are quick and jagged, and I force myself to calm down by acknowledging my surroundings. I glance at the desk, then the sunlight beaming through the windows, and paintings of ships and various city locations, and I sigh a breath of relief. Everything is as I left it when I fell asleep. I'm safe in a room on the third floor of the watchtower. Dureizen is not here to get me.

Dream or not, it felt so real, and I'm hoping Zier returns soon so I can question him. But what if Zier will be forever trapped in his father's clutches? If I don't see him by the end of the day, I will return to Dalgin to seek him out.

I head to the desk at the end of the room and begin to write. Aside from my journal entries, I tried my hand at writing a novel about two brothers becoming separated by some unknown power. Afterward, they reunite as enemies, and the story ends in tragedy. It's a basic concept, but it helps keep my mind at ease.

Jotting down the rest of my thoughts, I close the leatherback journal and put away the quill pen. Still no sign of Zier. It must've been hours since I started writing.

Unfortunately, my journal is the only entertaining thing I found in this barren abode. After exploring the building, I only found weapons, armor, millions of papers regarding the comings and goings of supplies, and dead people. There is also a dungeon under the first floor filled with even more dead people.

I sigh as I approach the window and examine the outside world. By the time I fell asleep, there were several dead knights out front. Now, countless suits of armor surround this desolate inn. Only a few people exist in the distance, but it's clear many of the villagers must be afraid to leave their houses. Understandable.

Using another window to view the ocean, a ship bobbles up and down near the horizon. It's not moving closer. No doubt they're afraid to dock. If they don't bother me, I'm content with their position.

"It seems my spell is doing the trick. Not a scratch on you."

I jump and see Zier in the window's reflection, and I momentarily forget all my questions for him.

"What's with the face? Scared to see me?" he asks, but I'm not afraid of him.

"You need to be straight with me. Are all my dreams real? The ones with my parents and I, and the two with you and Dureizen?"

He scratches his head and answers, "To some extent. Obviously, the one with your parents was fake."

"And why are you showing me these?"

"Well . . . as for now, I want to convey what kind of demon Dureizen is like. He's dangerous and cannot be trusted, and you need to understand this moving forward. You *will* encounter him in the future. You must also assume his strength is similar to mine, but this is not the case. I'm powerless to prevent his ambitions."

"So, if those dreams were real, how did you get out of there?" I ponder. "Your father tried to crush you!"

"Don't call him that! Not anymore. That creature doesn't understand what love really is."

"Fine, then explain to me how you escaped."

"When your consciousness faded—don't understand how he knew you were watching—I . . . told him I would never help you again, then vanished when he dropped his guard." He moves next to me and stares at the ocean outside, where we trained yesterday. "But who cares what that thing wants. I took some time alone, considered my options, and ultimately decided to stand by you and travel down your path. I will try to convince Dureizen to see reason again, for if he obtains what he craves, I don't believe you will survive."

I fidget with my clothes and stare at his chest, refusing to meet his gaze. "And what is it he wants?" I mutter.

"Now is not the time to tell you, but I need you to trust that I will protect you from all this. Do you have faith in me?"

"Trust takes a long time to earn. Even then, I will never trust you until I understand everything. Still, I enjoy your company more with each passing day."

"I guess I should have expected this answer." He walks away and adds, "Meet me outside when you're ready. Today, we are building upon yesterday's lesson."

"Zier," I stop him before he leaves the room.

"What?"

"Can you tell me why you shown me my parents? In the dream, I mean. They're dead, but why would you recreate them to be . . . better?"

He grimaces and responds, "Selfishness and sympathy. You lived so close to me, and I saw how your parents raised you like an object. Sure, they showed some love, but not enough. I guess a part of me wanted you to understand what real parents were like."

He exits and I ponder my life alongside the pain in my heart. Are real parents not like my own? It feels like my life has always been fake, and only when Krolas dug me out of my grave did I finally see what the world was like. And yet, my heart yearns to belong somewhere—a place which doesn't exist.

On this path toward revenge, I'm itching to conclude my misery and push on. Enzo killed the one who showed me the light, a radiance now accompanying me as a burn. Also, if what Zier says is true, I still love my parents even if they never felt the same. I have Zier to thank for showing me the truth. It brings me peace. Nonetheless, he and I are . . . two people who don't belong anywhere, not anymore.

*   *   *

After my preparations, I meet up with Zier near the gate of the watchtower. Like I saw from the window, every living person is avoiding this location like the plague. The piles of dead knights give a nasty aroma further deterring visitors.

We then travel to the ocean to begin my next lesson. We don't speak very much on the way there, which is fine. There's enough on our minds anyway.

When we arrive, I'm glad the large fish from yesterday has better things to do besides bothering me. The ship in the distance doesn't get closer either.

We confirm my knowledge on creating death shards and manipulating fire—the strain remains the same as before.

However, it's easier to execute my skills this time. And with that, we move on to our next lesson.

Zier teaches me how to use magic with greater force. I don't think I can kill anybody with it at my current skill level, but it will be advantageous to affect a large area and disable my enemies. He shows me the correct way to use my black powder blast—an attack only possible when allowing my emotions to dip so low. If only Krolas could witness my mastery of the skill. Additionally, there's also a new spell where I can use a powder blast on a distant enemy, emitting an explosion from their body and damaging the minds of those in close proximity. This attack seems to have little effect on Zier, likely because he's a demon.

All the spells today focus on fighting against larger parties. It's a strategy I had little practice with. Back then, I only partook in one-on-one battles since what kind of army will enter a small cave altogether? Aside from current events, we'd never see more than one visitor per one-hundred years, at least. Still, I can't wait to use all these attacks on Enzo. He will be at my mercy the moment I lay eyes on him.

"So, you're ready to test your skills tomorrow?" Zier asks as we make our way back to shore.

"You mean you weren't bluffing?"

"Nope. There's a small army coming from Lirium to check the status of the trading port. This will be your time to demonstrate what you've learned."

I consider what a small army could mean and produce a wicked face. "Is Enzo joining in on the fun?" I question.

"Not this time. A king like Enzo has more important duties at home to take care of. Controlling citizens, appeasing those around him so they don't consider betrayal; the dreadful package coinciding a kingdom's takeover."

"Then what's the point of staying?"

"Phoenix, I need to know if you can handle a largescale battle alone. You're a magic user, and you must continue growing in power. Of course, since you're unable to heal yourself, I'll be supporting you by your side."

"You won't fight?"

Zier frowns and says, "Not my place. How will you get stronger if I slaughter everyone in your way? How will you improve by only training and never facing the real thing? You've never killed a human, so why not establish a grand spectacle to commemorate the occasion?"

Judging by his words, he has a point. All my training with Krolas led to his death and my failure in battle. There is no excuse for such an outcome. I have the potential to be the most fearsome magician known to this world, and I couldn't defeat someone like Enzo.

"Alright," I growl. "Tomorrow, I'll show you my strength."

Zier pats me on the head like I'm some sort of pet. "Good. And when you succeed, I will have great news to share with you."

"Like how we're finally going after Enzo?"

"Well, I cannot spoil the surprise! I'll see you later tonight. I have more recon to attend to."

"And will I have another dream tonight?" I ask, unsure if I'm ready for Dureizen to tear me to shreds again if he notices me.

"Count on it. And as for your suffering, I'll pull you out of your dream if things get hairy. But tonight, Dureizen will change his mind with this final attempt. Our fate is written if I fail." He looks down with his eyes half open. It's clear he's miserable, but before I can stop him, he teleports away.

Alone, I watch the ocean's waves tirelessly caress the sand. The dedication for such compassion is inspiring. It reminds me of Zier and I, Zier being the ocean and I the sand. He's so powerful and has the capacity to destroy me without a second thought, and yet, he cares enough to protect me from the sun's rays and provides what he can. Still, the sun is relentless and unstoppable. I doubt he will change Dureizen's mind considering his last attempt, but I'm honored Zier is determined to save me.

I return to the watchtower, clean up, scour for food, and then write the night away. A group of soldiers will mean nothing to me tomorrow. I have full confidence in my ability to kill them all, but I'm curious what Zier's good news will consist of. I can only assume it is time for us to charge into Lirium and kill Enzo. But what if that *king* is already dead? It would make me so angry if someone else got to him first. No doubt he has more enemies than supporters.

The moon shines bright through my window, and I know Zier won't return tonight. Does that man ever sleep? Maybe once I'd like to spend time together outside of training.

I finish jotting down my thoughts and head to bed, preparing for another horrific dream where Zier claims his father will see things his way. I don't know how he'll do it, for Dureizen only does as he pleases, but I need to see the outcome. Even if Dureizen reaches out to me again, I'm confident I will be safe from harm. It's just a dream while my body is here in Sivertin. The worst possible situation is needing to brave the temporary anguish inflicted upon me until I wake up from the nightmare.

27

Dureizen, the black shadow demon, mimics the shape and size of a human. His arms rest behind his back. The face he bares is still unnerving as usual—eyes and mouth smiling wickedly through their empty space. He's waiting like he's expecting someone but doesn't spare me a glance.

As if on cue, Zier enters the picture with an aggressive gait. His blade appears from thin air, and he holds it toward his father threateningly. This scene appears to be a continuation of yesterday's events.

"Dureizen, this is my final request. Allow Phoenix to be free from your goal and use me instead." Zier announces. Is he actually planning on taking my place? Is he going to die for my sake? No . . .

"Silly, silly boy," Dureizen responds, unwavering in his stance. "That is impossible. It is not your purpose."

"Then make it."

Dureizen laughs and waves his finger back and forth. "Impossible for a demon. I require one who has an affinity with death magic but is also human. You should have known that. If there was any other way, I would go about it to spare you the heartache, but each time you enter my home, my attitude toward you changes. You are becoming a nuisance. You are no longer useful."

Zier takes a step back and lowers his blade. "If you believe my usefulness has run dry and are unwavering in your goals, then I will no longer be your son. You will have to find another who will clean up your dirty work. I'm done."

"Not a problem for me."

The black mass of Dureizen expands like a balloon, but it doesn't pop. As it inflates, the spikes on his body grow longer and sharper. One touch will cause uncontrollable bleeding from the looks of it.

Zier backs away slowly, refusing to lose his ground. I'm unsure if this is what he had in mind, but his plan isn't working.

When the black mass takes control of half the room, Zier strikes one of the many spines on his father. The shadowy mass comes clean off, reminding me of my first encounter with the demon, as the spikes are what grant the blood magic blessing.

Red goo pours from the wound. Dureizen's body does not recognize that it's been injured, and the face in the air still produces a gleeful smile. It seems he's a masochist and a sadist.

The balloon swells ten times faster now and forces Zier to retreat. Before the blackness swallows me up, my vision fades to black, and I find myself in the watchtower once again.

28

If Zier had no luck changing Dureizen's mind, perhaps I can try? Then again, doubtful Dureizen cares about the opinions of one he wishes to use. The only option Zier and I have left is to figure out a solution to avoid the shadow demon.

When the sun nears its zenith, Zier finally emerges from thin air. I wait for a few seconds to let the tension between us grow, then I close my book and glare at him.

"Took you long enough," I antagonize. "I thought for sure this *small army* you mentioned would arrive before you."

"Well, I—"

"Your plan failed," I cut him off before he can make any

excuses. "What were you trying to achieve anyway? You waltz into the lair of the most powerful demon in the world and tell him you will take my place? Then you insult him."

"I was trying to help you. There's no reason why I shouldn't take your place," he explains, but I know better than to believe him.

"And I will choose where I belong myself. You have no right to take away my freedom. Now tell me what this demon wants from me, or I will leave you. I have better things to do than constant training."

"Like getting yourself killed by Enzo? What good will that do for me?"

"For you!? I've had enough of your secrecy and selfishness. I'm marching to Enzo with or without you."

"Wait! I will tell you what he plans. Just give me—"

A loud, deep howl echoes outside our window. We both exchange glances and look outside. A group of fifty bright armor knights, holding swords by their sides, stand at the gate. The individual leading them returns his horn to his belt loop and raises a pole with a black and white banner, much like the one on this watchtower. He must notice us because he tilts his head to the third-story window.

The man exclaims, "Oppressors of Lirium! Demons to

the crown! The havoc you dealt on this town will be paid in blood! Now come out and accept your fate!"

Zier pulls me close, and we teleport out of the castle and onto the grounds. I freak out and pull out my blade from its sheath.

"Don't mind if we do," Zier mutters. His face morphs into those deep, black eyes and horrific smile, glaring at me as the knights scramble in preparation. "Phoenix, show them death."

I cut a healthy portion of my arm and blast an arrangement of shards out of my palm. It's always best to start with this so I can rile up my emotions. I feel the toll on my body, but the moment the shards begin to penetrate my enemy's armor, a sadistic pleasure brings me balance.

One by one, the knights drop their weapons and hold their heads. Some scream, some talk to themselves, and others fall to the ground. About thirty knights avoid my initial attack, and they move around to try and flank us. Their armor ignites into darkness, much like Rufus back in Lirium. It's a power that enables body regeneration, but it's no matter. They will all be dead in seconds.

Another slice upon my arm causes my enemies' wounds—bleeding black from my shards—to explode into a black powder. The mist surrounds the entire area. I feel like I want to throw up. Nonetheless, all the first knights who still have their complete armor sets fall, while the others freeze in place.

Zier seizes my arm, heals my wounds in a heartbeat, and is again careful to leave my burn. He nods at me, and I take the cue. My knife licks my skin just enough to penetrate it, and I use the energy source to increase my speed. I rush ahead and stab the necks of those standing defenseless, a guttural noise coming from each of them, confirming their offering to me, death.

The remaining knights must've shaken off the negative urges within them, and they rally and charge at me. I follow suit and enter the fray, cutting myself once more to reinforce my skin. They try to kill me, but I deflect every one of their blades with my knife. Those who manage to find an opening fail to do me any harm, and I laugh at their attempt. When I find openings, I stab the gaps in their armor: arms, hips, knees, neck. Everything.

But despite all those I've killed, more of Enzo's knights surround me. My power begins to weaken, and I feel new wounds brandish my skin. They are slight, but I realize I cannot do this all on my own. How can I when I failed to rescue Krolas? How can an orphan girl save a kingdom when she couldn't save her parents?

Suddenly, all the knights fly back into the air and land on their backs. The sound of metal screeching together is deafening. I look ahead and stare wide-eyed at the one I blame for halting my demise. Zier.

"Not too many left, Phoenix. Kill them and keep check of your emotions." I find his encouragement pleasing.

Him and I are partners. Demons, that's what we are to this world, and I will show them what it means to challenge one.

I make another cut, one which will test my capabilities.

All the dead surrounding me and memories of my horrible life take control of my mind and envelop my body. I feel my emotions swell, and black powder explodes from within me, cloaking the area with an even thicker cloud. The remaining knights tremor and collapse. Their bodies are so negatively impacted. I feel their weight itching upon my skin. I manifest that weight into my thoughts and cut myself a final time. I clench my hands together, and my enemies howl in pain. Never stop. Never stop. They will die.

Their cries become screams as a pleasing, gooey popping sound spreads across the field. I do not need to see what's going on for me to know. Their muscles are exploding, and they are bleeding out. This is what it means to cross me.

I take deep breaths to try and calm down. One after another. They all got what was coming to them. I didn't even notice I killed the guy with the flag. These knights are nothing to me.

"Before you ask," Zier mentions and grabs my arm from behind me. We fade away and reappear in the middle of a bustling town full of shop stands, colorful stones each radiating every neon hue imaginable, millions of people conversing with one another, large buildings, small castles, and giant glass orbs in the sky. "Welcome to Crystalline."

29

Without hesitation, Zier brings me into a strange place unlike any other. Right after I've slaughtered all those soldiers! No thanks, no appreciation, nothing. What's here that could be so important to our goal?

I push Zier away and question, "What are we doing here? What about my stuff?" I let my anger fuse with my voice so he knows how fed up I am. This is not Lirium.

"Oh, Phoenix, I remember when you were so curious about this city. You considered visiting at the edge of Zwelis, despite Krolas' displeasure of the idea. Don't tell me your revenge is more important than this."

"And what if it is? Don't tell me this is your surprise!"

A couple people stare at us as they walk by, but most seem to be focused on their own conversations. Besides, I can hardly talk over these people.

"Surprise!" he exclaims, and I glare at him. I consider if my magic can create curses, perhaps making him realize what he's done. Regardless, he must assume my intentions toward him because he walks away and gestures for me to follow.

I cross my arms and accompany him as he adds, "No, there's something else here I believe is more important than Enzo. Let me explain over lunch. I know just the place where we can eat."

I growl at his idiotic nonsense. At least the people walking by pay no mind to the bloodstains on my hand. Instead, everyone continues about their day, traveling in all directions, seeming to have no clear goal in mind. I can see why Krolas hates this place. The only redeeming quality is how strange and beautiful everything is. I've also never seen anything like the see-through orbs in the sky, seeming to have no support except for a thin, concave beam of glass below it. I want to ask what they are, but I'd rather wait until it's quieter and Zier and I are alone.

The colorful rocks covering the concrete ground and the walls of buildings grant an elegant light to the city. I've never seen anything like them before. Guessing from how they glow so brilliantly, they must be infused with magic of some sort, but where did they come from? There's not a single color I cannot find among them. Some are green, others blue, many are red and yellow. If I only knew about Crystalline when I was younger, I would've loved to visit just to view the stones, maybe even take some home.

"Then you would've fallen into his trap," Zier states. He keeps walking forward, so I must push past the few people who can't walk straight to keep up.

"What do you mean? What trap?" I investigate. It seems Zier knows something about Crystalline that I don't.

Zier speaks louder so I can hear him. "Dureizen created this city to function as his playground. Many people came here to have fun and see the sights, but it became a cage where people suffered, struggled, and drowned in fame while others were shoved into the deepest pits of darkness."

"I don't understand."

"Don't you see it?"

"No."

He refuses to follow up his theory as we walk through the streets. Typical of him. Half the time he ignores me when I have a question.

Eventually, we arrive at a large, single-story wooden building with open, glass doors in the front. Zier walks in like he owns the place, and I follow. All the annoying talking muffles away the moment we step in. Nobody follows us in here.

Throughout this space, tables and chairs are spaced evenly apart, much like the bar Krolas and I lived in. A few couples, eating bird, pie, or fish, are seated at tables covered in a white cloth. Everything smells great. My stomach rumbles as I realize I skipped breakfast.

A man blocks our way to the tables, delaying when we can eat. This guy appears to be in his thirties, with his hair slicked back and his mustache trimmed. He's standing erect and wears a black suit. On one of his arms, he holds a white cloth as a formal gesture. I furrow my brows. This place is strange, and this man wears attire unlike any I've ever seen before. Is this a demon café of sorts?

"That's an insult," Zier responds to my thoughts, then turns to the man. "Two please."

"Very well," he answers. "Payment please."

Zier presents his hand, and a brown bag of coins appears. The silver clangs together to show it's genuine.

The man raises his eyebrows and states, "Works for me," then takes it from Zier. He then leads us to a table in the middle of the room. "Please enjoy." He walks away from us, and we are left alone.

The room is quiet, except for the low talking the other visitors participate in. Everything looks barren. The walls are pure white, and there seems to be a backroom where people dressed like the employee are entering and exiting. It's an eerie place, yet I'd take this environment over the people outside.

"What is all this?" I whisper loud enough so only Zier can hear me.

"The finest restaurant in all Crystalline. You will know the rest when your food arrives."

"And what are we doing here?" I push. "What is this surprise?"

"Agnes is here."

"Who?"

"The one who killed your parents."

My breath stops. I grab my knife's hilt out of instinct and scan the room. Any one of these people could be Agnes.

Zier snaps, and I turn back to him. He tells me, "Stop being so paranoid and take a break. She's in Crystalline, not here in this restaurant. As the wife of Rufus and a spy for Enzo, she's earned a vacation to her demise after a job well done."

I grip the table and grind my teeth.

"Stop and relax," he repeats to me. "First, we eat, then we enjoy the rest of the day. I still need to locate her. We deserve a break in the meantime. Tomorrow, we can kill her."

"Fine."

"More important than killing Enzo?"

"Hardly."

A newcomer approaches us from the backroom, carrying two metal dishes with covers. When he arrives at our table, he places the dishes in front of us. Afterward, he leaves without a word.

Though I'm hungry, I need to learn more about Agnes in order to strategize her death with make-believe scenarios. I question Zier, "Does she know blood magic? Is she going to be any more of a challenge than those knights? We will find and kill her tomorrow for sure, right?"

"Relax, Phoenix. To put it in simple terms, she is as weak as a human. If we catch her off guard, she will be at our mercy in seconds. Now, remove the lid."

I take it off, and an intense array of sweet aromas embrace my senses. A small cherry pie and what I believe to be boar meat begs to be eaten. My mouth waters, and I am taken back to when I was a child. There was a time when my parents gathered a sum of money through unknown means and spent it on a night of delicacy. They brought me the leftovers, but they were the best dishes I've ever smelled and tasted. I was angry for so long when we never experienced anything like that again. Without a doubt, there is no fonder memory from my childhood.

"I knew you'd like it," Zier smiles.

"Did you order it? How did you know?"

"I didn't know, nor did I care too much to discover your favorite food. Instead, this place promises its guests a divine experience. Magic, to some extent, but truth be told, they only have the fanciest foods here. When we walked in, the boss made a bold prediction about what we would enjoy most."

"Is the boss the man who took our money?" I ask.

"No doubt about it."

"Well, what did you get to eat?"

Zier removes his lid, and I try to hold back my laughter. His meal is identical. Those dark eyes gleam with amusement and meets mine.

"I guess he believes we're one and the same," he comments.

I take a bite from the boar, and it's even more delicious than I remember, and the pie is the best thing I've ever eaten. It's clear Zier also enjoys his food. While we eat, I have time to reflect on what all occurred during our battle in Sivertin.

Between bites, Zier says, "You fought very well today, Phoenix. I wasn't expecting you to surpass my expectations."

"Had no choice because someone didn't help me kill a single one," I add playfully.

"True, for the most part, but look at you! Your last attack impressed me. I thought killing with your skill level was impossible, but you acted like a demon. Did you take inspiration from me?"

"Kind of. Our magic becomes stronger with added negativity. At the time, I felt as though I could break through any barrier. I felt a connection with the end of life."

"I can only imagine the toll on your body. I'm glad we're

on the same side. Also, I'm sorry for leaving your stuff behind—your journal, to be specific."

I shrug and tell him, "It's not a big deal. I left another journal at the bar where Krolas and I stayed." Looking at my palm, I remember all the negative words I wrote about my old mentor, but his company was appreciated. "If anyone finds my journal, they can learn about my life and perhaps discover another piece to the puzzle in Sivertin if they are curious enough. I'm sure I will find another book elsewhere."

"How about this, then?" Zier offers me a leather journal enwrapped with a thick string. Flipping through the pages, the paper is pure white and thicker than usual.

"It's perfect. Thank you. You've given me so much recently, like my clothes and teaching me how to properly fight with my once lackluster spells. I've been meaning to ask, why are you being so nice when before you were scaring me?"

"Emotion is the best way to evoke strength." I take another bite of food as he adds, "You being fearful of me should've triggered something within you. Perhaps it did, but now the situation has changed. I was forced to work alongside you because of current situations."

"Because of your father?" I inquire.

"Sure, but let's not spoil our food with sour conversation.

We can discuss heavier topics another time."

"I agree."

We enjoy our meal and pass the time with idle chatter. He takes my journal, makes it vanish, and he explains how I only need to ask whenever I wish to write. Probably for the best since I keep leaving them everywhere.

Throughout our conversation, every time I think about Agnes, Rufus, Krolas, and Enzo, I push those thoughts aside and let them dwell within me until tomorrow. I didn't know how tense I was ever since I met Krolas. Even before I met the king, I was uneasy. But now I can relax for the first time in forever.

After every scrap of our meal is gone, I sit there and let my food settle for a little bit. This is the first time I've eaten like this. My body feels fat.

Zier leans back in his chair and stares at me.

"So, what sounds appealing to you?" Zier asks. "We can visit shops, weapon shops, and more weapon shops."

I roll my eyes. "I can tell what you want to do."

"Nah, just suggestions. If none of those sound fun, there are also sparring tournaments we can attend, a theater specializing in song, and of course, the rooftops where we can view most of the city. I recommend visiting the rooftops when the sun descends."

"Let's do it, but I don't want to deal with the millions of people outside and the noise they cause. Can we just teleport around?"

"If that's what you desire, then I have no complaints."

He stands and makes his way around the table. Nobody's paying attention. Even if they are watching, the wise ones will avoid confrontation. Zier touches my shoulder when he reaches me, and we fade away from existence. We embark on our journey to enjoy Crystalline's many attractions.

30

What a life I have missed.

Zier and I first stop at the weapon stalls alongside the road. His reasoning was that we already had our peace in the restaurant, so the first thing we should do is go back into the chaos to avoid having to do it again later. Still, the obvious truth is he really wants to see those weapons.

Five stalls are parallel to each other, each with its own merchants showing off various blades to any passerby who comes too close. The first seller we approach stares at us with bright eyes as we examine his wares on the counter.

After glancing over his products, this specific stall seems

to only sell knives and swords. Zier picks each of them up and examines them in greater detail. As for me, I'm content with just looking. Each blade has different colors: red, orange, blue, and everything besides black, for whatever reason. Maybe it's to avoid conflict with the royal family's black steel weapons? That's the best guess I have.

The following merchant sells obscure weapons I've never encountered before. Scythes, flails, and spikey metal gloves in various sizes pique my interest, but they are too much for me. I'm curious what sort of warriors use them, and if they trained specifically to handle such bizarre weapons. Maybe if I ever get bored using a knife—which will never happen—I wouldn't mind learning how to wield a scythe. I think I would look cool swinging such a formidable blade around.

Afterward, we move on to the next stall which sells even more knives and swords, but unlike the weapons beforehand, these blades all have razor-sharp jags. They seem so dangerous. Zier confirms my suspicion by lightly touching his finger to one of their edges, and the prick causes him to bleed a little.

"Hey, what are you doing!?" the seller interrogates. "Don't dirty my blade unless you buy it!"

Zier ignores the pleas as he bends the sword's blade to

test its durability. Then he states, "How do I know the quality of the weapon if I don't—"

The sword snaps in half with an ugly metallic crack, and I jump and stare at the merchant. He furrows his brow and his skin turns red. I'm speechless.

"You . . . You!" the man's voice carries among the crowd. I feel like everyone is staring at us. A crowd forms. The man begins to walk around the stall to likely try and kill us, and I hit Zier to get his attention. We need to escape. The seller closes in on us. Instead of paying attention to the emanate danger, Zier puts down the two sword fragments and rubs his chin, continuing to ignore me.

"Zier! Come on!" I yell and punch his gut.

He displays no sign of pain, and instead grabs my arm and says, "Fine, spoil the fun."

We teleport away just in time to search for a new attraction. Aside from the dangerous situation, the crowd was starting to get annoying anyway. Even though nobody was pushing us around, I can only handle so much people. Besides, I couldn't help but believe the locals were inching closer to us with each passing minute. Still, it was fun to see all the different weapon types that exist.

After we emerge from the nothingness, we find ourselves

in a large, dark room with colorful, glowing stones along the floor, walls, and ceiling. The lights in the darkness promote a serene atmosphere, and I can't help smiling and taking in all the sights. I scan the room repeatedly as my eyes adjust to the lighting. I first make out a few people walking around, then see how expansive this room is, but still, there's nothing of significant interest yet.

Then I see it. Various works of art hang from the wall, each seemingly painted—due to the precise brush strokes. Each one depicts large animals I've never seen before within beautiful landscapes. Many walk on four legs, a couple on two, and there is one drawing with many colorful fish swimming in the ocean's deep.

Surrounding these art pieces, many rocks which reflect the background's shades help bring the paintings to life. It looks like the creatures could walk or swim out of these if they so choose.

Zier whispers, "This room used to be favored by magical artists who wished to bring their paintings to life. As you could guess, each one of these portray animals in their natural habitat, and by influencing these illustrations with spells, the creatures would materialize into existence. The crowds were always ecstatic, especially when the animal's likeness was accurate. Kind of silly, really. All these artists did it out of greed. Still, I'm glad to see new artwork being produced to this day."

"It must've been difficult using magic to design animals," I respond.

"Very much so. Nonetheless, it was their job, and these artists were passionate. It took intricate skill to recreate the lines in the paintings through link magic, fire, or any other spell or combination."

"Did you kill them all?" I speak quieter so nobody can hear me.

"Like I said, they were greedy. It also got to the point where I was sick of everything and wanted to eliminate anything Dureizen influenced."

"I understand," I say half-heartedly. It must've been an unpleasant time for Zier, but did the artists need to be killed? These paintings are excellent, and I would've loved to pay money to see them come to life.

We browse the artwork for a while longer until we view every single one. Once done, we teleport again into a large, crowded room with many people relaxing on cloth seats.

Everyone's speech is quiet—which is welcome—and we come across a couple open seats near an empty stage.

"What is this?" I ask once we sit down.

"There's a musical tonight. I don't want to spoil it, but you'll enjoy the event."

I smile and mouth a 'thank you' and then focus on the stage as multiple actors emerge from the shadows. These people enter from opposite sides, wearing two different armored uniforms: red and blue. Everyone wields swords and shields. Additionally, men and women are performing in this battle, a representation I was not expecting.

Both sides stand eye-to-eye with each other. The colorful stones inside this building add an appealing effect to the stage as well. It must be nerve-racking to be up there in front of everyone.

Then it begins. Many of the soldiers strike one another. Cries and the clashing of blades resound across the room. Before the conflict can prolong, one of the men in blue leaves the scene and moves closer to the audience. He's quiet as he stands still and stares at the floor. What is he doing? They're in a war, aren't they?

His silence disappears as his voice emits a low hum gradually becoming brighter with every passing second. The sound forms into words as he begins to sing. His voice carries over the audience, a tone not too high or too low—pleasing to the ear.

The actor sings about a battle for land and how neither side wishes to fight, but they must because their kings force them to. I wonder how Krolas might feel about this. I'm sure he would've hated Crystalline even more.

My attention switches to the people in the background fighting each other. The metal clangs of steel-on-steel are dull compared to the singer's voice, which helps the battle not be too distracting.

When the fighting ceases, everyone on the blue side appears to have died, except one woman who approaches the singer and holds him close. However, the sentiment is short-lived, and the man is attacked by another soldier and dies on stage. The girl screams and is taken hostage.

The red army removes all the dead bodies, except the girl's lover, from the stage. While this occurs, the woman soldier sings about her dismay and how it's the end for her. Her voice is just as beautiful as the man's, and I feel sorrowful for her situation. I want to help her, but I understand this is all for show. Nonetheless, I lean forward with anticipation on what happens next.

All the soldiers left alive walk off the stage. Only one man, the dead lover, remains. I'm curious as to why. The show can't be over, for this is a horrible ending!

Then suddenly, the dead man begins to sing where he lies. A song about death and dismay emanates throughout the room. Each lyric involves a lifetime of suffering, only to be repaid with misery. He desires and deserves a second chance.

The crowd cheers as a dark figure, almost like a shadow and strangely resembling Dureizen, appears and touches the dead man. I look at Zier for confirmation, and he grimaces and looks away. I guess that answers my question.

Rising from the floor, the man shifts his tune to be more aggressive. He now speaks of revenge, and the black shadow disappears into the background. His song gets louder as the soldiers in red return on stage. The captured woman looks shocked but overwhelmed with joy for her partner's return. When the man notices her and the soldiers, he flaunts his weapon and charges forward to save her.

The enemies are confused and don't know how to react, and they all fall one-by-one, dying from a single swing and unable to fight back. Once all these villains die, he unbinds his lover, and they sing together. Their voices complement each other with perfect harmony. A song of sadness is now one of triumph and love.

In the end, the lovers return to their king, who is dressed

formally in robes, and they tell him they will no longer serve him. Before he can exile or arrest them, they vanish off stage, smiling.

The other patrons and I clap. I'm so glad this story got a happy ending. In fact, I feel a strange warmth in my heart. For whatever reason, this musical reminds me of Zier and I in a way, even though none of the events reflect our situation. Still, I'm happy to have experienced this, and I'll treasure this moment forever.

After we leave, it appears sunset is fast approaching. Zier looks at me and asks, "Anything else you want to do before nightfall?"

"You mentioned tournaments are held here. Is there one going on right now?"

He nods and touches my arm. We then teleport into a crowd of people. They all seem to be cheering. A few of them look at us funny, but I don't think they question our arrival much for their focus is glued to the arena below.

The arena is covered with dirt, probably to soften the landing if someone falls. Currently, there are two competitors dressed in white, a man and a woman, who are both wielding swords.

They clash their weapons together and hold them there

for more than a couple seconds, dire time to kick the opponent down or push forward to knock the other off balance. Instead of doing any of these things, they back up and clang their swords together like they are in sync.

"Alright, I'm bored," I tell Zier, and he raises his eyebrows.

"I thought you wanted to watch a tournament."

"This feels fake when compared to an actual battle. Look, they're not even trying to hit each other!"

"Smart girl. What once used to be battles to the death is nothing more than showmanship and skill with a blade. Unfortunately, this is the best you'll find in Crystalline nowadays."

"Lame," I comment. "Let's do something else."

"Then allow me to lead the way this time. I want to show you how beautiful Crystalline can be when the sun goes down."

I smile and touch his arm this time, and he teleports us to a place of tranquil awe: the rooftops of Crystalline. The sun descends past the horizon, and I observe the glorious city as people begin to turn in for the day.

31

After this day, I feel much closer to Zier. A part of me believes we've known each other forever. Knowing how he's always been around since I was a young girl on the other side of that bloody door back home makes me feel nervous but familiar with him. Were we always destined to meet? Did Dureizen always have plans with me, and did Zier just decide he didn't agree with them one day? Who knows.

Nonetheless, he and I are one and the same. I've come to realize Zier's father wants him to be bound to his ideals and do his bidding for all eternity. My parents wanted me to guard that door for a lifetime. Both Zier and I would receive backlash if we resisted our superiors. Zier already proved that with his father, so why would it differ from mine? They don't care about what we want for ourselves. They just need us to be a part of them.

The multitude of orbs in the sky spark green like magic. One after another, a flame rises from the bottom of the glass supports and into the various heights of the orbs. Once they reach the top, the green fire stays lit and surrounds the inside. It's a beautiful sight. The light gives the entire city an unreal glow which casts away the darkness.

It's a full moon tonight, and I must thank Zier for choosing the perfect time to see this city. Despite our real reason why we're here, I'm sort of glad Agnes chose this as her tomb. Being here has allowed me to experience a new side of reality I've never known about. Best of all, I got to experience it with a friend.

Below us, rocks and flames color the city in all sorts of patterns. It's all so surreal to know something like this is possible, even if Dureizen is to blame. Still, the green flame might not be his doing. Zier did only mention the colorful stones attracting newcomers. Why would Dureizen do more than the bare minimum? Perhaps the tall fires are a byproduct of what people came up with afterward.

The intense crowds below are nowhere to be seen. Most

locals are likely trying to get some sleep at this hour. From what I can tell, only a few shops remain open, and the only available attraction now is enjoying the scenery. Most people might be used to this ambience and don't care to enjoy it anymore. It may be second nature to them, but if I lived here, I might never sleep. Aside from the rambunctious crowds during the day, everything is too perfect at night. This is just right for me.

I join Zier at the rooftop's edge and lean over the metal railing. His face invokes concern, for his eyes are shut, his forehead wrinkles, and he bears a frown. It's not often I see him like this.

"What do you think about Crystalline?" I ask him. He grunts and refuses to open his eyes. "We had fun today. The musical was phenomenal, and I feel like I'm an extraordinary fighter when compared to those people at the tournament." Still refusing to respond, I fear the worst. "Are none of these things actually interesting to you?"

"They are." He opens his eyes but refuses to meet mine. "It's just . . . I can't shake the feeling."

"Of Dureizen's influence?"

"No. The sensation of slaughtering all those people for years. They were all wasted lives that did not need to be tainted with magic. I was a dog who ate the scraps my master fed me. Nevertheless, I can't help but question Dureizen's intent. What benefit was there in giving all those people powers? How hard could it have been for him to bless those who wish the world good? Do you think he did it all for me? Making me kill so many people so I would eventually become numb to murder. Or do you think he did it for sadistic reasons?"

"I couldn't say."

He grips the balcony until his knuckles turn white. He then adds, "Of course, you wouldn't know. I can conceal my emotions for so long, but here, I can only think about that insane demon I used to call a father."

"Tell me more," I suggest, placing a hand on his cold arm. "It might help you feel better. Now you have someone you can talk to. Besides, the more I know about him, the better off I'll be too. Tell me everything."

I don't expect him to obey, so I watch the lonely city that tries so hard to please others. In the night, the true wonder of this place reveals itself, but only to the few people who care to enjoy it. In the day, everyone disregards the beauty and focuses on entertainment. People live strange lives.

"Very well," Zier mutters. "Get comfortable because I'm not stopping until I feel much better or worse."

Not releasing his arm, I put most of my weight on the balcony and watch the city. I don't want to make him uncomfortable with my staring—not that he'd care—but I'd like to hear about his past.

He clears his throat and begins:

"Before living in Dalgin, Dureizen was a demon who wandered the world for new and *exciting* adventures—since being alive for a thousand years plus must become boring at some point. This journey brought him to Lirium, where from my understanding, he made a deal with a commoner who became the first king.

"The terms of this pact would allow Dureizen to create a flourishing kingdom for the poor soul in exchange for the demon's freedom to wander and do as he pleases. Dureizen's one obligation was to never harm the hierarchy. However, the first king was smart, forcing the demon to create a large deposit of black steel ore under the castle. Any weapon forged by this ore was far stronger than any normal blade."

"Can these weapons harm Dureizen?" I interrupt.

"Anything can harm him. Black steel weapons just make the job easier. *If* you can land a blow. Nonetheless, they were meant for Dureizen if he stepped out of line and broke his contract. Assuming nothing of the sort would happen, even though it did, then the demon would be free to travel throughout the kingdom's territories.

"To make his so-called freedom not require so much travel, he also fabricated Crystalline from the ground up near the kingdom. People would visit. People would suffer and die. These events are why the glowing stones were formed. These rocks, the discussion of magic, and the attractions all worked together to bring in new faces and to trap the old. Despite all the horrible events people heard about, everyone wanted to be a part of the cursed, beautiful city, even if it meant their death. In Dureizen's eyes, what good is a playground if everyone's too afraid to visit it?

"Since then, Dureizen began granting blood magic to more people each day. There were times when five people received it, when others only one."

"I can't imagine having more than a few in this world," I consider aloud. "If there were more Enzo's, I couldn't imagine killing them all."

"And that's what I had to do," Zier shakes his head and touches my hand. Despite wearing gloves, I can feel the icy cold coming from his body. I worry he might try to kill me here, for this is the first time Zier discussed so much on his mind, so I hold still and refuse to move away.

"At worst," he continues, "people would use magic for revenge. Revenge leads to torture. Other than that, I remember those who used spells to improve their voices in song, to become stronger and win competitions against non-magic users, and other petty nonimportant things. There's one time I remember entering a tournament against a three-time reigning champion, an arrogant magician. When I challenged him, I killed him in seconds. After the event, no more magic users dared to enter that tournament for a year. I was glad my efforts weren't wasted. Nonetheless, I regret showing off. I believe I entertained Dureizen by doing so."

Zier walks away, releasing his hold and forcing me to let go. He then grasps his head and yells to the world, "I haven't slept for three days because of him!"

I don't pursue him. Instead, I try and calm him down by commenting, "You look great for staying awake for so long."

He turns to me and gives a ghost of a smile. "It's a demon thing."

"Well, look at this place. I understand how you must be upset being here with all your memories, but isn't your father's influence all gone?"

"Everything still exists from those days. Not much has changed. Sure, Dureizen is no longer torturing souls and forcing me to clean up his dirty work, but it's impossible to separate myself from the memories. I constantly think I'll turn around and see him, smiling, towering over me alongside the large crowds. I continue to believe he's somewhere in the shadows stalking me. Despite my confidence in dealing with awful situations, the concern of a new magic user showing up and attacking us or another leaves a sour taste in my mouth."

I shiver at the thought of another user, someone I can't kill so effortlessly. "But you don't truly believe there's another one besides us and Enzo, right?" I mention, and my heart aches from another problem arising. After Enzo's death, I plan on traveling the world, not wasting my life away hunting others down.

"No. Dureizen still seems content living in Dalgin. He had his fun here, and now he's moved on. Still, it annoys me how people focus solely on their lives here as if Dureizen never left. These people don't notice anything around them and just pursue their goals without concern for others. This is the falsehood of purpose. There are so many negative connotations toward living this way, and people from all over the world are drawn to it like those dark days. There's no life here."

"How long ago did he leave Crystalline alone?"

"Right before the reign of the fifth king," he answers without emotion.

I can't tell if he's calm now. Even so, I move the subject away from Crystalline so he may relax. "Why did he leave?"

"Don't know." He returns to me and looks into my eyes. His pupils reflect a million colors, and I believe mine are doing the same. "Perhaps he just got bored and wanted a change of pace, but maybe, just maybe, he saw what he was doing to my mentality. Perhaps he went into hiding to repent and spare me from killing every day, cleaning up his needless messes."

"Well, regardless of the past, Crystalline is still a place I enjoyed spending time in with you. Despite its darkness, there's a beauty I've never seen anywhere else."

"I guess you're right," Zier mutters. "Without magic, none of this would exist."

"All this talk about your past reminds me of something I meant to ask you. What's your preferred name?"

He takes a small breath, holds it like he wasn't expecting the question, and then replies, "Just call me Zier. I don't like my old name."

"Why's that?" I inquire.

"My real family isn't really mine."

"What do you mean?"

"You love worming your way into my life, don't you." I look away and become fearful I've gone too far. Then, before anxiety overtakes my body, he adds, "If you care this much, let me just say that after obtaining blood magic, my biological father had already forgotten me and had another boy. It didn't bother me at the time. I didn't know I was meant to be this boy who would eventually inherit the kingdom. This is the first thing I saw when I turned sixteen, the time I was released from my imprisonment in Dalgin's cave: where Dureizen raised me whenever he came around to take care of me. Sixteen is also when I received blood magic. A strange coincidence, don't you think?"

"It seems to be a notable age, I guess. I do have one more question on my mind though, and now that we're alone and tomorrow is the day I'll inflict vengeance on Agnes, I need an answer. What is my purpose? Why are you keeping it hidden from me? I need to know in case your father breaks out of his sanctuary to find me."

"He won't."

"But he can," I retaliate.

"There's nothing to gain from knowing, but—"

"No buts. You and I are very much the same, and I'm

sure you would hate someone hiding important information about your life until it was too late."

He utters a low growl and stares at me. I return his gaze and refuse to let up.

"Tell me, now," I command.

"If you insist," Zier hisses. "Dureizen desires to cause more chaos with your help. At some point, he wants to take you and turn you into a monster, as you are the only human with an affinity with death magic."

"What kind of monster will I be? A demon?"

"Don't count on it. As you should know, Dureizen only cares about himself and puts others last. He breaks promises and causes suffering for amusement. Whatever he desires from you will bring you lifelong misery. He may even kill you. I want to keep you safe from those outcomes, for you deserve the freedom I've never had."

"Why did you keep that from me?" My eyes become glossy from tears. "Why!?"

"Because I didn't want you to defy him and try to kill him. Not yet. With my help, I can keep you safe. Judging from my interactions with him regarding the subject, he only wants you after you kill Enzo, which will prove you're ready to be of use."

"Then why did you train me?"

"Maybe because I care about your desires!" he blurts out. My breath stops. "Maybe I see you as someone who can free me from a miserable life. I'm one-hundred-sixteen years old, and I've never met another death magic user. You and I have similar lives; you're a treasure I refuse to lose. Killing Enzo, Agnes, and Rufus will make you happier, so I want to help you, but I'm afraid of the cost. I don't want Dureizen to take you away."

"I—" I try and find my words. "I don't want to lose you too. All this misery afflicting my life leaves me feeling alone, but this loneliness becomes a little less every day. I'm with you because I see you're like me. I just wanted to know the truth, and I wanted you to not hide it from me, to trust me."

"And do you trust me?" he retaliates.

"More so than yesterday. Aside from our terrible introduction, I thank you for these pristine clothes, the journal you gave me, and your protection. I would be dead without you too. Krolas' death," I look at my burn, "is an event that will haunt me forever, yet you cared enough to let me treasure his memory on my skin. You saved me from bleeding out, and even if I survived by some miracle, I would still be the wimpy magician who thought she could achieve anything.

"Even though you kept my purpose a secret until now, I

understand why you were cautious about bringing it up. You didn't want me to be afraid and act unpredictably by charging headfirst into Dureizen's clutches, or shy away from my freedom due to fear. No. Instead, you've opened my eyes to a whole new perspective. I still desire to kill those who've done me wrong, but I'll do so with you by my side. Together, Dureizen will never capture us. We will kill my wrongdoers and escape."

He offers me a hand and asks, "You still wish to kill Enzo, even if it means a higher chance of getting caught? We could always run away now and get a head start."

Brushing away his hand, I walk into him and hug him. His muscles tense, but he returns the kindness. In his arms, I feel a warm misery connecting our sorrows, and it helps me accept the darkness within this world. I no longer have to do anything alone, for I have a demon by my side.

The full moon rises, and the stars shine brighter than the city's lights. These stars don't sparkle as prominently as the ones in Dalgin, but they are just as beautiful. I can stare at them forever.

Here in the arms of death and in the most magnificent city in the world, I have found my purpose. I will be the one . . . no . . . we will be the two the world will learn to fear.

Dureizen will never catch up. My purpose after Enzo's death will be freedom.

After another hour, we sleep together on the rooftop under the skies. I dream about lying in fields of white flowers under a blue sky. The sunlight produces small shadows among me.

Another dream involves living in a large house with Zier. We cook boar, bake a cherry pie together, and laugh about our time in Crystalline. It seems dark everywhere else in the home except the kitchen where we are, but my vision keeps the focus on us.

The last dream allows me to fly high in the sky. I can touch the clouds—fluffy and soft—and can observe the world below. A house surrounded by a large field of white flowers exists below me, a residence combining my two previous dreams. I think I make out someone within the shadows of the home looking up at me. They're as dark as the void, but when I try to focus in on them, there's nobody there.

32

Agnes: Ezno's spy, murderer. You're going to feel the pain you wrought upon me. A week after my parents disappeared, I had no clue what happened to them. I believed they might've abandoned me, but the longer I waited, I realized how cruel this world can be. When I found the truth about who was to blame, I knew I would avenge their death in one way or another.

I hope you're ready to pay for what you've done. Death is on my side.

When I open my eyes, Zier's lying beside me and watching

me. He and I exchange smiles, then he stands up and extends a hand.

"Ready?" he asks. "I found her location."

I take his hand and get up. Typically, I would be groggy, but last night's events and my anticipation for today fuel me with vigor.

"Where's she at?" I ask.

"Underwood Inn. Spending her time with another man aside from her husband, Rufus. She gets around if that increases your drive to kill her."

"It's all the same to me. I just need you to support me, and I will make quick work of her. Let's go."

He keeps ahold of me, and we teleport to our destination. When we arrive, the environment is far more unique than anything I've ever seen before. We are in a sizable room with the usual wooden tables and chairs, but this time, two staircases lead to the upper floor where the living quarters must be. Above us, large roots are hanging from the ceiling, giving me an awkward familiarity of home. There are no windows to allow natural light in. Instead, wall torches extend chaotic shadows across the room. Although I feel comfortable here, I've moved past this phase in my life and despise walls that aim to cage me in.

"Underwood Inn, an underground area on the outskirts of Crystalline," Zier confirms my uncertainty.

"Let's go."

We head for the right staircase. The one who must be the owner is cleaning dishes behind the counter. He pauses and stares at us. In response, I cut my arm and watch him as we continue our path.

"Excuse me, what are you—" the owner stammers, but all the dishes on the shelves crash onto him and shatter. The noise is overbearing, and he cries out as he falls to the floor on impact.

I stop and turn to Zier. "What are you doing?" I yell. "Now Agnes is going to know we're coming!"

"You think we want to waste our time and search all the rooms? We will lure her out. Look."

Following his finger, five weary people yawning and rubbing their eyes exit the doorway above. I realize once again I have no idea what Agnes looks like.

"Is she one of them?" I ask Zier.

He shakes his head. "No. Time to generate more

ruckus."

The supports under these people snap, and the platform crumbles to our level. Everyone screams as they fall to the floor, and dust flies high into the air as the wood and stone rubble scatters everywhere. The noise echoes throughout the room. Anyone within five miles must've heard that. I raise my collar over my nose to prevent breathing in any of the smokey air.

"The one in the black cloak," Zier states, and I squint and see a few more people peer out of the doorway, undaring to fall to the floor below. Only one of them has a black cloak, a figure with a slim and tall outline.

"Get me up there!" I command, and Zier grasps my hand and teleports us to her location.

I slash my weapon ahead of me the moment we materialize behind them. It connects to someone, and they cry out and join the others in the rubble. Another man jumps down, and a satisfying splat follows. The remaining woman must be none other than Agnes, distinguishable by her black cloak, brown hair, and a disgusting, piercing glare.

She grins at me and waves just before she drops below. I try and stop her. I need to be the one who kills her. Yet, no noise follows from her fall. She must be quick on her feet, disappointingly.

"She's trying to escape! Come on!" I shout, and we teleport back to Underwood Inn's entrance outside to try and cut her off. Nobody is running up the stairs, but somebody is running into the city. That's her. She's fast, but that only prolongs the game. Her survival will run dry.

I charge forward, but I'm forced to stop after a few steps. Zier stays put and bends over like he's tired already.

I make a fist and watch as Agnes is escaping because Zier is slowing me down. "You can't be that exhau—"

"There's something wrong," Zier cuts me off and breathes heavily. "Something's off. We shouldn't pursue her."

"Then you stay! I'm not losing her now!"

With the small amount of blood draining from my arm, I increase my speed to compensate for lost ground. I sprint after her with all I have. Some man walking without care gets in my way, so I shove him aside and continue. I scan the alleyways and growing crowds as I proceed further into the city. Despite her agility, she shouldn't have magic. I can find and kill her myself.

My body tears through everything in my way like a relentless bull, yet there's still no sign of her. Perhaps all the people in my way are slowing me down too much, but then again, it should've delayed her escape as well.

As I run, Krolas' lessons on overusing body manipulation come to mind, and I must slow down and take a small breather. I need a moment to observe my surroundings. But where could she have gone? My nails grind into my palms, and I grit my teeth. I can't believe I lost her.

The crowds brush past me in both directions. All I can do is scan the dark alleyways and bright streets for anyone who looks like Agnes. Perhaps I overshot and ran past her? What if she turned into an alley when I lost sight of her? Maybe if I wait, she will barrel into me, and I can stab her then and there.

Yet, she isn't anywhere to be seen. Everyone wears colorful clothes to match the city, while Zier, Agnes, and I are the only ones who seem to wear black. It should be easy to find who I'm looking for!

The hair on the back of my neck stands, and I sense I'm being watched. Out of instinct, I turn and see a woman in a cloak standing at the edge of a dark alleyway. Agnes. She waves at me again and her silhouette vanishes into the shadows, the darkness absorbing her figure. She wants me to follow her. No matter. Whatever tricks she tries, today is her last day on Earth.

I force my way through the crowds of annoying people talking as loud as the destruction of Underwood Inn. I hope she isn't planning on running away anymore. I hope this alleyway is a dead end. I hope she thinks she can kill me so I can laugh in her face.

It only takes me a moment to reach the edge of the darkness. My arm still bleeds. I'm alone. If she wants to fight me here, I plan to make this a quick battle.

"Phoenix," the blackness beckons for me. "Come on in and kill me."

"How do you know me?" I demand an answer, but Agnes doesn't reply.

I create another cut that extends upon my previous one. If I bleed too much, I will stay alive out of determination and rage. I blink, and the darkness appears gray. It's enough for me to see into the pitch-black space. Yet, nobody's here despite the voice sounding so close.

Stepping forward, I keep my eyes and ears open for any threat which may approach from the rooftops or a hidden passageway. There seems to be nothing. Maybe she already left? I grind my teeth at the thought.

"That's right, Phoenix, come closer," she begs for her demise while trying to act mysterious. Her voice gives the impression of being everywhere and nowhere.

I do as she commands. I'm confident she doesn't know I can see in the dark. She cannot hide from me. If she tries to ambush me, I'll be ready.

"How do you know my name?" I question.

"Because," her eerie voice replies without hesitation, "I was warned about your arrival."

"By who? Enzo?"

"Not even close."

"I'm sick of your games. Come out here and fight me!" I scream out. This blasted woman is the one who killed my family? She's more annoying than ever.

I continue to provoke her by adding, "You're a coward for killing them. You couldn't even last in a fair fight, so you had to sneak up and murder them!"

"Who are you talking about, Phoenix?" her voice sounds closer, and I keep my guard up in case she rushes toward me, but she's nowhere.

"You know who! Ashen and Flare!"

"Your parents? Oh, yes, I remember they couldn't put up a fight as my beautiful knife shoved into their backs, just like I will do to you now."

My heart pounds as something slithers across my ankle,

but nothing is there when I look. I slash out around me but hit nothing.

"Come on! Show yourself!" I demand.

Something moves in front of me, a shred of darkness which isn't gray, and I follow it as it melts into the ground. I step back. From where the blackness is, a head emerges from it, then arms, then legs, until the newcomer is shaped into the likeness of a human. Judging from the coat, it's none other than Agnes, but she isn't supposed to have blood magic!

She pulls back her hood and gives me that same disgusting smile of a pointless criminal. "Confused, you impudent child?" she mocks. "I know you can see me. My sources already informed me about what to expect from you if you became bold out of nowhere. What happened to the girl who couldn't save a single soul?"

"I'll show you."

I strike at her torso, and she dodges backward and opens her cloak to reveal a multitude of knives. She grabs three of them and throws one toward me before I can react. It penetrates my stomach, and I keel over. I taste blood coming from my throat. My chest heaves, and I cough and look up at her. She's approaching me, but I hope she doesn't believe my hatred runs so shallow.

She laughs at me and says in the most ridiculing way possible, "Silly girl, you are going to die just as pathetically as the ones who share your blood."

I rip out the knife stuck in my stomach and throw it at her. She dodges like she expected it. No matter, she's only delaying the inevitable.

From the bottom of my heart, where my fear of defeat resides, as well as the anger which claws its way out, I guarantee a painful death for such a snarky woman. I hold my stomach wound and clutch, mustering all the energy I can.

"I will not just give you death; I will make you suffer physical pain too," I pronounce, and a bloody flame ignites in my palm. Where Krolas' burn is, I imagine he's bestowing the energy I need. I will produce a blaze worthy of his teachings. It grows and grows, and I present it to her. She steps back from me, and that horrid, sharp smile becomes a lovely scowl.

The newfound light doesn't affect my exceptional vision. I'm bleeding out, but I don't care about my pain. I need her to suffer, and if this means I must endure agony alongside her, then so be it.

I release the pent-up energy within my palm, and a blast of fire—like a dragon's breath—erupts from my hand and spits onto Agnes. She dodges most of it, except she forgets about her cloak being flammable. She removes it before the flame can lick off her skin, and reveals a white undershirt with black pants. I will stain those clothes with crimson.

I rush forward, deflect one of her knives with my blade, and then catch the other in my left hand. It makes me bleed, but I refuse to let go. From my new blood, I use it to lubricate my hand to slide it closer to hers. Its agonizing being hurt this way. Nonetheless, the moment I feel her tense muscles, I smile.

The blackest death spews out of my left hand and onto hers, crawling farther onto her body. Her eyes widen, and she tries to slash at me with her free hand, but I drop my knife, grab her blade, and then release darkness through that one as well. She attempts to kick me, but she's a dying animal, so her leg only goes up by a few inches before giving out. She cannot let go because of the connection. She falls, and I inch closer to feel her dying breaths upon my face. The corruption transforms her skin into an inky black, stretching onto sections of her head and the entirety of her arms.

"Please, no!" she begs. "I'm sorry."

Laughing, I'm aware her body's dying. I then force my spell to explode in whatever capacity I can manage. She screams as her body bursts into pieces, and I let go. Judging from my work, she's still alive and bleeding out but only has pieces of her arms still attached. She is also missing most of her chin. Satisfying chills run through my spine. I will enjoy her fluids draining onto the stone until her eyes gloss over. Even then, I will marvel in my victory.

"Phoenix, get away!" Zier yells, and on instinct, I stumble backward. I realize my body is weak from all the wounds.

My vision detects the unusual darkness connected to Agnes' disappearing trick, and it melts into the stone ground beside her. Zier grabs me and heals my wounds, and my vision begins to restore itself. Just before my eyes fully readjust, I notice long shadow hands reaching for the dying woman and dragging her down below.

"NO!" I scream and push away from Zier. However, I'm too late. She is no longer here.

33

I failed to kill her. She will come back to haunt me unless I can finish the job. She underestimates me. I'm not like her victims. Where she molds herself into the shadows to hide and cower, I am that which she tries to be. Her end is nigh.

Before I can retaliate further, I find myself with Zier on rolling green plains. There is no sign of Agnes. He tosses my knife at me, and I pick it up. Then he rubs his forehead and watches me like I made a mess of things. Although, it's quite the opposite. If it wasn't for him, Agnes would be dead. Why did he have to take her away?

"That wasn't me, Phoenix," he tries to explain.

"Don't give me that crap. Who else could've done that? Where is she!?"

He ignores me like he always does and looks ahead toward an array of houses and busy townspeople living their pointless lives. I don't recognize this town, but I'm confident Agnes isn't here.

I push him, and he stumbles backward. He then turns to me and snarls.

"What more do you want?" he asks like he doesn't know the answer.

"Where is she!"

"Dureizen took her to Lirium's Castle." I pause and wait for him to elaborate, yet he doesn't. Instead, he returns his gaze back toward the town.

Turning him around, I get close to his face and mutter, "What do you mean he took her? What could he want with someone like her? Besides, shouldn't Dureizen be in Dalgin still?"

"You look very pretty up close," he smirks.

"Answer me!"

"Fine! You want to know the truth?" He knocks me back

and sits on the grass. I stare down at him as he challenges my gaze. "Dureizen is making his move early. He expects you to follow Agnes to the castle with my help and capture you there. Your revenge will be what plunges you into his trap. Either we run now or never escape."

I answer, "You already know what I want. Remember what we discussed in Crystalline last night? Tell me that wasn't for nothing. Together, we will always succeed."

"Just as I expected. Against a demon like Dureizen, the most powerful creature in this world, you think we can kill him and get your revenge without any consequences. You're insane."

"I've come to realize that, thank you. It's what this world turned me into."

Snickering, Zier's eyes brighten a little. In response, I offer him a hand.

"Come, let's show this world what we can achieve," I suggest. "If Dureizen is waiting for us, we will run. If we cannot run, we will prove to him what it means to underestimate other demons."

"Confidence," Zier comments and takes my hand, and I pull him to his feet. "You're not even a demon."

"Eh. I feel like one. With you, I am stronger than all these other people. Enzo stands no match. Dureizen will be the same."

He shakes his head and motions for me to follow him into town. He then explains, "Don't get cocky. Dureizen will kill you if you see him. But your mind is made up, and even if it brings us to the brink of death, your confidence is inspiring."

"So, what are we still doing here?" I ask, then my stomach rumbles louder than I want it to.

"You should ask yourself," Zier laughs. "Come on, can't go on a murderous rampage without sustenance. Might be part of the reason why you struggled with Agnes."

Glaring at him, he begs for mercy by holding his hands in the air. Still, I must agree with him. I'll only stomach what I can for now, then kill Agnes before she can recover.

We eat a simple meal of bread and water on the outskirts of town, just enough to sate our appetite. After Crystalline, I'm done dealing with people for a while, so I'm happy we chose to eat here.

"Do you know the name of this town?" Zier asks between bites.

"No."

"Kuemarin. If you'd like, we can meet Rachel Kuemarin, the one from the stories who helped create this town. In case this is your last day alive."

"Shut up. We are the ones close to death, so you can say we're already dead. After we win, meeting Rachel can be on our bucket list."

"Fair enough."

This whole ordeal is obviously bothering him, judging by how he holds himself. This man who is above danger is now afraid. Nonetheless, I can never be complete without revenge, and he is courageous to join me against such impossible odds. I can only hope Dureizen will leave us be. After our enemies die, we can run away forever and explore the world as we see fit. Zier's powers will keep us safe, and my strength will compliment his.

We prepare ourselves once our meal is finished. I confirm I have my weapon, test my skills by creating an abundance of shards, and Zier and I hug once more as we teleport to our destination. I've been ready for this day ever since Krolas' death. Finally, all my enemies—Agnes, Rufus, and Enzo—will be cowering together in my benefit. This will not be the day I die; today is the day we bestow death to undeserved life.

When we emerge from the nothingness, I find myself standing on a red and blue carpet. Two knights stand before us in front of a wooden door. Before they can react, Zier slaughters them like the ones in Sivertin. They scream as their armor crashes onto the stone floor.

Behind us, below a sizeable downward staircase, knights prepare their weapons and charge at us. I almost injure myself, but Zier snaps his fingers, and the knights die where they stand. Their bodies roll back down the way they came.

No other sentries come to the rescue. There are multiple passageways around us, but I can only assume the downward staircase marks the entrance. Zier pats my shoulder and points at the wooden door, now protected by two globs of gore.

"Throne room is through here," Zier states. "I can sense Enzo and Rufus are alive and well behind those doors. Agnes is still close to death, which surprises me. As for Dureizen, no sign of him yet."

"Will I have to worry about anyone disrupting our meeting?" I feel the blood rushing to my face and my body filling with energy so intense that I shake ever so slightly.

"You worry about your revenge, Phoenix, so we can get

out of here quicker. I'll keep intruders at bay like in Sivertin, and I will support you in battle."

I manage a smile through my adrenaline and remark, "Just don't kill my targets. They're mine."

"Deal."

I step over the knights and enter the throne room. As Zier predicted, Agnes is a bloody pulp at the edge of the stairs leading up to Enzo's throne. Rufus is holding her close. And Enzo's head rests on his fists as he leans over and watches me enter. He anticipates our reunion—just as I.

34

It's strange. Aside from all the horrible things Enzo's done to me, I don't know much about his life. Are there any redeeming qualities for this man? . . No. He deserves to die.

The room is freezing, causing goosebumps to form on my arms. It makes no sense, for outside is sunny and warm, but here, Enzo's cruelty must transform this room into an uninhabitable hellscape.

The false king's outfit resembles the one from that horrific day. The black ponytail, red jacket, dark brown pants, and black boots with gold accents engulf my body with so much rage. It's like he never changed. Everything's the same to spite me.

His brown eyes watch me as I approach his barren throne—which he doesn't deserve. I can only imagine how Krolas would appear sitting where he belonged, but no, this disgusting person stole his title.

As for Rufus, he doesn't even spare me a glance, but as I approach the throne, Agnes initiates a grunting tantrum with whatever strength she must have left. No doubt due to fear. I chuckle under my breath. Her misery is satisfying. The grunting shifts into cries of terror, so much so that Enzo turns away from me and stares down at her.

"Oh please, you can't say you're afraid of this incompetent fool," Enzo dares to comment.

I use the opportunity to show how much he underestimates me, and I slice my arm and blast a ball of fire toward him. The speed at which I can produce flames and launch them surprises me. It must've been less than a second. Perhaps Zier is assisting me from behind, or maybe there's so much tension inside me begging to burst like a balloon.

He doesn't notice the fire and instead continues to judge Agnes for being rightfully afraid. However, the moment my attack reaches the staircase leading to the lifeless throne—his grave—a blue sheen of light surrounds the area where my enemies are, causing my magic to dissipate.

Zier walks forward and touches my shoulder, reassuring me. He calmly says, "Don't worry, I'll destroy the barrier. I won't let anything delay your revenge."

My partner clutches his hand. Enzo turns to watch us since Agnes is now mumbling in pain instead of crying. Nonetheless, the blue sheen still exists, separating the space between us and them.

Zier growls and changes his face into those terrifying, deep black eyes and long, sharp teeth. "Perhaps more power will suffice," he states and tries ridding the force field again, yet nothing happens.

Enzo announces, "Please, Phoenix, Zier, I want you to enjoy yourselves here and experience the drama instead of attempting to kill your host. No breaking the barrier until the show is complete."

"How do you know my name?" Zier demands.

The room drops in temperature as a shadow emerges from the back of the throne and grips Enzo's shoulders. Enzo doesn't look afraid, yet Zier freezes in place and isn't moving a muscle. Then, the shadow's head reveals itself with its open eye and mouth holes, and I feel the hair on my arms and neck stand up.

"I'm to blame for that," Dureizen mentions. "I got so lonely after you stopped seeing me, so I craved to connect with new friends."

Stepping back, Zier grabs my arm and shifts his gaze between Dureizen and me. "Why isn't it working?" Zier panics. "Come on. Work so we can get out of here!"

Dureizen guffaws and says, "No teleportation for you either, my son. All your powers are rendered useless here. Every single ability except healing because our poor Phoenix can't do so."

"She still can't!?" Enzo snickers. I want to smash his face in.

Dureizen turns to the false king and adds, "Don't be rude to your guests. Phoenix here is special. In fact, all of you are special. For you, king, have eyes expressing determination and ambition. Your skin gives signs of hardship, and it appears you have achieved your goals through struggle. What a sad being."

I ask Dureizen, "What are you doing here? Why are you away from the cave?"

The creature peers quizzically at my eyes. He then explains, "I'm not some caged animal who's never allowed freedom. My interests bring me here."

The demon melts into the air and reappears next to

Rufus and Agnes. Rufus falls backward, and Agnes tries to escape but can only produce a small yelp. He lifts both of them up with his long shadow arms and pushes them close together, Agnes' blood getting all over Rufus' armor. Agnes cries out even more from being moved around. Dureizen ignores her protest and observes the couple.

Announcing over Agnes' wails, Dureizen says, "What a sorry sight for an ugly soul. This girl, Agnes, your slim figure and black outfit allow you to sneak around undetected and do anything for anybody. Mostly horrible things: murder, eavesdropping on royalty, and only performing jobs that get you higher up the ladder. How you've let yourself deteriorate."

"Hey, she's not—" Rufus fights, but Dureizen cocks his head to him like a hungry bird, and the knight freezes.

"What a white knight you are," Dureizen continues. "Your deeds have been blackened with fear and greed. One wrong move, and you will fall into a pit of despair and be thrown away by your king. No scars or blemishes either. Quite fascinating you are. Did you have to work to get where you are, or were you just born into it?"

"Well, I . . ."

Uncaring about his answer, Dureizen drops them, and Agnes cries out again when slamming onto the floor. Rufus groans, and moves closer to her and attempts to comfort the dying animal.

Afterward, Dureizen appears beside Zier and me, then mimics my partner's devilish smile with newfound, long, uneven teeth. He grabs us by our backs and lifts us up. I try to break free, but his grip is firm. Attempting to use my knife on him would likely get me killed too, and my reasoning is justified by Zier refusing to fight back.

"Zier," Dureizen says, "or should I say, Zayn Malfester. Let me fix your face." Zier's expression returns to normal in a blink of an eye. We really are up against the most powerful demon in the world.

Dureizen continues, "You have the body of a sixteen-year-old, but your lifetime makes you an old man of one-hundred-sixteen. It's nice to see you're still wearing the same black and red armor, even though nobody can hurt you besides me. Your experiences have altered your spirit into a ruthless killer, and for what, to please your master? But now you've changed. Your black eyes now show a bit of light, and this girl is to blame."

Enzo cuts in, "She is nothing. How can someone like her amount to anything?"

I don't look at him; instead, I look straight at Dureizen who returns my gaze.

"Oh, she's important," Dureizen acknowledges. "Ever since I met you, Phoenix, at my eternal resting place, I saw immense purpose from one who claimed to have none. I saw someone who reminded me of my son. Nonetheless, there was one problem with you. You were weak. Now, that is no longer the case. You are useful now."

"What do you want from me?" I mutter. "What can I do for one who is immortal and all-powerful?"

"To have you join by my side and expand on this world's possibilities."

Zier growls, "Leave her alone. Take away my powers if you must, so I can take her place instead."

Agnes continues to wail, tears streaming out of her bloodshot eyes. Dried blood surrounds her, as it should for someone like her, and new blood exits her arms. Rufus looks at Enzo, who gets off his throne and approaches the couple.

Dropping us on our feet, Dureizen returns behind the blue sheen of magic, where Enzo, Rufus, and Agnes are safely behind. He watches the false king with wide, hollow eyes, and I find myself doing the same.

Enzo stares down at Agnes, who increases in volume after seeing him tower over her. The false king claims, "You never shut up, do you? I'll just shut you up myself."

"What a nice turn of events," Dureizen mentions.

"Please, King Enzo Malfester. Please save her," Rufus begs.

"What's the fun in that," Enzo responds. "I have no more use for her with a demon on my side."

The false king stomps on Agnes' neck and crushes it. A spongy snapping sound resonates throughout the room, and everything falls silent. Finally.

"You monster!" Rufus huffs and scowls at Enzo. The knight then unleashes his blade from his scabbard and prepares to strike.

Dureizen extrudes one of his arms and pushes Rufus far away, out of the protection of Enzo's force field. The knight falls to the ground and stands back up in one swift motion, readying his sword toward the false king once more. Enzo doesn't seem to care about Rufus' attempt to kill him, for he stares at Agnes' corpse.

This is my chance to kill Rufus. He's beyond any protection now. Furthermore, it's great to see the knight lose his lover. Even though I desired to kill Agnes myself, Enzo finishing the job is fine by me. Betrayal is beautiful against one so cruel, for their 'king' shares no sympathy for either of them. I already gave Agnes so much suffering. Enzo only offered mercy.

Resting my blade upon my arm, I refrain from using magic and see what will become of Rufus. I desire his death, but to have him be betrayed like Krolas and I is a much better punishment. You're getting what you deserve, old friend.

"You're a liar, Enzo!" Rufus screams at the top of his lungs. "No matter what I did for you, I never got anything in return. Sure, I got stronger, but for what!? You killed my friends, and now the only family I had left!" Rufus begins to blather through his tears and swollen eyes. He points at Enzo, then to me. "You were supposed to heal her when she arrived!"

Enzo fails to conceal a grin and waves his hand, gesturing toward Agnes' corpse. He replies, "Oops. I guess she lost her purpose."

"What!?"

"Yes, fewer problems if your wife's dead. She will no longer try to sleep with me for my goodwill. And now that I have all the pieces lined up: Dureizen working for me, Krolas is dead, I have the crown, and Phoenix is here, I have no use for a loser like Agnes."

"Then you leave me with no other choice." Rufus walks toward us, and I watch for any sudden moves. Although, he returns his sword to his scabbard and holds out a hand for me to take.

"Phoenix," he speaks in a low tone, "I'm sorry for all the trouble I've caused. Keeping Enzo in the loop led to Krolas' death and your suffering. Now I've seen the wrongdoings of my ways, and I hope we can work together to kill this horrific monster. I can't do it alone, so I ask that we all work together."

I nod and take his hand. We shake, and he turns away and stands between Ezno and me. He's exactly where I want him.

Then the knight extends his sword toward Enzo and declares, "You bastard. You will die for—"

His voice drowns in the blood gurgling in his throat. One stab is all it takes. A betrayal from everyone he's worked with, along with the death of his wife, is all too perfect. He is left with nobody as he dies.

Crumbling to the floor, Rufus grasps his neck and gazes

into my rigid eyes.

"You deserve this," I tell him, and I get down and decapitate him so he cannot regenerate like last time. Sure, I can slice him to bits like he mentioned when he became a traitor, but no human can survive losing a head. I observe his eyes glossing over and his body becoming limp. Rufus is no more. One less problem for this world. Only two left. Enzo, the one I strive to kill more with each passing day, and Dureizen, the demon causing Zier's eternal misery.

"Pathetic method to kill someone," Enzo chimes in, triggering my teeth to grind together. "What could you even want with a weakling like Phoenix? You should use me instead." The false king looks at Dureizen. "You and I make a great team. Our interests are similar from what I can see. We both desire power and freedom, so let's achieve this goal together!"

"Hmmm . . ." Dureizen swirls around Enzo as if he's observing him. "Well, how about we run a test. I want to acknowledge Phoenix's strength, and if she fails, we can determine the future from there." The demon snaps his fingers, and the force field shatters. Enzo raises an eyebrow toward Dureizen, to which the creature responds, "How can we have a fight if you're invincible."

"I'll make a joke out of her."

"Just try it," I remark and cut my arm and let the blood splatter across his carpet.

Zier adds, "I got your back, Phoenix."

"Will you be joining me in this fight, Dureizen?" Enzo asks, but the demon shakes his head.

The shadow responds, "Phoenix needs Zier because it would be unfair without a healer. A strong king like yourself should be able to handle two young meddlers in your kingdom. Yet, I advise you to only focus on Phoenix since she is your competition."

"Enzo," I announce so he can cease this pointless discussion and fret upon his real threat. He looks at me, and I form a second cut on my other arm. "I will be the last thing you witness as I snuff out every ounce of your life."

35

This is the end.

Dureizen moves to the back wall to watch. He doesn't spare a glance at Zier or Enzo. His nothing eyes instead stare into my soul, making it difficult to look away. It seems I'm moving closer to him. Deep greens of a forest and bright yellows like the sun swirl around my peripheral vision. All I can focus on are those eyes as they loom ever-closer.

Something trips me, and a cold blast of magic scatters above where I stood. My eyes return to focus, and I see Zier offering a hand. I take it and stand up.

"Focus on Enzo, I'll let you know if Dureizen interferes,"

Zier commands, and I give him a nod.

The large amount of blood flowing from my arm presents endless possibilities, yet, Enzo launches another spell at me. Out of reflex, I move my hand in an arc, forming a black aura that absorbs the attack before it hits me. Then I fire back at Enzo with my own link magic.

Of course he dodges just in time, so I blast more shards at him. He deflects the rest of my spells with a new, blue sheen in front of his body. Afterward, Enzo's makeshift shield expands until it exceeds his mass. The magic morphs into a mighty creature, matching the likeness of a dragon.

"Remind you of anyone?" Enzo antagonizes.

Zier heals my wounds with a quick touch. I understand my partner's message and release a fresh flow of blood to switch tactics.

The dragon unleashes itself from its user and rushes toward me as fast as Krolas' phoenix. I doubt my magic can block it, so I manipulate my body and jump over the spell milliseconds in time, the icy frost of the monstrosity burning a bit of my elbow.

As the dragon dissipates behind me, I've realized fighting another magic user can mean death at any moment. I must get closer to Enzo, for attacking from afar seems to have no effect. In the corner of my eye, I see Zier rushing toward the false king, so I propel myself forward once I touch the ground again and join next to him.

Enzo's black steel sword and my knife clang together as they connect. Zier joins the fray a second later, forcing Enzo to parry my blade and sidestep away. I rush in again before he can retaliate, but he's faster than me, and swipes a clean cut on my leg. I fall over, and Zier fends him off as I prepare an explosion of death.

The false king's black blade slices into Zier's arm. My partner returns the favor by splitting Enzo's shoulder open. They both take a moment to heal, and I release a dense purple cloud directed at my enemy.

My magic puffs out of my body at an insane speed. Before anyone can react, it absorbs Zier and Enzo. I know my partner will be safe, but as for the human . . .

Then, everything goes quiet as the fog's thickness continues to thin over time. Zier approaches and heals me, and I stand up and see Enzo staring at the ground. I got him.

Without wasting time for the false king to recover, I swing my blade at him. However, my heart lurches violently, and I fall to the floor. My brain is flooding with flashbacks of Krolas. This is what it must've felt like to fight against your mortal enemy and lose. All this time preparing myself was pointless. My efforts are in vain, for Enzo killed Krolas and my family, so he might as well kill me too.

Someone is trying to speak to me. It sounds like Zier. I look up and see Enzo grinning and pointing his sword at me.

"You fell for the same trick my foolish brother stepped into," Enzo's voice mocks me. His words are clear as day, speaking over the other voice trying to reach me. "A delayed reversal. Seeing you look so grim relieves me, for if I got hit, you might've gotten a good strike on me. I'll admit one thing: you've gotten stronger. Still, you'll never be powerful enough to kill me. Nobody will."

"Death is where my magic thrives," I respond as I recognize his trick. Where Krolas burned alive from his fiery attack, I'm deteriorating from the inside. My own spell is trying to kill me. Though I feel terrible, I know what I must do to end this once and for all. I let the darkness inside me overtake my body and fuse with me. My hands and arms become black and purple with power.

Enzo strikes downward, and I squint my eyes and accept

my fate. I wait for the blow to connect. Yet, nothing happens. When I open my eyes, I'm still alive. His weapon fazed right through me! I stand up, clench my hands like I'm holding an invisible sphere, and produce a being I've felt connected to ever since Krolas' death. The only fitting weapon that can kill this monster and let me die happy.

Flames spark, evolve, and rise between my hands. It grows and expands as it takes over the entire space leading up to the ceiling. The air is difficult to breathe as the room makes my skin boil, and Enzo's cocky smile adjusts to fear. His eyes wide and his mouth agape, he witnesses the creation of a fire phoenix, the last spell Krolas used against his brother. This time, I will succeed where my mentor failed.

"What's this bird without death?" I comment. The raging phoenix ignites into a purple hue. Bones can be seen throughout the creature, and its eyes are now blood red. This divine being is half Krolas and half me. Nobody can stop it from devouring our sworn enemy.

Enzo tries to run, but he doesn't get far. I release the spell toward him and fall back, but Zier catches me so I can watch. My skin returns to normal as he holds me.

The blaze erupts into blackness as it connects with Enzo

and swirls around him. Trying to see the results while they're occurring, I notice some of Enzo's flesh is gone, and his bones expose themselves to me. The longer the phoenix swirls, the less skin he has. This is the end of my torture. This is what Krolas meant for you.

As the flames dissipate, Enzo still stands and looks toward the sky. Most of his clothes are destroyed. One of his hands is primarily bone with muscles hanging off it. His skull is partially visible. There are patches of muscle and bone across his body. The only skin left on him is charred black, begging to flake off. I can't believe he's still standing.

"Lunestre," Enzo's voice is dry as he speaks nonsense. "I have failed you. You saw great things in me compared to that fool, Krolas, and now I am nothing anymore. Just how things were. How my life was wasted for a week of glory."

He then crashes to the floor. Bones scatter across the stone. One of the smaller bones reaches me, and I put it in my pocket. It will serve as a memento. His failure will bring me pleasure moving forward, and I will always be triumphant over those who wish me harm. My revenge is complete. I've avenged you, Krolas Malfester. May you be at peace knowing your brother's dead.

I look at Dureizen to witness his reaction toward Enzo's death. The demon is still leaning against the wall and staring at me with his unemotional expression. It's almost like he wasn't paying attention to the fight.

Then, those hollow eyes furrow into an angry scowl. My mind feels lighter. I feel tired. Zier tries to say something to me and lays me down, but I drift away into sleep as he drops me.

36

Plunging into the rippling waters of sleep, I find myself stranded in the middle of the ocean. The water is cool to the touch and drenches my clothes. Small waves cause me to bob up and down. The sun is shining so bright above me, reflecting off the water's edge and burning my eyes as I try to search for land.

Below, three large, gray fish circle me. I'm afraid. I'm alone. I've never had any experience with swimming, so I doubt I can outswim them. Even so, I must try.

I swirl my arms and legs in whatever way possible to help me move, but it doesn't seem like I'm getting anywhere. Those fish are still near me and are getting closer. I thrash my arms and legs to gain speed, yet it's no use. I can't swim away!

One of the creatures becomes brave and breaks out of the circle and swims right for me! I panic and try to splash it away, but it doesn't care. I scream as it bares its teeth and opens its jaws. It can swallow me whole!

A dark shadow envelops the sun and lifts me out of the water. Zier has come to save me! We quickly ascend, and I see the fish bite at the water where I once was. I release a wavering sigh of relief.

Now that I'm out of the water, I'm shivering from the cold. The wind intensifies my discomfort since I'm soaking wet.

I look up at my savior as we rise above the clouds. Zier is a black mass with wings bringing me to safety. I never knew he could do something like this.

Where we are, I can see the ocean expanding far across the horizon. There is no land, so I ask, "Can you teleport us to safety? Somewhere where I don't need to be cold preferably. I'm also sick of being apart from solid ground. I don't like it."

Zier's black shadow stops midair. I wonder what he's doing. Why aren't we moving? Then, a strange mass protrudes from the shadow, revealing a face which causes all blood to drain from my face. This shadow isn't Zier. It's Dureizen.

He releases his grip on me, and I close my eyes and scream as I undergo the sensation of freefalling. I continue to descend further and further for a full minute. I'm going to die the moment I touch the water. Those fish are still there waiting for me! Zier, please save me!

"He's not going to, but I will," Dureizen's gleeful voice emits right above me.

I open my eyes with caution, unwilling to experience my inevitable demise. The moment I do, the wind no longer whisks by me. I'm floating in the sky above the clouds, standing and facing a humanoid version of Dureizen.

The demon exhibits his hollow mouth and eyes, but his body mimics the anatomy of some of the men in Dalgin. He has no clothes—not that he needs them, for he's just a shadow. His eyes continue to stare at me like before. This time, however, I no longer perceive the motion of being pulled into him.

"What are we doing here?" I ask Dureizen.

"You don't enjoy the view? The freedom?"

"Not particularly. I—"

A sudden environmental change disrupts me. I'm still high in the sky, yet it's so hot. I feel like I'm melting from heat despite being drenched in salt water and sweat. The sun beats down on me, and below, a grainy, yellow texture extends for miles. Spiky, tall green plants exist to break up the dull landscape.

"Perhaps you can dry off in this," Dureizen says. "I must congratulate you on your strength. You've grown stronger faster than I expected, but that's all the more useful for me, for I have a proposition for you."

"And what is this proposition? Zier believes you mean me harm, so tell me what it is. If it's promising, which is unlikely, I may accept it."

The demon points down toward the earth. I don't know what he wants me to see since I just looked at it, but he appears persistent in his still stature. Following his finger, I now notice a sizeable, yellow animal treading this barren landscape. Some small, black creatures are now scurrying about. A few people walk over a hill, each slouching over with their arms hanging in front. They look exhausted.

"Those people are suffering from lack of energy," Dureizen observes.

"What about it?"

"With my power granting you true freedom, you can save people."

I blink a few times and inquire, "Are you going to transform me into a demon?"

Dureizen chuckles and says, "Never. Two demons are already too much for this planet. The power I wish to bestow you goes beyond a demon's capabilities. Instead of saving people who are living, you will be able to rescue the dead."

"Like Krolas!? You're saying I can bring him back? Same as my parents?"

"Feisty one, aren't you," Dureizen remarks, modifying the world once again into a bleak, rainy meadow.

"So much for being dry." The rain is much colder than the ocean. Here, I'm being blow-dried by freezing air. The wind here causes the rain to smash into my body. It's difficult to hear anything besides nature's force.

Dureizen points down again, and I see tombstones across the entirety of the meadow. So many people. All dead. Does he want me to save them all? But why?

The environment disrupts again; I am above an extinct forest this time. Ashes, much like Krolas,' blanket the dirt.

The trees are all dead, leafless and soiled black. Any hope for survival is no more. Still, this place doesn't appear to be Zwelis, which relieves me a bit.

Dureizen resumes, "Krolas, yes. Your parents, no. Not that you'd want to save those ones. My power is only limited to blood magic users. Krolas can be revived for your sake, and if anything happens to Zier, you can bring him back too!"

The demon walks up to me and wraps an arm around my shoulder. He makes me uncomfortable. He can stab me at any moment, just like my first meeting with him.

"Will I have a choice of who I bring back?" I question. "What's the catch to all this?"

The demon smiles. "That depends on your mental capabilities. You can bring back anyone you desire, and that's it. No catch. I'll leave everything up to you." I raise an eyebrow to show my distrust in him, then he adds, "I just want to make up for all my mistakes. Zier had to kill so many people because of me, and this is my way to apologize. Will you do this for all our sakes?"

I refuse to look at him, for he may influence my decision with his otherworldly gaze. Everything he offers sounds promising, but there must be some sort of catch. There always is. I don't trust Dureizen, but I want to bring Krolas back and protect Zier like he protects me. Wouldn't that make him happy? Make me happy?

"I . . . I decline your offer." I answer.

"Hmmm?"

"I don't want your blessing."

Dureizen's face gets close to mine, and he whispers, "But what about Krolas? Won't you miss him?"

"More than anything."

"Then why?" he spats. The sound rings in my head.

"This power comes at a cost, which you refuse to tell me. Zier doesn't trust you either, which is enough to question your motives. I deny your offer. This is my life to live. Working with you is not something I wish upon myself. I desire complete freedom to do as I please without anyone tying me down."

"Poor Phoenix, you don't have a choice."

Something sharp stings the back of my head. It feels like a long needle penetrates my skull and implants a pulsating migraine. My head is being stabbed. It's scratching deeper. I fall to the ground and clutch my head to alleviate the pain, but the horrid sensation keeps swelling. I can't think about anything else. It hurts.

"I'll put you to sleep to ease your mind," I think Dureizen says.

"Just make it stop!"

"As you command."

The pain dulls as I lose consciousness. If I must be asleep to end this pain, so be it. But why did he harm me in the first place? What is he hoping to gain from it? I just need my suffering to quell. I just want to be in the comfort of Zier. Whatever Dureizen does to him, I'm sure he can counteract his heinous desires and manage without me. I'll join you when I can, so there's no need to wait for me.

37
Zier

I shake her body to snap her out of it, but she becomes limp in my arms, and I know it's too late for her. Dureizen gives me his same old petty smile. I'm done with his crap.

"What did you do to her!?" I question him, for I can only assume he had a role to play in her demise.

"She's still alive if that's what you're asking."

"Then why is she like this?"

Dureizen, as he likes to demonstrate things instead of giving a straight answer, approaches Enzo's corpse and holds the dangly mess up like a puppet. Then he says, "Look at this worthless fool. Just a bag of bones with no more use for me.

One could say this carcass results from Phoenix's ambition, but I find it lacking."

"Cut to the chase, and tell me what you did to her!"

"Hmm . . ." Dureizen moves Enzo to the throne and drops him like trash. "I think I did enough favors for my son. He's been too disrespectful toward his elders as of recent, so I'm going to take my leave. Just take care of her. I don't want anything to happen to my prize possession."

"Dureizen!" I yell, but it's too late. He's gone. I'm left here all alone with Phoenix's cold body.

I attempt to heal her, but I have little hope of success, for Duriezen's magic is superior to mine. Staying with her in this room, I spend a couple hours trying to figure out what is wrong and curing whatever wounds I can find, but in the end, my theory is correct. She's lost. Dureizen has a curse on her. At least she still breathes. Nonetheless, it appears she's in some sort of eternal slumber. Why would he want to do this to her? If he planned on killing her, why keep her in this state?

I whisper, "I guess it's time I return now. Phoenix, I'll find a way to bring you back. Just give me some time to figure out a solution."

All my powers have returned. Since Dureizen's gone, so is his influence on me. If only I had my abilities sooner, then maybe I could've prevented this and gotten us out the moment Enzo died.

Hoisting her onto my shoulder, then grabbing Enzo's black blade, I teleport us out of the castle. We arrive back in Kuemarin: a small town with lively people, the new home of Phoenix's companion, and where she and I would've visited after escaping my adoptive father. It just feels wrong to return with her unconscious.

I approach Rachel's house, a magnificent two-story building with white and gold flowers across the yard. The closer I get, the more people gasp and point at me, obviously thinking I killed this poor girl and am dragging her around with a sword for attention, but only if they knew. At least none of them approach me. I'm not in the mood to deal with others. There's only one man who can help me now.

Arriving at the residence, I knock on the door and wait for someone to answer. Nobody heard me. I knock again, this time louder so someone can open this door already. Then finally, the latch unlocks, and a tall, burly man who I saved only out of kindness toward Phoenix reveals himself. Krolas Malfester.

"You seem to have gotten used to living here, seventh king," I observe as his yellow eyes become dull with concern.

"Shaving your beard, wearing your baggy clothes, and maintaining hygiene. By the way, this is for you."

I hand him his brother's sword, then he ushers me inside and locks the door behind me. I'm sure the crowd watching me continued to develop the longer I was out there.

Krolas asks, "What's happened to her? What happened during my absence?"

"You know, I was expecting your first words to only revolve around how much you hate me for taking you away. Or maybe about what happened to your brother."

"Phoenix is more important right now. I'm sure Enzo is already dead." He holds up the sword as evidence, then places it on the table. "As for now, I want to know how I can help."

"Well," I say scornfully, "as strong as I am, I think Phoenix needs a more comfortable resting place. Afterward, we can discuss all the details."

Krolas nods, and we head upstairs to a room with a woman in a white and blue dress and golden hair. She's crocheting in a chair next to a plain bed. This is no doubt Rachel, though I've had no interest in seeing her myself. She looks like an older version of Phoenix, except this woman grew up without the intense struggles that she and I had to suffer.

I avoid meeting her gaze as I gently let Phoenix down from my shoulder and onto the bed. She looks pale, so I put a blanket over her and turn to Rachel.

"She's sick," I tell the woman who stopped to watch what I was doing. "I've never taken care of anybody before, and I have to discuss matters with Krolas, so can you watch over her in the meantime? Just ensure she won't starve or become dehydrated, and let me know if something goes wrong."

She gives me a ghost of a smile and responds, "There's no need to stress. I'll take care of her while she's here. Judging from your attire, you must be Zier. Krolas couldn't stop talking about you and Phoenix."

"I'm sure. Anyway, thank you. I'll be back to check up on her later."

I leave the room with Krolas and head back downstairs. The idea of being around someone who requires care produces a strange feeling in my stomach. I want to be there for her, but I don't want to burden her with trivial matters between Krolas and me—even though she won't hear it. At least I'm here to protect her.

Krolas and I sit at the white table where Enzo's blade rests. The moment we sit, Krolas stares at me with judgmental eyes, and I know I have a lot of explaining to do.

I start before he verbally lashes out and explain, "You know I saved you once Enzo left, then moved you here so Phoenix could learn how to defend herself. You see, her power is stronger the worse she feels, and if she ever learned about your survival, it would've taken more time for her to become a formidable fighter."

"Well, maybe if you brought her here—"

"Then maybe we could've all stopped Enzo together," I cut him off. "I know. Except this time Enzo was not the biggest threat. Dureizen was."

"What? Why didn't you tell me?"

"Because I didn't know what to do myself. Phoenix learning to wield her spells would've helped her stand up against him, and with my help, I had a sliver of hope that I could kill Dureizen and save her life. But I was sorely mistaken. That blasted demon is just too powerful. He always gets what he wants, and of course, his plans included Phoenix."

Krolas crosses his arms and leans back in his chair. "But you're his son. Did you try to persuade him otherwise?"

"Too many times to count," I lean forward and stare at Enzo's blade. I can't recall a time when Dureizen listened to my desires and fulfilled them.

"Do you know what's wrong with her? Can she be saved?" He asks me like I know everything.

"I won't ever give up on her if that's what you're asking. As for her illness, Dureizen placed her into a deep sleep, but he refused to tell me why. Healing her doesn't work, but there are so many people in this region and other parts of the world who know medicine, so maybe one of them can offer us a lead."

"Nothing but wishful thinking," Krolas points out the obvious. "The only one who can save her is Dureizen or you, and knowing who gave her this curse, I'm betting Dureizen is the only cure."

"That's too bad because I'm not going back. Knowing him, he will continue to sicken her. In time, she will become his pawn."

Krolas growls under his breath and commands, "Tell me everything."

We discuss the notable events: training with death magic, Agnes' death, and Rufus and Enzo's death. I also let him know why Dureizen targeted her instead of me. As an added detail, I also tell Krolas how much she misses him and how I wanted them to reconnect before she got vengeance, just in case things went south. But unfortunately, she was resilient and insisted we return later instead of wasting time.

Krolas sighs and says, "Sounds like her. Still, you could have forced her to visit. Could have prevented this tragedy."

"Like I said, Dureizen was making things complicated. Phoenix's constant desire to get revenge convoluted things. Sure, we could've met up with you and ran away together, but the likelier outcome was that Dureizen would've killed you to force Phoenix to break. It's just the kind of thing that demon would do."

"You still could've—"

"Phoenix is capable of dealing with any threat!" I fight back. "Dureizen is undefeatable. This would've happened no matter what we did. Still, if you could see her in action now, she is no longer the weakling she was before."

"Very well. Either way, what has happened is done. Did she ever learn how to heal?"

"It's impossible to heal with her type of magic. Although, do you want to know something? Everything she did since your disappearance was for revenge, mostly for you and her parents. She never stopped craving it. If it wasn't for you . . ."

Krolas leans forward, his chair snapping from the front

legs slamming into the hardwood, and he moves his face closer to mine. "And I regret involving her in all this," he adds.

"You were going to use her as a sacrifice," I challenge. "I remember that."

"Things changed. I learned to care for the girl despite her bloodlust."

"A healthy bloodlust. It's only natural for—"

I pause as a large shadow covers the doorway. It stands there, unmoving, as if waiting for one of us to open the door. When we do not, three heavy bangs cause the barrier to shake and threaten to come off its hinges.

"Are you expecting someone?" I ask Krolas.

"No." He grabs Enzo's black steel sword and approaches the door. Rachel comes barreling down the stairs, and Krolas signals her to go back with an aggressive gesture.

The shadow sways and speaks incoherent words in a sinister tone. It pauses, then speaks louder, the words still unrecognizable. Then it tries to form words again. This time, the voice is distinctly male. The intruder's next attempt at speech is distinguishable, and his words cause my body to shiver. "Oh, Zier, I have sniffed you out."

The door breaks free from its hinges and flies toward me.

Krolas dodges out of the way, and I duck as it crashes into the table.

Green magic pulses from the outsider's hands as he smiles at me. He looks familiar, but that's impossible. His face is covered in scars, his eyes are full of greed, and his black hair is as sleek as I remember.

This man . . . is a spellcaster from Crystalline. More specifically, the one I challenged in a tournament. Scarsguard.

38
Zier

I'm writing in your journal to keep track of events while you're asleep. I never told you this, but I have been fond of your hobby since the day we met. It's a great way to pass the time when feeling uneasy. Furthermore, I enjoy looking back and reading all your entries. I wonder if you will enjoy reading mine when you wake up.

One day you will awaken. Until then, I will keep you safe and continue seeking a cure for your coma. Many lands may offer leads, and if it comes down to it, I will kill Dureizen for the answer to your awakening. I miss you. Without you, my life is endless with a silly king who won't stop pestering me. I don't understand how you could get along with him.

As for now, just understand you will not miss a single day of your life while I write in this journal. Your day of revival will come.

The past has come to haunt me. How did he survive? I know for a fact I killed him. There was nothing left of him after I finished the job.

Scarsguard and I lock eyes, and I know he's only after me. "Krolas, he's mine to take care of," I mutter. "Stay with Phoenix."

The king nods and backs away upstairs. Now it's onto unfinished business.

"You mean the girl?" Scarsguard asks.

"What do you know?"

"Nothing. Except I must thank her for helping me find you."

I snap my fingers, and his arm blasts open and covers the floor with gore. He screams and cries as he falls to the ground, nursing his wound and attempting to halt the bleeding. After a moment, he uses magic to clot the flowing blood and patch up his maim. Nevertheless, his arm is gone.

I declare, "This is what I did to you in the tournament, except I destroyed your entire body. So how are you back?"

Glaring at me, he responds, "Say my name, and maybe I'll tell you. You must remember me. I've come back from the pits of hell in order to kill you for what you've done to me. So, tell me my name!"

"Hmm. Something with a scar in it, I'm sure. I just can't say you're important enough to remember." It's a lie, but I can't offer this weakling any satisfaction. He's a cheat, only received Dureizen's blessing to win money, and I put a stop to it. I can do so again in a heartbeat. As for now, I require answers.

He makes a small incision on his face with his fingernail, then charges at me and produces a deep yell. Green magic extrudes from his hand and swirls around him. I should kill him now, but he still hasn't answered my question. How can he be back from the dead?

A makeshift sword of energy forms in his hand, and he slashes at me. Instead of letting it hit me, I teleport behind and kick him off balance. He lands on the ground with a thud, then turns to look at me with some effort.

"My name is Scarsguard! Scarsguard! After you heard it a million times in the stands, you tell me you don't remember!?"

"Already forgetting it now. Maybe you should've named yourself something else besides what's on your face."

He stands up again, makes another cut next to his eye, and attacks me with his energy weapon. I entertain his determination for my demise, and deflect his decorative blade with my knife. After he loses his balance again from missing a solid blow, I kick him back down, and he crashes into the pots and pans hanging near the table. It's clear his magical weapon can pack a punch, but I can hardly tell the difference between him and a child with my power.

He cries, "I only heard your name once, right before you blasted me into smithereens! You said to remember it, Zier. I've carried your name to my grave. Now you're going to kill me again, aren't you!?"

Ignoring his desire for me to end his pathetic life, I repeat, "What do you know about Phoenix? How are you back? Answer me." My face molds into my favorable demonic one, and he cowers away.

"I met her not long ago, and her presence brought me to

you. I could feel the connection, the familiar energy coming from this house. It fuels me with hatred, and I knew I would find you."

"Is that really all you know? No idea how you came back to life?" I question.

"Yes. I don't know anything else."

"Then I tell you, remember my name and never return from the grave again. Know Zier is the one who will always kill you on this earth."

His whimpering grows louder, and I snuff it out before he can annoy me further. His body blasts apart with a snap of my finger, and I clear up my face to make it more presentable. As for the new stains covering the walls and floor, I evaporate them into the air, saving Rachel and Krolas the trouble. The broken door and fallen kitchen supplies should be the only telltale signs of battle.

"No need to keep anyone alive who will place Phoenix in harm's way," I state and head upstairs. Upon entering the room where Phoenix rests, I catch Krolas by the door, ready to strike with Enzo's blade. I put a hand up, and he relaxes and sits on the bed with Phoenix.

"What was that about?" he questions me. "Friend of

yours?"

I shake my head and respond, "Just an idiot from the beyond who's come to haunt me. Might be Dureizen's doing to screw with me, but his arrival may be linked to Phoenix."

"You mean to tell me the dead can be revived?"

"I guess so. No idea how."

"Well, this complicates things," Krolas adds and looks at Rachel. "If these people know our location, this town isn't safe anymore."

"Agreed. We must leave first thing tomorrow morning. Need to find a place where Dureizen or any other undesirables won't discover us. My main task is to keep Phoenix safe, and I might as well scour these lands for a cure. Will you be joining me? Having a friend who's another magic user would make travel easier, and a lot less boring."

Rachel looks at Krolas, and Krolas looks at the floor. He then responds, "Rachel and I have been thinking. We've decided that after Enzo falls, we must return to the kingdom together and fix Enzo's wrongdoings. There is also the matter of Lunestre, my mother, who still lives in the castle. I need to know what became of her while I was gone. So, as much as I care for Phoenix's wellbeing, I need to be with my people, or else this kingdom will shatter. Regardless, know you have an ally in Lirium who will always assist you when you need one."

"I presumed as much," I state. Moving to Phoenix, I brush her hair back and rest my hand on her cold cheek. "Phoenix. Phoenix, wake up." She doesn't even twitch. I shouldn't entertain the idea of things being too easy. "I'm going to save you. Trust me. One way or another, I will drag you back from hell, for we are partners in death."

"It must be strange to have the same magic," Rachel remarks.

"Very much so. There's a connection that should've never existed. Nonetheless, I'm glad we share it."

I head out the door and turn to Krolas. A question has been on my mind for a while, ever since learning about my history with royalty.

"Krolas," I start, "why did you receive a black steel knife instead of a sword like your brother? Doesn't that make you a weaker king? Perhaps you're an undesirable leader, according to your parents?"

Blinking a few times like he wasn't expecting such a question, he answers, "The knife is given to the kingdom's rightful ruler. It's supposed to symbolize how kings or queens don't need a large weapon to compensate for their strength of heart and skill. So, take that into account in whatever way you want, since I know you have a black steel knife as well. As for Phoenix, she has the makings of a leader and a hero. Once she awakens, you and her will no doubt achieve great things."

Speechless, I materialize my weapon from thin air and examine it.

"Oh, and one more thing," Krolas adds.

"What is it?"

"Thanks for not killing me."

"Well, let's just say your purpose now lasts a lifetime as a friend and the rightful ruler of Lirium."

He nods and turns to Phoenix and Rachel, and I exit the room and continue to stare at the black blade in my hand. Tomorrow we will part ways, Krolas. We both have our destinies to achieve. You don't know how grateful I am to have someone I can rely on. Whatever challenges we encounter, you will restore your kingdom, and I will save Phoenix.

39

Dalgin is quiet as usual. A few people are out working and shopping, a couple birds are chirping in the distance, and a cool breeze saddens my aching soul. The weather is foggy, and there's only a rough sun outline in the sky. It's strange to be back after seeing a portion of the world and encountering new friends.

But nobody is here with me. Krolas is dead, Zier has disappeared, and now I have no one to travel the world with. Sure, I can explore and find happiness, but after meeting Zier, being alone doesn't have the same appeal. I have nothing to look forward to each day. Besides, Zier told me we would travel together. I just don't understand where he might've gone.

I wonder if Dureizen may know where he's at. He must have some idea. Despite harming me the last time we met, he cured me afterward and brought me here, meaning we are on okay terms. Zier might even find me before I find him, which would solve all my problems.

Returning to the cave, everything looks as barren as the day I left it. The lanterns are no longer lit—must've ran out of fuel days ago—so I cut my arm to see better in the darkness. The door at the end of the cave is no longer there, my parents are gone, and there's no strange visitor who will visit me one random day. I am alone in a place overflowing with ill memories.

I walk to the end of the cave, through the hole in the wall, and then down the endless passageways. Many paths lead to dead ends. When I reach one of them, I turn back and try another route. Krolas must've had some guide he followed, for there are no telltale signs on where to go.

When I eventually arrive in Dureizen's sanctuary, there's nobody here. Once again, I'm by myself. There are three small shadows in the back of the room, none resembling the demon with their lighter color, and when I approach, they disappear.

I try yelling out Dureizen's name, but all that comes out

is a whimper. Something must be stuck in my throat. Speaking again ushers the same effect. Nonetheless, I'm happy I don't hurt anymore, so I don't question it. I will just have to continue my search elsewhere.

Exiting the cave after another eternity of cramped passageways, I wonder where to head next. It's been a while since I ate, but I don't feel hungry, thirsty, or tired. So, the only option left for me is to retrace my steps.

*   *   *

Zier joined me at the bar where Krolas and I stayed. Perhaps he's waiting for me there. We've defeated Enzo and escaped Dureizen, so why wouldn't he linger at a place we are familiar with?

I open the door and walk inside. There's nobody here either. Krolas' ash pile is still where I left it, and the number of bloodstains across the floor is disgusting. Strangely enough, this place doesn't smell like it used to. Here, it smells just as good as an empty meadow. I don't understand why, but I'll take it.

Upstairs is no different. My room is just how it was, and my old journal is still there alongside the other books. Still, the bloodstains remind me of my failure. Constant practicing and failing. Becoming unconscious from blood loss and trauma.

381

Horrible.

Krolas' room layout is identical to mine, except there are no bloodstains here. How he was lucky to not need practice in his spare time. Maybe extra training would've saved his life? Who knows. It's evident Zier isn't here either, but the book, 'How to Live With My Out-Of-Control Partner,' rests on a table. I have no interest in reading it. The sour memories of Krolas showing it off whenever I was around are now visions of loss. If only he could come back from the dead. If only I understood how to achieve this feat. Even if it meant he must read that book daily, I would be so happy to see him alive.

When I leave, I think I see a group of shadows like the ones at Dureizen's sanctuary, but when I chance a second glance, they're gone. I swear I saw at least twelve of them. It's no matter. Lirium's castle is my next destination. Maybe Zier is waiting for me there, unsure where I disappeared after our victory.

I proceed through the empty streets. Every building around in this quiet city looks the same. Nobody is out, even though Enzo is no longer terrorizing them. It's uncanny to see a large area like this be so vacant.

The drawbridge across the moat is already down for me, and there are no guards to stop me from entering. I prepare my weapon just in case there are remaining Enzo supporters who wish to ambush me, then I walk across the wooden path and open the front gate.

The large door is heavy, and it feels like something is blocking it. I continue to push, and after banging it a few times, the door finally gives in and opens enough for me to enter. The culprit behind the secure door is none other than more dead knights Zier killed. He really is something else.

I walk into the throne room and see Enzo's corpse, leaning over the chair with his limp body. His companions, Rufus and Agnes, are dead in front of him. It's a glorious sight. The rotting king commands his deceased followers. That's what they get.

Nevertheless, as lovely as this is, Zier isn't here. I search around the castle and find a library of books I have no time for at this moment—once I find my partner, we can spend a week here together. He isn't in the training room, or the hallways, or the living quarters, or even the windy rooftops of the towers. This man is impossible to find.

I head back downstairs and check the throne room one last time before leaving. Zier must be here. I open the door and fall backward as a shadow rushes into me. It leaves the room, and I need a moment to calm down. Though I don't understand what these shadows are, this one felt familiar. Its negative presence offers me nothing but loathing. If these are ghosts, then I want nothing to do with them.

In the end, Lirium is just as disappointing as Dalgin. Where else could Zier be? He wouldn't be in Sivertin back at the watchtower, right? I can only imagine how many knights must be there at this point. Shrugging, I know my remaining options are limited, and I can't leave a single stone unturned.

*   *   *

Here in Sivertin, I'm beginning to get used to the emptiness surrounding me. The last three places I have gone to are mostly desolate. The same can be said for this one. Nobody is outside being productive. This is even worse than when Zier and I stayed here!

The tower is no different. Aside from the corpses constructing a makeshift morgue, no conscious people are to be found. It makes no sense. Maybe we killed Enzo before he could send another party over here to investigate? Either way, it's not good if Lirium's trading port is dysfunctional. I wonder what's going to become of this place.

My old journal is here at least. Although, I see no use in carrying it around. I hope we find each other and you can give me my current journal. As for now, I don't feel like writing anything. I'll stay awake for days and search for you until every corner of this world has been checked twice.

The last familiar place I can explore is Crystalline. Zier hates the city, but he may know I want to revisit it someday. It's a stretch. After I search there, it will be time to scour every obscure location across the world.

*   *   *

Despite all my wandering around today, the endless sun still shines, and I'm not hungry. Surely it's been more than a day, but the sun never lies. Maybe I'm just becoming delusional.

Crystalline is empty. The bright stones in the city sparkle in the sunlight. But as usual, there's no sign of Zier.

I don't understand what's going on with the world. Where did everyone go? I love being alone more than anyone else, but this is too much. I feel like I'm going crazy searching for someone who's impossible to find.

"You're looking for someone, aren't you?" a gray shadow looming in an alleyway speaks to me. I approach it, for this is the first time someone has talked to me today.

I stand in front of the strange mass, then the shadow adds, "I'm the only one around here who's brave enough to approach you, but many of us need your help. If you awaken me, I will assist you in your search. Coincidentally, I'm looking for him too."

"Zier?" I croak.

"Yes. Yes, that's him! Quite the coincidence indeed!" The shadow wiggles with excitement.

I'm happy I'm not the only one searching for him. Having help at this point is what I desperately need. At this rate, I'll never find Zier.

The shadow pauses and says, "Touch me, and I will manifest. I'll help you find him when you do this. It's a promise."

I do as he commands. What do I have to lose? When I poke the shadow in the alleyway, it becomes darker, dissipates into the air, and leaves me. Just like everyone else. I clench my fists. He got my hopes up for nothing, and now I'm left alone again, wandering this empty world of ghosts. I hope he keeps his promise, assuming he didn't just evaporate from existence—even though it looked like he did.

* * *

I close my eyes on the rooftop where Zier and I stayed the night. I'll take a break in Crystalline for a few days to recuperate, and maybe I'll get lucky and find who I'm looking for. Everywhere I've visited has been nothing but a failure, serving as a joke to make me angrier. I just need to relax and concentrate on where I can find him.

Still, my mind always ends up blank. The more I think about him, the more I forget. I keep my eyes closed and examine the darkness, searching for something that may or may not exist. I'm forsaken, rejected. I always have been alone. This isn't the freedom I desire: wandering ghost towns and aimlessly searching for something. Sure, the world is beautiful, but it's a beauty I wish to experience with another.

"Phoenix," somebody whispers in the sky. "Phoenix, wake up."

The only problem is I'm not sleeping. Whoever's voice enters my head can go away. All you are is another shadow trying to lie to me again.

"I'm going to save you. Trust me. One way or another, I will drag you back from hell, for we are partners in death."

That sounds familiar, and I stare at the cloudy sky for an answer. Could it be Zier? Is he looking for me?

Maybe it's time I leave Crystalline. If I can hear whispers, I will continue forward and find a way to him. He exists somewhere. I hope you search for me too, so we can be together again.

AUTHOR'S NOTE

I want to begin by thanking you, the reader, for experiencing Phoenix's dark tale with me. As you may know, this is my first published novel, a story which has gone through many revisions since 2014 as a passion project. Now, here we are 12 years later, truly kicking off my writing career with a story I am deeply proud of.

There were times I believed *Fester* would never reach completion due to how long development took. I remember when this novel started out as a competition between my siblings for who could write the best book. Something like that takes a lot of time and dedication, and before I knew it, I wrote my first draft with the title, *All That Remains*.

It had conflict, intense battles, foreshadowing, and . . . it was terrible. It was so atrocious where I could not bring myself to edit it, for it would require me to either restart or spend way too much time on the manuscript to maybe salvage it. In the end, I gave up on the draft and took a break from writing, trying to discover who I wanted to be in life.

A couple of years after high school, 2018, I became inspired once more after becoming emotionally attached to an anime called *Death Note*. The story within this show included many layers involving emotion with high stakes—how could I not fall in love with it? This got me wondering if I could also create something so impactful for others, and in turn, I decided to rework from scratch, *All That Remains.*

The manuscript was slow to develop, but it was a huge improvement upon the original story I made some years ago. At this time, I began to read more and learned how to incorporate my thoughts onto the page better. Everything was going so well. In fact, I decided to go to college with a focus on Creative Writing to further improve my skills. However, working and going to school ended up slowing *All That Remains* to a halt, and after a year or two, I realized I would have to start this story over again. I forgot so much regarding what I already wrote. My style had drastically changed from when I first began writing this version. There was no way I could continue it.

Eventually, I began my third draft of the story. Untitled, none of the original characters, now including magic, a heavily parodied version of the original story. The only thing that stayed true to the original was the tone—dark. In the end, after many edits later, I finally came up with the title of the completed manuscript, *Fester.*

The feeling was surreal. After so many years, I was able to grasp my dream turned reality. So, I want to say once more, thank you for experiencing this journey with me. I hope you will look forward to what's to come in the future. Fresh, enthralling experiences revolving around the complexity of human emotion. Darkness, love, passion, fear. A multitude of projects are currently in development.

And . . . where will Phoenix's journey take her next in *Together: The Shadow Blood Tale?*

ABOUT THE AUTHOR

Zaven Boswell is an Iowa author who studied at Des Moines Area Community College and Iowa State University with a focus on creative writing. After becoming inspired by the great fictional stories that exist in today's media, he strives to create dark stories with an incentive on emotion—tales which allow readers to immerse themselves within the overall plot. In his pastime, he enjoys reading and watching movies with his fiancé and cat, as well as playing video games such as *Kingdom Hearts* and *Final Fantasy.*